THE GAMES OF THE DEAD

THE GAMES OF THE DEAD

MATTHEW THEISEN

THE GAMES OF THE DEAD

iUniverse books may be ordered through booksellers or by contacting:

iUniverse
1663 Liberty Drive
Bloomington, IN 47403
www.iuniverse.com
1-800-Authors (1-800-288-4677)

Because of the dynamic nature of the Internet, any web addresses or links contained in this book may have changed since publication and may no longer be valid. The views expressed in this work are solely those of the author and do not necessarily reflect the views of the publisher, and the publisher hereby disclaims any responsibility for them.

Any people depicted in stock imagery provided by Thinkstock are models, and such images are being used for illustrative purposes only.
Certain stock imagery © Thinkstock.

ISBN: 978-1-4917-9995-6 (sc)
ISBN: 978-1-4917-9996-3 (e)

Print information available on the last page.

iUniverse rev. date: 06/13/2016

ACT I

The Paranoids are After Me

As he sorted through the realities, dreams, and screen-world dimensions in the community's collected consciousness, he watched representatives behind them emerge to place their respective members in allocated systems according to various, and sometimes- what seemed to him- trivial effluvium: birth-names, surnames, and occupations; then further segregations according to crimes, racial backgrounds, religions, and most watched television programs, until the groups became splintered into dualities of staged contests that were easy to contrive as psychic energy was manipulated into pointless but exciting debates and combats, depending on the levels of consciousness and sub-consciousness.

Pablo Nuri, atop the hierarchy, suddenly felt the presence of older generations who had seen or been through similar experiences, and were a bit resentful at having to barter with the young in order to pass along whatever wisdom and essence the elders had garnered and considered important. To the young, the benefits for their investments seemed as dull as a movie without sculpted steroid torsos and graphic effects' explosions.

Pablo commiserated with the elders, yet he also desperately wanted to escape from them. He was a not-so-starving poet on Food Stamps who had recently read T.S. Eliot's essay encouraging writers to study traditions and then go one's own way; and the irony occurred to Pablo, in his state of sifting, that Eliot's works were no longer taught in the education systems. Intrigued by the humor, Pablo tried to shift into college potency to discover, perhaps

3

by some telepathic means, if indeed there was no awareness of traditions to break from after close scrutiny of them.

He felt zapped by a raider who interfered with the spokespeople representing the sundry groups; and Pablo was streamlined to the inner-workings behind the crusades against obesity, illegal drugs, and bullying: he clearly saw the subliminal messages that coerced an audience with fast-food restaurant commercials, and while they were in a fully-laden stomach stupor, be plied with advertisements for pharmaceuticals.

He had spent a distasteful summer working at a corporate chicken farm with immigrants struggling to achieve American status; and when he mentioned he had three years of college, his fellow-workers either thought him very loco or a slumming braggart. It had been his last summer of freedom, if it could be called that only because he could walk away from the job and not worry about responsibility to anyone except himself until autumn classes began in August.

Estella, though, had become more affectionate and began telephoning him every evening after work. Pablo was suspicious, despite his fondness for her, yet his mind worked in such a manner that he believed if he played too detached she would let him go his own way; then, when she was independent or had another man, he would miss her psychic energy and again want her attentions. So he tried to develop a certain amount of vagueness with her that still showed interest. He based this particular approach on Thomas Aquinas's theory of potency and form, as well as on Pablo's amusement after reading that Leo Tolstoy created his own religion after studying Christianity; and, prior to the rise of the Soviet Union, people made pilgrimages to Tolstoy's Russian estate.

The matter of how long Estella would stay to adore was resolved on the day Pablo began outlining his senior thesis on taxation in the American colonies, and Estella told him she was pregnant. He was audience to the plotting maneuvers crumble into disorder, and stirred in his sleep as he heard Estella say, 'What are you going to do with a degree in history and writing? You read books your professors don't teach and barely glance at the ones they do. What kind of references will they give you for grad school? You're the one who said college is about sex, money, and career-connections, and everything else is accidental.'

Pablo jolted awake on the far side of the bed from Estella, and lay looking at the clock. He had searched through three pawnshops for a non-digital clock and finally found one with luminous hands, and dots indicating the hours. He watched it until time seemed to move backwards, then got up, used the toilet and went to the small living room.

Pablo rubbed Hector's head absentmindedly as the boy ate cold cereal with 1% milk. His tears over a bowl of oatmeal and powder milk were too unbearable for his parents, so though Hector occasionally exceeded his daily portion of 1% milk, Pablo had learned not to enforce that particular house-rule too strictly. Besides, Estella would side with their son, so what was the point of being a villainous taskmaster from a Dickens' novel, especially if Pablo failed at it?

While Estella's gourmet coffee percolated, Pablo set up his writing tray-table and rolled a few cigarettes. If she complained of him raiding her beloved beverage, he could offer her three or four tailor-made cigarettes from the pack he bought once a month and kept in a generic airtight sandwich bag to keep them fresh.

Hector, with hopeful and determined innocence, said, "Last night mom said we can get cable TV soon."

Pablo replied, "Your mother says a lot of things." Without adding the thought: That doesn't make her the Word of God.

"Yeah," Hector said, scooping a mouthful of cereal to hide his enthusiasm. Lately his papa seemed to take a curious delight as audience to Hector's extravagant imaginary spending, only to bluntly say 'No' when Hector was certain victory was at hand. Hector swallowed, then asked, "When can we afford it?"

"As soon as we balance our credit we can afford more debts," he replied; and when his heavy sarcasm had no visible effect, he added, "Counting reincarnation, that'll be four or five lifetimes." Pablo saw crestfallen Hector and said, "Oh, that's right: I'm supposed to give energy to your wishes and that'll make them come true. Okay, I'll do that as long as you don't start saying prayers for more goddamn channels." He looked at the screen Hector had tuned in and said, "The little blocks sure are appearing this morning. Maybe each one leads to its own scene and if you trail it back to the source you'll find God."

Hector concentrated on the screen for a moment to see if that was true, then commented, "Mom said the government sold all the airwaves. Is that why I see ghosts?"

"Could be. As long as they're nice, don't tell anyone. If they turn nasty, we'll take you to the health clinic."

Pablo read the last two journal entries he'd written the past week and muttered, "All reruns." He turned to Hector and said, "Beat it, knucklehead, and get ready for school."

Pablo read a short chapter of Sinclair Lewis's *Babbitt,* and with new material in Pablo's mind, he decided to make a quick journal entry to be expanded when he had more time; but as he wrote, ideas flowed and a vague resentment grew that he didn't have two hours of privacy. He had learned to use epigrams for his journal from a novel he liked to think of as the slackers' *Bible,* the lead character much more interesting than Ignatius of Loyola and his foundation, The Society of Jesus. Pablo scribbled furiously, hoping to get as much down as possible to be reformed later from its golem-like state with only a dysfunctional trickle of consciousness:

Tell me, Muse, of the man of many ways, who was driven far journeys, after he had sacked Troy's citadel.

-Homer *Odyssey* I: 1-2

She went to consult the Lord, and he answered her: "Two nations are in your womb, two peoples are quarreling while still within you; but one shall surpass the other, and the older shall serve the younger."

-*Genesis*

When I had journeyed half our life's way,
I found myself within a shadowed forest,
for I had lost the path that does not stray.
Ah, it is hard to speak of what it was,
that savage forest, dense and difficult,
which even in recall renews my fear:
so bitter- death is hardly more severe!

But to retell the good discovered there,
I'll also tell the other things I saw.

-Dante Alighieri *Inferno* canto I: I-9

Chorus: Two households, both alike in dignity,
In fair Verona, where we lay our scene,
From ancient grudge break to new mutiny,
Where civil blood makes civil hands unclean.
From forth the fatal loins of these two foes
A pair of star-crossed lovers take their life...

-William Shakespeare *Romeo and Juliet* Prologue 1-6

Ghost: Now, Hamlet, hear.
'Tis given out that, sleeping in my orchard,
A serpent stung me. So the whole ear of Denmark
Is by a forged process of my death
Rankly abused. But know, thou noble youth,
The serpent that did sting thy father's life
Now wears the crown.
Hamlet: O my prophetic soul! My uncle!
Ghost: Ay, that incestuous, that adulterate beast,
With witchcraft of his wit, with traitorous gifts-
O wicked wit and gifts that have the power
So to seduce! - won to his shameful lust
The will of my most seeming virtuous queen.

-Shakespeare *Hamlet* I, 5: 35-47

It's like being in Vichy France during the Nazi Occupation of World War II when the German high-command looted museums and private art-collections because Nazi culture was so poorly crafted even its perpetrators were weary of it; we're hostages to the very forces that destroyed the global economy through manipulation of mortgage funds by high-finance institutions, and can only prevent utter ruin by caving in to their demands, which will soon include no government regulations of current or future schemes and scams. Yet if Obama and Georgie Bush Junior had not hired- at exorbitant wages- the architects of the financial disaster to fix it, they would have gladly and capriciously pulled the world's structure down, then used their fortunes to resurrect it in their own images; so American taxpayers borrowed from China to bail-out global conglomerates, which could inspire a conjecture those world corporations now owe more allegiance to China. That's when Georgie Bush Junior became unpopular: he could've waged all the insane wars he wanted, but by god don't mess with our personal finances. He went from a ninety-three percent approval rating in the polls to seventeen, which is about the percentage of eligible voters who supported him in the 2000 elections.

America wasn't hit as badly as other nations whose elite oligarchs were foolish enough to invest in the scams and now find social revolutions and outright civil wars rocking their countries, particularly in the Mideast and North Africa, where the Muslim fundamentalists are better organized than the more liberal parties. It's easier to form a group if everyone is on the same page of a Holy Book. However, even nations like Greece have fascist politics, especially in regards to the influx of immigrants fleeing civil wars. Italy certainly doesn't desire another Hannibal from Carthage, Libya invading their territory. He may have been the enemy the Romans loved to hate, and it did focus their attentions from massacring each other, as was proof that once Hannibal was gone the fasces came out and whipped on the people to choose their dictators. Not much of a choice: war at home or abroad. After Georgie Junior invaded Afghanistan and Iraq, the fundamentalist Muslims also took their shows on a world tour, and the next thing we knew, we're bombing and arming so many different peoples it reads like Plutarch's histories wherein everyone switches sides according to ambition, wealth, supplies, and munitions. Choosing one's hate to purchase and consume has become a lucrative trade, with about as much sincerity as I showed on hangover mornings when I had to apologize to Hector and Estella, promising to never do it again.

If we are liberated, will we turn on bank-tellers as collaborators with the high-finance institutions like the French publically humiliated Nazi-lovers by shaving their hair off and marking their foreheads with swastikas to be reincarnated as Manson Family girls chanting and singing outside the courtroom where their cult leader was being tried for attempting to instigate a racial revolution? The dopey popular-cult songs The Family read deep meaning into, helping to inspire their ambitions (like a soundtrack to the Cause), are now being carefully studied and analyzed by academicians being paid to teach America's youth the secret Biblical-like codes of throwaway tunes. We'll soon have four successive generations with the mentality of the murderous 1969 Charles Manson protégés, only the former will be in charge of nations and corporations; cults are easier to control when they're institutionalized. Just ask Manuel Noriega about how he was bombarded by vociferous stupid ballads from American troops while he took sanctuary in a Roman Catholic church. Panama's president learned a hard lesson from dope-dealing with a member of the Bush Family.

I prefer representing myself, despite my sometimes crafted contrary images; but Americans are obsessed with acting, probably since the early colonists dressed as Indians to dump English tea into the harbor; and the British have always loved pageantry from Shakespeare to modern royalty. As a culture, we inherit or invest in roles that become variations of tradition, yet are considered unique and original as new products to be consumed. There is something in us that compels collaboration. It behooved Julius Caesar to go deeply in debt to creditors so as to afford theater rites and coliseum games for the public, thereby winning their utmost support, which furthered Caesar to his destiny as emperor. Perhaps I worry too much about my audience, yet what do I hope to gain by pandering to any of them? Or do I wish to be an oracle?

George Babbitt, a booming 1920's real estate leaser, believed in the order of industrial accouterments of convenience and status trophies. Did his creator, Sinclair Lewis, envision the forthcoming Great Global Depression of the 1930's which would help spark World War II? Babbitt was a sort of Achilles- I think *Babbitt* was published the same year as James Joyce's *Ulysses*- who loses his best friend and tries to go solo, despite the counsels of a poet, who wrote commercials for various consumer items, and another crony named Vergil.

However much modern critics denigrate American television programs of the 1950's, I keep in mind that it was a new medium and the confident elation of recently defeating the Nazi Empire of Entropy was something to be mass-produced. The audiences of those programs didn't call the shows art, unlike our era wherein people are so heavily invested in escaping the third-dimension that they feel obligated to defend it by calling it genius. They're like a mass of conscious unconsciousness waiting to be exploited and aimed at the enemy of the hour.

A quote from a speech by President Franklin D. Roosevelt, "We must be the great arsenal of democracy." Order is presented to different sections of populations, and depending on investments, new traditions rise and fall. Perhaps Americans do not consider that their taxes create the neo-wealthy in other, unstable, nations which can only maintain their pseudo-democracies through munitions; or, worse, believe we can buy enough loyalty that the new-rich in those nations will not mind taking the kind of risky chance President Ngo Dien Diem of South Vietnam did; though even Hamid Karzai of Afghanistan, who has bought as much trouble as he can with Americans' money, is realizing we might have him killed if he doesn't play the schizoid role we've fit him and his family with and are funding like a badly-made Hollywood project, which entails making foes of his countrymen. The new-rich in other countries realize this, at least if they're half-smart they do, so the money we throw at them they kick-back to buy our politicians (and corporate support) especially around campaign election seasons.

It can be too much for people to study closely and realize what makes up the new traditional packages and to what destination the vaunted visionaries are guiding their followers; especially in a frenetic-paced society where milk and honey are promised right around the corner if people hurry enough instead of vacillating due to inherited obstinacy. Yet since the "old ways" are perpetually resurrected in new guises, why not stubbornly hold onto aged traditions until they're popular again? Stick around long enough and one can be the craftsman (or woman) who is ahead of the crowd, and therefore hailed as a genius.

Even Josef Stalin is popular in Russia again, and he was Georgian, like Alexander the Great was Macedonian, not Greek; or Napoleon was Corsican, not French, and Hitler was Austrian, not German. Barak Obama's foes are still saying he was born in Africa, not America. Of course the Jews' mythical Moses was only adopted by Egyptian royalty (with the irony being the Jews adopted much Egyptian culture).

The Mideast nation of Dubai is now adopting global conglomerates (and their incestuous subsidiary bastards), like Dick Cheney's oil business, Halliburton; the incentive is Dubai does not tax Great Corporate Houses. Aaron Burr failed in his propaganda blitz in trying to get America to adopt Mexico by force, but Cheney succeeded in destroying Iraq's infrastructure, which America slunk away from after Halliburton moved to Dubai and people realized the war in Iraq wasn't going to pay for itself in oil, which is instead sold to China. Who will Karl Rove remold like a gold calf in America's next major election for a mass exodus of corporations to new promised lands?

Pablo stopped writing when Estella and Hector emerged from the short hallway, ready to leave. She kissed Pablo on the crown of his head, saying, "I cleaned the bathroom so don't make a mess."

"I'm not sitting down to pee."

Hector quickly aped, "Neither am I."

"I'm not asking you to," she said; "I just asked to keep it clean. I scrub enough toilets at the dorms. Give me the EBT card so I can buy lunch."

"I thought we were going to brown-bag it the rest of the month."

"I didn't have time to make lunch this morning."

He took out his wallet and handed her the card, saying, "We only got ten bucks left on it and we need rice."

"I'll pick some up on the way home. Have a good day. Don't be late for work because of your brain-child."

After farewells, Pablo took a quick shower, wondering if it was worth arguing about hot water rights in the household. As he dressed, the landline telephone rang and he hoped it was *Mood Food* either offering more work hours or giving him the day off because business was slow. A four-and-a-half hour shift seemed pointless torment and ruined most of the day.

"Hello?"

"Hey dummy, I just called your cell-phone and Stella started yelling at me, 'Who is this?' Fortunately, I have your apartment number memorized."

"Hi, Simon. Sorry I didn't warn you about that. She only let me tell a few people about her taking over the cell-phone."

"Why'd she claim it?"

"She said I use too many minutes."

Simon laughed, "Well, that's new: a chick telling a guy he's on the phone too much."

"The real reason is she's trying to encapsulate me and Hector away from you renegades."

"It's cheaper than having another baby."

"Where are you?"

"Sioux Falls," Simon said. "Can you make it here tonight?"

"I don't know. It's kind of tight around here for gasoline; and it's her car. Her brother gave it to us."

"Just tell her I'll pay for gas."

"Well, to be honest with you, Simon-"

"Oh, no: here it comes."

"I was trying to be diplomatic. I have to live with her and I don't want to deal with the stuff between you two."

Simon said, "Listen, stupid, this is serious merde. I know all about Stella and that's why I'm not coming there. But this is a family matter that can't be talked about over the phone."

"Oh." Pablo hesitated. "Then I suppose it's too sensitive for an e-mail."

"What're you going to do? Go to the library to read it?"

"Yeah."

"Great," Simon said, "and while you're there you can e-mail the covert agencies my last known address, which they probably already have. *Athena's* at six tonight. I got business there so I can wait an hour or so."

"Okay," Pablo said. "If I can't make it, I'll call."

2 Hunting the Predators

Pablo walked into *Athena's* and immediately felt conspicuous. He saw Simon at the bar, walked over and said, "Let's get out of here."

"Why?"

"Come on." Simon shrugged and slid off the stool. He followed Pablo, who muttered, "Christ, you deserve to get busted, doing your business in a place like this. In case you haven't noticed, this passes for sophistication in South Dakota among white folks."

One of whom brushed by Pablo and shouldered into Simon. Simon's reaction was fast, "Watch it, you turd-headed mook."

The offender returned and stepped close to Simon without touching him, and said, "Did you say something?"

"What, you got sauerkraut in your ears?"

"You want to tangle, let's go. Only I should warn you I know karate."

"Yeah," Simon said, "and I know your sister in the Biblical sense. What of it?"

Pablo knew better than to get between them, and watched from the door as the bartenders dispersed the brewing brawl.

"Geez," Simon laughed as he went into the warm April evening with Pablo, "I forgot this city is run by Nazis."

"They're Norwegian Quislings," Pablo replied. "All they want is business as usual. Where should we go?"

"Let's drive to a grocery store with a deli we can eat at."

"There's one down the street. Let's get a chicken and go to a park. I'm not getting into a car with you." They walked a few blocks and Pablo noticed something: a part of the scenic decorum was missing. They passed a liquor store and Pablo asked, "What happened to all the street-people?"

"Jail. Sonia told me after the safe-house was built the cops got federal funding, probably from Homeland Security in our War Against Terror, and used it to clear out the street-people, which means court for things like an open container of alcohol. If they don't show up for court or pay the fines, there're arrest warrants issued, and extra time in jail for expenses and warrants. They're learning the horrors of overcrowded jails for having terrorized the populace by panhandling for beer money."

Pablo asked, "What's the safe-house?"

"Right next to the jail the county built a place for the chronically homeless. There's cameras all over the joint, they serve jail-food there, and no one can enter another tenant's room. It's too depressing to think about, but at least it got Sonia's dad out of the gutter. Oh, by the way, she gave me a peace-pipe and some kinnick kinnick you can have."

"What're you talking about?"

"She's on a Native American kick," Simon said. "Clean and sober eight months and she's Mrs. Hiawatha. Her brother makes pipes, and there's an Indian art gallery that sells special smoke."

"It's not that synthetic dope is it?"

"No, it's all natural. She said not to use the pipe for my dope so I have no reason to keep it. Like, it's something spiritual or god knows what. You can have it and I'll tell her I lost it on my journey. She said there's some great art at the shop, too, though expensive."

"Hell, I can't even afford a comic book for Hector."

"Graphic novel," Simon said. "Catch up with the new lingo, Pablo. A few years without the Internet or TV and you'll turn savage."

"When are you leaving?"

"Heading east tonight. I only stopped to see Sonia and you, and take care of some business. Anyway, the pipe hasn't been blessed so you don't have to do the whole Four-Directions' ritual for a puff without being cursed. You still on the wagon?"

"Yeah," Pablo said. "Five years now."

"Good. Apparently, you're supposed to keep the pipe away from booze, so after I get drunk tonight, you can take it out of my car."

"You sound superstitious."

Simon nodded, "I've been around. Some of it's bull-merde, like when I wanted to be a priest. Bad karma can stockpile though, like overfilling the jails on petty ante charges so the legal system can brag about the wonderful job they're doing. All it does is make people mean and desperate. There's no vocation in being a desperado anymore with the computers linked around the world. Hell, I bet Rapid City would expedite an extradition from Malaysia on a public intox charge just to prove they could."

"So why are you still in the business?"

"For the money. We've made a lot of cash since you retired."

Pablo thought a moment, then said, "I don't want to be around you if you start boozing."

"I can wait."

Pablo tried to be reasonable, "But you're leaving tonight and you'll be drunk driving."

"I left my protégé at Sonia's. He'll drive."

"Oh, that's smart: two Hispanics with California license plates, one drunk and the other probably high, driving though the Midwest on an illicit business trip."

"Don't worry about it."

Pablo shook his head.

Simon bought a cooked rotisserie chicken, kettle potato chips, and cold soda, and they went to a nearby park they used to frequent. They sat at a picnic table and began to eat. Simon watched Pablo a moment, then said, "Do you remember that argument you had with Blatz?"

"What?"

"The English teacher. Over a book."

"Oh, *The Scarlet Letter.* Jesus, what made you think of that?"

Simon laughed, "You're the only one I know who thought the guy, the doctor who learned the dark stuff from Indians, did the right thing."

Pablo shook his head, "Oh, yeah: Chillingworth. I don't know if he did the right thing but it was the human thing. Americans think only good people should get vengeance. Actually, I kind of liked him until he repented."

"There's nothing as shameful as a person getting what he wants and being unhappy with it."

"Estella and I joined a computer site book-club when I first sobered up. I quit after 500 pages of *Anna Karenina*."

"Why's that?"

"She cheated on her husband, blamed him for not loving her with enough passion, then my audience got mad at me for understanding the husband wanting revenge. Yeah, he was a cerebral, officious ass, but she only stayed with him for his money and wealthy lifestyle." Pablo shrugged, and added, "There were some good farm-themes in the book about wealthy landowners not caring about anything except pleasure and prestige via quick, easy money, which I suppose was a sort of warning about the Russian Revolutions that took place some fifty years later; people won't put up with being sharecroppers in an industrial society as long as they will in an agrarian culture because there're too many temptations to play the Almighty of one's own *deus ex machina*. Driving past all the flooded farmland on the way here, it dawned on me how far out of touch we are with things as basic as food-supply."

Simon said, nodding approval, "I don't understand all your terms, but it's too bad you dropped out of college; you got a good head for things like revenge. I truly doubted you'd be able to stay sober and leave the business."

"My drinking and drugging got worse while we were losing the house and our jobs, which of course only multiplied our woes. Estella stayed with it, though. I mean, me. So now, when she wants me to toe-the-line, I usually go along with her."

Simon smiled, "Which means not making literary enemies, eh?"

"We had to give up the computer anyway." Pablo felt uncomfortable, so asked, "What's the big family matter you need to talk about?"

"You remember how broken-hearted everyone was about Henrietta disappearing?"

Pablo was surprised, and rocked back a little on the picnic-bench. "Yeah. It's not something to forget even if I wanted to."

"They found the people who did it. One of them, anyway: my cousin, your second-cousin, Rico Mendolza."

"What?"

"He was running a human trafficking business," Simon said. "You can't tell anyone. Not even Stella. The only reason I'm telling you is your dad helped get my grandma out of those massacres in Guatemala. So be on the watch."

"For what?" Pablo asked. "If they have Enrico, what do I have to worry about? Hell, I ain't seen him since I left California, and he's never met Estella or Hector."

"Hugo swore to wipe out that side of our family."

"Henrietta's dad?"

Simon nodded.

Pablo thought a moment, then asked, "Will he do it?"

Simon shrugged, "All I know is I'm tucking-tail and running. He ain't been right in the head ever, and those extended mandatory tours of duty in Iraq and Afghanistan didn't exactly make him better. He complains about it, but kept re-enlisting and wanted to make a career out of it, so what was the Army supposed to do?"

"No. This is all wrong."

"Isn't it, though?" Simon sighed. "Goes overseas to fight for a democracy women can vote in and comes home to this."

"Holy God. How could Enrico do such a thing?"

"Simple," Simon replied: "just snatched her off the street promising her candy or something."

"But...his own people."

"Terrible, isn't it? But you're a history-buff. You know people always start on their own before branching-out. If you can get the people closest to you to trust you, that's a base to build on."

"What about Henrietta?"

"No one knows," Simon said. He sniffed, then explained, "There's a lot of legal maneuvering going on. Plea deals and so forth. Rico might implicate everyone he's ever done business with."

"Yeah, but..." Words failed Pablo.

"We're all implicated," Simon said.

"How far back will they go?"

"Right to Original Sin when crimes flowed from one woman and man." Simon smiled and added, "The eyes of both of them were opened and they realized that they were naked."

Pablo became annoyed, "Cut the crap, Simon. His own niece. That's a helluva a lot worse than what we did. Or are you implicated?"

Simon wasn't irritated by the question, and replied, "Not in that. The rest, I don't know. That's why I left California and need to make some quick money to lay low."

"This is insane. The district attorney should know better than to fool around with stuff from almost six years ago. What the hell is he thinking?"

"She's part of a gung-ho task force bought by a group we don't know," Simon said. "All we do know is Asians invested in a bunch of global banks and high-finance institutions. They're moving a lot of stuff, and are smart enough to cover their proceeds with legitimate businesses that aren't just a mom-and-pop dry-cleaning shop. The officials like them because they aren't as hot-headed as Hispanics. Anyway, the district attorney wants to be imaged as an Untouchable, and we- unfortunately- are the modern Al "Scarface" Capone who are too stupid to hire Jews to handle our money."

"Yeah? Well, Eliot Ness got drunk one night after Prohibition ended and crippled someone in a car-crash."

"Did he?" Simon asked. "I didn't know that. Problem is, right now we got nothing on her. She came out-of-the-closet last year and now everyone praises her for being an honest lesbian. She'll probably write a how-to manual on how to be a queer public official. If you're going to come out-of-the-closet, might as well make a profit and call it an art-form."

Pablo laughed despite his agitated emotions. He nodded and said, "According to Plutarch, the ancient Greeks did that too, and were as greedily treacherous about turning on allies and breaking the peace as anyone else. It's like America's fascination with homosexuality has them think, perhaps due to screens' subliminal messages, that queers and lesbians are campy and honest, but the truth is, put a bugger in charge of an army brigade and he'll attack anyone, especially if his bleeding hemorrhoids are stirring up a mean mood."

"That's just it," Simon said: "we don't even know who owns her. The Asians sure as hell won't tell us."

Pablo shook his head in frustration, saying, "I don't need this. Both Hugo and Enrico? You didn't tell anyone you were coming here, did you?"

"A clean get-away, except for my apprentice, who blooded for me. They have Rico somewhere in seclusion. As he's talking, the Caesar will try to wipe out everybody Rico can trace back to the chiefs."

"Us," Pablo said. "And Hugo?"

"He tried to get mental disability from the Army but they said he might have had a pre-existing condition so he has to wait. I don't know how he's supposed to support his family. Maybe he can join a gang because if he gets a job, even as a gas-monkey to keep serving Halliburton, it would prove he's not disabled. The last I heard, three weeks ago, he walked off the job as a convenience store clerk; said reading the gasoline-gauges gave him combat flashbacks." Simon smiled, and said, "Irony is, he's one of the few of our childhood group who stayed legit. Well, mostly, if you can call drinking rum like a fish being legit. Now he's gunning for his relatives who were in the business."

"How deep in our family line is he going?"

Simon shook his head, "I haven't slept in two days. Everything I told you can be suspect, except the stuff about Rico selling us out and Hugo's madness. Oh, and being out-bid on the D.A. and her task force." Simon was quiet, then said, "I like you, Pablo. You were smart enough not to get blooded, at least as far as I know, and got out with a wife and son. You knew how to invest, well, not so much with the house, but you know what I mean. You should stay with Stella's...what was it? Encapsulation. Finish your college degree. Hell, that was supposed to be your way of staying legit, and now you're slinging hash."

"I work at the counter."

"Hashish or hash: not much of a choice. Come on," Simon said. "I want to see Sonia. I'll give you that peace-pipe and we'll go our ways, unless you want to meet some of Sonia's friends."

"No thank you."

Simon tossed the supper's remnants in a nearby garbage can. "Too bad," he said; "these Lakota women are like little earth-mothers. Ours have gotten too civilized."

"Is there anything else I should know?"

"How much do you want to know?"

Pablo considered a moment, then said, "Enough to protect myself and my family."

"We're all family, Pablo," Simon said, and began walking away. Pablo followed, resisting the urge to try and force his cousin from nebulous vagaries, because in Simon's way he wanted to keep Pablo from information that could be dangerous. Simon seemed to understand Pablo's frame of mind, and the former said, "Don't bother going to the library and looking it up on computer. They're keeping the story out of the Internet and news corporations until the task force makes the arrests. It won't save your life to know this, but maybe you can find some consolation in knowing Rico had no intention of going this far. He got involved with some dope cartels outside of our business and invested in heroin from Afghanistan. Most of the money was from buyers in America, then the poppy crop got blighted by... Well, hell, at this point it doesn't matter whether global pharmaceutical conglomerates did it or a green man from Mars who's pushing his own brand of grok. What does matter is Rico was deep in debt and was offered a way out by human trafficking."

"But we're nobodies. Just small time street stuff. Lieutenants at most, but just soldiers. Why would the Tsar worry about our family?"

"Some of us were promoted a few years ago because of our expertise. Well, that and some of the warlords had to leave America."

Pablo felt sick; he hadn't considered his old business relations to be upwardly-mobile. "What happened to the Diazo family?"

"All gone," Simon said; "and we took their places. Me, Rico, Antonio, Miguel, Ivan. What a name for a kid caught between the crossfire of suspected crazed Commies and democratic death-troops."

"I don't remember him."

"Well, he might remember you. Especially if asked by Torquemada." Simon hocked up snot and spit, turning his head so the phlegm sailed in the wind. "They got some real brutes that our former Attorney General would admire. One guy, just mention his name to who you're questioning and they'll tell you anything you want to know."

"Alberto Gonzalez as a role-model, eh?"

Simon laughed, "We Hispanics sure can pick them."

Family members had taken to calling themselves Hispanics since enlisting in Caesar's forces; it bothered Pablo but he saw no point in correcting racial terminology. Since his own past had been demolished and swept away, he found solace in others' histories and tried not to take a dim view of people's disinterest or reinvention of chronological occurrences. "And we can't get to Enrico?"

"Nope. And he's willing to sacrifice all of us. The whole idea of bringing a family into the business is to make it tight, so no one rats because of reprisals against loved ones. All of which is like the quantum theory that ran the global mortgage trade; and right now, I'm giving myself a bail-out."

"What about the others?"

Simon shrugged, "I didn't want to kill them just to prove I'm loyal to Caesar. They're on their own, just like us."

"I meant your wife and kids."

"Them too." Simon stopped abruptly and glared at some shrubbery moving softly in the breeze. "Just as I suspected: no God blessed ram there to sacrifice in place of my lineage."

"Jesus, you scared me," Pablo said, glancing around.

"I suppose Hugo feels even worse than me. The Tsar's men took Antonio into a room with Miguel tied to one chair and Antonio's wife to another. They said if he killed Miguel, Tony and his wife could live but only as outcasts, and have to leave the country. If he killed his wife, he and Miguel would be put somewhere safe until this is over."

"What happened?" Pablo asked.

"I've thought a lot about what our family went through in Guatemala. Scientists did studies with lab rats and discovered if they made a momma rat dysfunctional and not care about her pups, when those rats had their own offspring, gene-tags were passed along that made them not care about their ratlings. Does that answer your question?"

"I wasn't in Guatemala very long. When my dad went back to fight against...well, everyone who had it coming, my mom stayed with us. There was no right or wrong. I'm convinced America trained and sent in the death-troops, but adopted us when we came to the promised land."

"Schizophrenia is congenital too."

Pablo ignored the remark, and said, "So business settled in a way that the University Estella works at has athletic coaches who have logo apparel contracts with corporations that send the work to Guatemala sweatshops; at least until the conglomerates pack it in and move to China, which leaves the Guatemalans out of work so they'll come here and one will get Estella's job at a lower wage."

"What does she do there?"

"I don't know her official title but she's a janitor. We need the insurance package she'll get next year," Pablo said. "Actually, Sioux Falls is quite progressive when it comes to taking in immigrants and refugees, funneled in for the right price. There might be more Muslims showing up because of what's going on in Pakistan, Yemen, Afghanistan, etcetera."

Simon grunted and said, "I've come to believe America's military wants an all-out World War III. That's what their system and equipment is primed for, and it obviously isn't working in that long list of nations you just rattled off."

"I told Estella something like that a few months ago. Our troops there rely on natives' information, so a Taliban guy has a score to settle with a rival, for business or personal reasons, and calls in an American drone airstrike that blows up a Muslim wedding party. Or maybe he just wants to prove he can get the Americans to serve his every whim, like Aladdin commanding genies."

"It doesn't look good onscreen, does it?" Simon said.

"Well, hell no. But in a major World War III attack, such a thing wouldn't even be in the news. Carpet-bombing cities would be acceptable then, so one strafed and incinerated party at a village in a remote mountain region would get less media attention than Afghanis becoming addicted to foreigners' pharmaceutical brands because the opium crop has been destroyed, and who the hell could live in a warzone for twelve years and not want some kind of escape from reality?"

"I can imagine the stress they're under," Simon said. "If hostilities break out between China and America, our more patriotic corporations might return here, because by then all the trade and labor unions will be broken and cheap workers will be available, which will cripple China's economy; like what happened in Japan when America started hauling-ass out of their islands in the 1990s."

"Difference is, Japan didn't have a military except what we forced on them. Thanks for the dinner," Pablo said, "and the peace-pipe."

"Unfortunately, it's every man for himself from here on out." He shook hands with Pablo and said, "Good luck finding a scapegoat."

3
The Patronage of the Snopes'

Two nights later, as Estella and Pablo prepared for bed, she watched him from the doorway to the bathroom as he brushed his teeth. When he had finished and rinsed, he said, "It's revolting, all of us using the same tooth-glass. When was the last time it was washed?"

"I'll take care of it," Estella said. "Let's go into the living room. I don't want Hector eavesdropping."

"He can hear us from there, too. These walls are made of corrugated cardboard and genuine composite sawdust. They're so thin I think they were manufactured in China. Good thing we don't live in an earthquake zone."

"Never mind," she said as they sat together on the sofa. She had pointedly shown no interest in Pablo's trip to Sioux Falls, so he was surprised she asked, "How did your visit go with Simon?"

"There're things you shouldn't know, Estella, but it didn't go well."

"Did you make any money?"

"He bought dinner and gave me gasoline money."

"You know what I mean."

Pablo's voice lowered to edginess, "I know what you're saying, Estella, and I'm telling you no."

"Oh."

He peered at her in the dim light of the low-watt bulb, and said, "You sound disappointed."

"They told me today they're cutting my hours."

Pablo absorbed, then said, "I thought you were at the top of the list."

"They said it was a clerical error. I won't even be able to draw unemployment benefits unless I fight the University. They said maybe I can get some hours during their sports' camp."

"Oh, that's great," Pablo said without vehemence. "They'll dish-out money for professional athletes to make appearances and we're lucky if you get to clean up after them."

"What're we going to do?"

"I don't know."

"Could Simon help us?"

"He can't even help himself," Pablo said, and sighed. He didn't mention Rico turning snitch and the likelihood of Pablo being put on the authorities' watch-list. "It's bad, Estella. Really bad."

"But your old connections. I mean, I met someone today who can move it for us."

"What're you talking about?" Pablo blinked and rolled his once-mighty shoulders. "You want to do that?"

"Well, no; but maybe just for the summer. If I don't fight the University, they'll give me hours again and not try to get rid of me."

"Where'd you meet this person?" Pablo asked.

"In the student union pub. The maintenance guys closed our break-room for the day to clean it, so I went to the pub for lunch. It was crowded so he sat at my table."

"What's his name?"

"I forgot," Estella said. "His nickname is Ras, from some Russian novel."

"Raskolnikov," Pablo laughed. "*Crime and Punishment.* You had lunch with a wannabe superman who's too stupid to hide his alter-ego."

"Anyway, he's as desperate for money as we are. He had food pantry charity potatoes he cooked in the pub's microwave oven, and then piled on condiments from the salad buffet."

"Well, we're not that desperate yet."

Estella became more animated but not convincing. "He's graduating in a few weeks and wants to make some money to leave town. Everyone will be celebrating the end of the school year, and he knows buyers."

"What's his major? Pharmaceuticals?"

"He said something about computer graphics."

Pablo shook his head, "Will his degree have printed on it: 'High-tech Coloring Book Artist'?"

"This is serious, Pablo," Estella said. "Can you at least talk to the guy?"

"I'm getting paranoid just listening to your crap," Pablo said, staring into her eyes until her gaze dropped. He lit a cigarette, puffed a moment, then said, "Don't you find all these coincidences oddly arranged? And none of it is to our benefit. Everyone in this city serves the interests of the University corporation, legitimate or otherwise. When I stopped dealing, one of my old connections tried to get me back in the business; then he turned state's evidence against all his associates: turns out the college and the cops were compiling a long list of names through him, which miraculously didn't include me. Just think of all the tax-free money the University and cops got by dealing through him."

"I don't think they're that corrupt," she said quietly.

"Don't make me call you naive or stupid, Estella. You think all the interference and nosiness by college officials is somehow benevolent. But it's not. The only reason schools came down hard on binge-boozing was to evade lawsuits from upset parents whose idiot eighteen-year-old did twenty double-shots of pure grain alcohol and choked to death in barf. It's not compassion or kindness that motivates colleges." He shrugged, then his voice became more emphatic. "Why would I trust a business partner who goes to college to be poor? He can't even afford goddamn potatoes. Let me enlighten you some: they're trying to manipulate you into being a dope-dealer to get to a major pipeline, and they're saying they're doing it for your own good and because they love people. Just like what you're trying to do to me right now."

"I'm not doing that," she said, wiping her eyes.

"Then what are you trying to do? We can't even afford to move out of town right now. Even if we could, where would we go? We'll just have to take our lumps here."

"But if what you say is true, we can't trust anyone."

"Well, at least they won't be shooting at us," Pablo said, fatalistically. "We may be targets, but if we serve the University corporation in legitimate ways, maybe we'll be rewarded. For instance, that locally-owned liquor store near the campus: when a franchise grocery store announced plans to build a booze shop right across the street from the family-owned store, the president of the University said she opposed it, and the city wouldn't sell zoning permission. Do you really think she did that for the students? Geez, three months later she showed how much she cared about them and the city by taking a better paying job at a more prestigious school."

"What're you saying?"

"That maybe we can earn legitimate protection too if we don't get on their hit-list."

Estella shook her head, "You make it sound so corrupt it hurts."

"That's because it is," Pablo defiantly said. "Anything can be legalized or criminalized, Estella. When Hillary Clinton campaigned as a presidential nominee, she couldn't even bring herself to say she made a mistake supporting Georgie Bush Junior's invasion of Iraq based on warped intelligence from covert agencies, not even after the massacres of Iraqi civilians by mercenaries America hired to do blood-work; then Obama rewarded her with an appointment as Secretary of State to find a way to have America slink out of Iraq. That's her version of what it takes to make a village using "smart" power: leaving behind a fractured provisional government and taking with us a huge national deficit. It's somehow appropriate she ended up with brain damage, a mongoloid version of Thomas Aquinas's intelligent potency. Kind of like Ronald Reagan jinxing himself by saying, 'I don't remember' once too often regarding his Administration's schemes and scams so towards the end he didn't even know he was president. Well, he's in heaven now: ignorance is bliss."

"You think women are as corrupt as men."

"Yeah, but they're better at making self-image facades of nurturing through business." Pablo smiled, "Sometimes they're so good at it they even fool themselves."

She leaned against his shoulder and he put his arm around her. She said, "It sounded like a good idea at the time, though I'm sorry I even suggested it."

"You're not Lady Macbeth," he said.

"Now I know why people go into even deeper debt: they hope to buy vacations from money woes."

"Those escape routes certainly get offered often enough," Pablo said. "Remember when you stopped by our bank last December to get a free calendar and the teller said you had to see a banker and do a survey of our account?"

Estella laughed and said, "We had $20 in the account, $8 in quarters for laundry, and 38 cents in Food Stamps and the banker was trying to convince me to buy a house, or at least a car, with a credit card he offered. He was some young guy who was probably about eighteen-years-old when the global economy was ruined, and had no history of it while in college getting drunk every weekend. I think he didn't even look at his computer screen with all our humiliating information on it. If we couldn't afford a calendar, what made him do a sale's pitch to me for buying a house?"

"They also target the disabled," Pablo said, "because bankers and creditors know the disabled get a monthly check from the government. Besides it being morally reprehensible to prey on the mentally ill, it encourages financial irresponsibility."

"At least the crazies can't say they're discriminated against; they have the same opportunities to ruin their finances as everyone else."

Estella cheering up made Pablo glad they'd reconciled, albeit through finding an enemy in common, so he said, "It's easier to purchase respectability now that most of the objective study of history has been sentenced to death. That banker-fellow in Sioux Falls made predatory loans to low-income people at usurious rates; as soon as the Federal Exchange Commission threatened a government investigation into his loan-sharking, he sold the bank, bought a hospital and put his name on it and a coliseum featuring geriatric rock-n-rollers and ice-skating shows based on entertainment conglomerates' bad cartoons, spending a fortune on advertising."

"Oh," Estella said, "like that British television series, *Middlemarch*, I got from the library. The one you and Hector weren't going to let me watch until I threw a fit."

"Well, geez, Estella, as if we wanted to see 19th century provincial Brits in a mini-series. I couldn't even understand them half the time. You should've just read the book: it'd have been easier for all of us."

"Not for me," she replied; "it was too long. I'd seen about everything else. How many times can I watch the Ku Klux Klan ride to the rescue?"

"It's no worse than the Black Muslims; and they were Night Riders, not officially Klan members."

Estella asked, "Who's going to ride to our rescue?"

"The Four Horsemen of the Apocalypse," Pablo said. "They're due any day now. It's amazing to watch the media try to conjure them. The same day the government announced budget cuts in Food Stamps and low-income subsidies, they also said they'd throw money at Egypt's Islamist military government, which will use our funds to buy American weapons made in China." Pablo laughed, "Then, the same weekend, America and our allies did military strategic maneuvers off the coast of China and North Korea; but what really makes the media worry is China uses all the computer stuff they sell to Americans to spy on us."

"Well, China does censor its media."

"Exactly," Pablo said, "but look at the crap in our media. Is it worth fighting for?"

"We owe them a lot of money, too," Estella said. "Maybe provoking or inventing an attack by China would be easier than paying them back."

Pablo shrugged, "That was the Nazis' attitudes about reparations after World War I when the global economy was wrecked in the 1920's and 30's. They succeeded in getting other Germans to agree bread, work, and community spirit was the way up and out, which of course eventually led to war. We've got Food Stamps, and if the screen worlds don't blink-out people will have jobs, so it only makes sense for Obama to wage war by covert agencies pushing buttons because that's where our communal consciousness is: no one is alone anymore in our society."

"You always feel like you're being herded somewhere."

"It's due to a lack of choices, and I don't mean between different brands of peanut butter or cell-phones." Pablo sighed, "I could go back to college and a student loan would keep us off the streets, but we'd have to pay it back and what would I do with a degree in history but teach?"

"You don't want to do that?"

"The only way I could is to will my way through, and we both know how reasonable I am when functioning solely on will power."

Estella laughed, "You become the antithesis of a superman."

Pablo glanced at her, "Did I tell you that one?"

"You mentioned it when you were reading the philosopher the Nazis loved."

Pablo hugged her close, then pushed her away and said, "It was kind of funny in a pathetic way. He raved about how will power can function great without any kind of…input or potency; like doing the same thing over and over again, then giggle at the destruction and reconstruction of eternal reruns."

Estella nodded, "Hector laughs at all the sitcoms he's seen a hundred times. I don't know how to get him to stop imitating them, so I said we'd get cable TV to expand his repertoire."

"Was it a promise?"

"Kind of. That was before I found out about my summer hours being cut."

"Well, little Hector is just going to have to will his way through books instead. I'll take him to the library tomorrow." Pablo leaned to kiss her and she shifted her face downwards. He sighed and asked, "Should I sleep on the sofa tonight?"

"You'd better. I'm ovulating."

They kissed goodnight, and after fiddling a bit on the sofa, trying to not feel humiliated about being unable to share the bed with his wife, Pablo got up and smoked a few puffs of kinnick kinnick from his peace-pipe. Despite Estella's sincerest defense that she followed Roman Catholic dogma, Pablo felt certain her dislike of contraceptives was due to the effect they had on her body. To distract himself, he wondered about the Jews in the entertainment industry, and felt self-righteous in his critique of a movie from the library he and Estella had watched the previous week. The same year Adolf Hitler ordered Nazi Germany to invade Poland and partition it with the Soviet Union, which started World War II, the movie the Nuris had seen won several major awards in the self-congratulatory system of Hollywood. The movie centered on America's Southern states' glory of traditional chivalry, real estate, political self-determination, and the importance of enslaving sub-humans, who can occasionally be shrewd, but need to be kept subservient for the good of social order.

Pablo thought of all the Jews involved with the movie: financing it, renting a studio to film it at, and directing it. Did they feel as though they rightly deserved the guild's gilt awards at the ceremony that was a decadent party of gold calf worship? How many Poles, including Jews, were killed that year by Nazis and Soviets, who likewise carefully structured propaganda shows of invented history for their respective citizens? How many nations is America currently bombing and/or arming? America's entertainment industry rarely lack villains, but are screen-worlds running out of plots based on rabid Islamic extremists receiving their comeuppance in various entertainments? They are as fictitious as the reasons invented for invading Iraq. Maybe we just don't know who are enemies are, so Hollywood has become more diversified in selling shows to audiences, not just making villains Nazis or racists, but also homophobes. In former eras, anyone who talked and looked different was considered a likely foe; technology has made at least the appearance of diversity convenient. Satan, loosely translated, meant enemy; and anyone outside the Hebrew tribes was demonized. Enmity towards enemies once spanned decades, like America versus Communism; social media forums have sped things to The Enemy of the Hour. Soon enough, everyone will have been demonized.

Pablo went to his writing tray:

"Indeed you may believe that he, the bird who lives on prey and terrifies all other birds, was always a feathered thing- but he was once a man. The spirit's bent and bias are so constant that even then he was ferocious, set on battles, always keen for violence. His name- Daedalion; and he was born, like me, of Lucifer, the one who summons Aurora and is, too, the last to leave the sky. I care for peace: tranquility and family have been most dear to me; but what my brother loved was savage war. He had a daughter, Chione... Mercury could not endure delay, and with his wand that brings on sleep, he touched the virgin's lips. That wand has too much force: the girl submits, in deep sleep, to his godly violence. Then, when night scattered stars across the sky, Phoebus [Apollo] approached in an old woman's guise; and from fair Chione he gathered more of those delights that had been reaped before by Mercury. Nine months had come, had gone; from seed that had been planted by the son of Maia [Mercury], shrewd Autolycus was born: a connoisseur of wiles and guiles, an heir who passed off black as white and white as black, he fully matched his father's art and craft; whereas Apollo's son (the birth was twin) was Phillamon, much famed for lyre and song."

-Ovid *Metamorphoses*

My father named me Autolycus, who being, as I am, littered under Mercury, was a snapper-up of unconsidered trifles.

-Shakespeare *The Winter's Tale* 4, 3: 24-26

Autolykos came once to the rich country of Ithaka, and found that a child there was newly born to his daughter... "My son-in-law and daughter, give him the name I tell you; since I have come to this place distasteful to many, women and men alike on the prospering earth, so let him be given the name Odysseus, that is distasteful."

-Homer *Odyssey* 19: 399-400; 406-409

When the time of her delivery came, there were twins in her womb. The first to emerge was reddish, and his whole body was a hairy mantle; so they named him Esau. His brother came out next, gripping Esau's heel; so they named him Jacob.

-*Genesis* 25: 24-26

He answered me: "Not man; I once was a man.
Both of my parents came from Lombardy
and both claimed Mantua as native city.
And I was born, though late, *sub Julio*,
and lived in Rome under the good Augustus-
the season of the false and lying gods..."

-Dante *Inferno* canto I: 67-72

I didn't have to go to my job this morning, so I spent the day gathering literary, though probably not literal, lineages of various ancient great Houses (epics, scripture, poetry, theater) looking for a homeland and me taking them in as a historian of dubious qualities, and not too pleased about his bad reputation. Perhaps Lucifer, the Morning Star, resented being outshone by the light he heralded, at least in this solar system, and decided to multiply and be fruitful for colonial purposes. Some begin with twins: one rascally,

33

and the other perhaps more dignified or at least not sinking to the level of stealing and conniving to further lineages and wealth's inheritance. Is this all I'll have to pass on to Hector?

To what do I aspire? Chione, mother of gods' twins, despite being a subspecies lived up to the pride of her grandfather, Lucifer, and said her beauty was greater than Diana's- virgin goddess of the hunt and moon- who promptly killed Chione. After she was slipped a date-rape drug by Mercury, Chione became the great-grandmother of Odysseus who became famous for his crafty wandering; when the Jews got back to the Promised Land from Babylon, they shaped the tales into holy scripture, brokering a deal with a desert deity to justify acts that were unjust; the Greeks were pragmatic about criminal deities, which the Jews learned from. Made in god's image, indeed: Jacob's daughter, Dinah, was raped by a non-Jew clan member who had his- and his entire tribe's- wand shortened through circumcision in preparation to unite with Jacob's family legally and religiously (property and land included). The chumps were all killed by Jacob's tribe while recovering from the painful operation. Medication time, boys... medication time. I never discovered if Dinah begot a line that her brothers killed the progenitor of. I know Diana was sister to Apollo and aunt to the sons of Chione. I suppose we're all born into the midst of family struggles, inner and outer.

The grand scale of culling the human herds is also a business with built-in temptations to image oneself as a scourge of god and leveler of karmic justice. Perhaps deities use opposing gods and goddesses to separate the chaff from the wheat, putting them to work, as it were, to purify their own system; and, in turn, having to be employed themselves in gaming other orders to liquidate the assets and do away with the bad stock. In other words, the Nazi deities were used by Yaweh to cull the Jews, and the Germans were culled for the Nazi gods by Christians, Communists, and other members of the Allied forces. To play god of all the systems would make one schizophrenic, but also be a temptation that, with the proper backup, would be appealing to someone who thrives on collecting others' ambitions and discontent at having to work within a system where there is not much hope for reward because they must pay their dues for having previously played lords of their own order and are more than willing to follow someone who promises them great things. Is it better to have people invent imaginary resentments, for instance a video game reward that is stolen by another player, than a global industry focused on murdering each other for the spoils of the planet like World War II?

Convenient Diversified Death

To form a political connection,
a young and ambitious Missourian
applied to Ku Klux Klan's racist schism,
who lynched blacks in devious plot or whim;
the recruit submitted enrollment fee,
but with spurning Rome's Church did not agree,
so was rejected by the Ku Klux Klan,
then became President Harry Truman.
He dropped atomic bombs so they could zap
the imperialistic yellow Jap;
despite racist howls to the contrary,
he integrated the military.
Patriotism fades, but franchise stores
shape equal death in corporate world wars.
People now select their own chosen folks
to dominate with or bear heavy yokes;
yet regardless of how we pray and laude,
a human's solemn oath does not bind God;
so please understand the battlefield curse:
the great can be killed by those who are worse.

4

God Told Me
To Do It

Hector tagged along as his papa browsed through the tiny Classics' section of the public library. Hector's knapsack was full of comics and young adult books, which Pablo had already censored, ruthlessly rooting-out those he considered brain-rotting entertainments.

"You know what I'm going to do instead of getting you a pet?" Pablo asked.

"No."

"I'll find you something to put your mind into as a companion that won't turd on the floor. Aren't I a good dad? Always thinking of others, that's me."

Hector wasn't too certain of those self-accolades but kept his opinion to himself. He sighed as his papa sifted through the tomes that looked thick and incomprehensible. The previous night, while Hector was watching television, his papa abruptly stood in front of the screen and said he was going to express more interest in Hector's education. Hector wasn't quite sure what that entailed, though he vaguely associated it with his school's library offering books about children who had two dads or two moms, which Pablo had seen broadcasted on the local news.

"Oh," Pablo said, "they've got H.P. Lovecraft. I might get that one for myself, though god knows why it's in the Classics' section. Ah, this is what I was looking for: a novel version of the *Iliad*. We'll wean you off this one until you're ready for more poetic translations."

Hector thought: Poetry? It can't be as good as the epic covering a year of chicken soup with rice. He had memorized that volume three years previous, and still recited it to himself sometimes as he laid in bed, waiting to get sleepy. He didn't express his doubts, yet his papa seemed in a cheerful mood, so Hector asked, "Can we get a movie, dad?"

"No." Pablo looked along the shelves, then said, "Come on. I want to check the computer and see if they have the *Bhagavad-gita*. If you do a good job of connecting all your buddhi to something other than a sing-a-long toothpaste commercial, we'll get you a movie next week." Pablo disliked using one-dimensional worlds as rewards and punishments, which had become a corporate trend complete with personal access to paradise states through passwords and secret codes. To Pablo, it really wasn't the younger generations' fault, because they didn't know any better, that the reward and punishment system was a complete mess; they were being raised by people who had been raised by a generation that rewarded and punished by allowing or taking away television and movie privileges. Pablo saw no point in raising his son to reward people in screen-worlds with flattering comments and pictures, and punish via videos of yakking in bed and gossipy rumors; yet at the moment, it was expedient to use a carrot to donkey Hector into some sort of progress his father approved.

"Dad, I can't read this stuff."

"I'm going to read it to you until you can go solo. Invite your buddies over and we'll make it a group effort."

Hector sadly watched other children who were getting all the things they wanted: even here at the library, where everything was free, his papa was being tight-fisted. Oh well, Hector thought: Maybe he's right and I'll end up smarter than everyone else and make more money than them and be able to boss them around. Though I won't be as mean as my dad, unless they make me mad.

Hector cheered up with that thought, and thinking of ways to punish malefactors who offended him, followed his papa to the religious/spiritual section of the library. Pablo hunted about, commenting, "If so many people know God, then why shouldn't they make some dollars from Its many good names? My sweet lord, they even have a volume of virtue by a former Drug Tsar. We won't get that one, though. We had conflicting business interests and he had the public on his side so I was out-numbered. Needless to say, I tried to avoid rendering unto his Caesar."

"What're you talking about, dad?"

"Something called the Drug Stamp. Maybe I'll write an historical autobiography some day and you can read it. Though I doubt a Falstaff with dope-induced violent paranoia would be humorous to most of my potential audience."

"But drugs are bad, aren't they?"

Pablo replied without looking at his son, "I'm doing my best not to give you mixed messages and make you neurotic, but you'll have to cut me some slack once in a while. I could probably match Georgie Bush Junior scoundrel-for-scoundrel in associations and business partners, though neither one of us rose to the occasion like Prince Hal; but at least I have the excuse of not inheriting a kingdom. Oh, here it is. Hare Krishna. Just remember, Hector, cartoons aren't the modern myths; at best, they're our era's folk-tales. It's hard to believe people actually pay to be advertised to, and pay even more to skip commercials, but the sooner you accept that, the sooner you can be free of burnt out cynicism. What I'm introducing you to are epics, some of which may have been based on folk-tales. At least the Hindus and the Greeks have the good sense not to call their epics scripture like the religions of Abraham do. What I'll read to you is part of an epic from India; and when you get older maybe you can study some Hindu scriptures yourself, their idea being it's something for the individual who's preparing to go beyond the scripted words on a page, so it really isn't meant for everyone. I suppose that's the right attitude but doesn't stop people from forcing it on others."

Hector nodded and stayed quiet. He didn't want a lecture, but could tell his papa was warming up to one; so Hector steeled his reserves and thought about school being let out for summer soon, and how he would spend the time with his friends.

"You see, son," Pablo said, "you have to learn to callous your mind without becoming too insensitive. As you go along in life, you'll find people who work and craft to get into your head to rule as kings or queens of pleasure and pain, and sometimes they mix those two. For instance, if you don't buy into all their notions of pleasure, they might- and probably will- become angry and resentful and resort to punishing you with pain."

"Like Mrs. Brown?" Hector asked.

"Exactly. Most people are craftier than your second-grade teacher was, but they can also act on whims like she did. She set up your buddy, Antony, as her kicking-board and was nice to him to lure him in and then turned vicious. He didn't know what he'd get from her, which is a hard way to live. So he rebelled. Maybe that was just his natural rascality, but it only made things worse for him and the entire class."

"She was mean to him, though, dad."

"I know she was, Hector. We don't talk about it now, but when you were much younger I was very cruel to you. And to your mom. That's why you should start trying to form your mind to be ready for senseless battles that try to control the mind through the senses."

Hector stayed quiet, then said, "I guess I follow some of what you say because we did a lesson on the senses in class last year, but we didn't...uh... go that deep."

"That's because they don't know what they're talking about and I do," Pablo said; then added, "Never mind that. My pride can go to extremes." He laughed, "Not only misguide myself, but any who are unlucky enough to follow."

"I don't think mom's going to like these books."

"She'll get over it. But you'll have to go to church with her and not complain."

"Is that the deal you made with her?"

Pablo tousled his son's hair and said, "Yep. You see, you're already caught in a battle and you figured it out right quick."

Hector didn't feel elated by his papa's praise; rather, Hector felt an abstract grudge that he was being used as a means in a game of faiths, and both sides were image-making through him, with him, and in him. Was Hollywood really so awful that his parents were trying to instill their own systems? Hector didn't think so. He hated it when his friends talked about programs and screen-games Hector had to abstain from due to Spartan economics. He desperately wanted his life and mind to be arranged like everyone else's, and sadly thought of how he was completely misunderstood. He tried to not blame his parents, but who else was at fault? Hector's mother and father seemed to want to make him feel guilty for his desire to conform, especially with his friends; but Hector was fairly certain he was not to blame for it. After all, during an argument between his parents, Hector once heard that Pablo had been part of a gang; or so Estella accused as an insult, which Pablo had not refuted. Antony was wild, but Hector didn't think his friend would become a gangster.

As for religion, Pablo seemed to believe God wasn't out to get him, but the professionals of various sects were, and they were dirty in-fighters capable of great mischief. Hector recalled what his papa once said regarding the Roman Catholic Church: 'They mess up a lot of people, which makes more souls to be saved. Keeps them in business.' He felt even worse scornful loathing towards politicians, which appeared unreasonable to Hector; yet despite Estella's moderating influence, Hector understood his father's obsession with following the money-trails behind the scenes, because so little of it reached Hector. He did not consider himself greedy, but did think he was greatly inconvenienced. It was a vague distinction which Pablo both encouraged and tried to curtail, depending on his mood and what Hector may desire at the given moment, which currently was self-pity.

"Dad, why are you doing this to me?"

"Aha," Pablo said, "just the question I was expecting. It ties in with what I want to start teaching you, and that's the questioning of your ambition-"

"Ambition?"

"Your motives for playing different character roles. Do you do it for rewards, or attention, or to distract yourself?"

"I don't know, dad. I just do it."

"Right," Pablo said. "And I understand that. But, for instance, your loyalty to your friends, which I know you have, can get you into a huge amount of trouble, just like patriotism can."

"Is this another 'think for myself' lesson?"

"Kind of," Pablo explained: "I'm trying to not talk above your understanding, and I don't want to tell you I'm doing this for your own good and you'll appreciate it later; or that you're doing it because I told you to, which would go against the whole point of it. You're old enough to start forming your own ideals and images beyond screen-worlds, and you may have to do some fighting to keep or evolve them."

"The last time I got in a fight I lost."

"Ah, but at least you gave him a black-eye and were smart enough not to fight on school property. Besides, that's a different kind of fighting, though it ties in with what I'm saying." Pablo paused in reflection, then said, "The characters in the books we're checking out have notions that gods and goddesses tell them what to do, and that's a very dangerous assumption, especially in a war. It happens nowadays too, and a lot of people get killed in fighting about whose god is bigger and better, or whose prayers are answered and whose denied. There're all sorts of names for it: Crusades, Jihads, Bans, Final Solutions. Americans tend to believe in vengeance by proxy, maybe that's so they can feel like gods themselves. Achilles's killing-spree in the *Iliad* is an exception; he wanted personal revenge, and actually it'd be wiser and safer to follow him into combat, in part because he did most of the work, instead of someone who's doing it on the advice of a prophet. That's not to say you shouldn't use foresight, especially when following a leader like Odysseus, who was kind of an Emperor Penguin on an ice floe pushing a buddy into the water to see if there were any sharks. You might admire their skill and craftiness but you could end up as a sacrifice to a monster. Come on, let's go get some popsicles."

"Are you trying to get me to question your authority?"

"Well you already do that anyway, Hector. I just want you to go to some peace beyond doubt."

"You get mad when I think I'm right."

"That's because you turn into a little righteous corrector without reason."

"I try to have reasons."

"But you don't have skilled reasoning," Pablo replied. "It's something to grow into from being arrogant when your mom or I thwart one of your desires, or want you to do something you don't want to do and you start running off at the mouth. I suppose some of it could just be laziness."

"Mom said you should get work doing construction."

"I'm too old for it. We built fantastic Mayan cities in Guatemala and I won't do it here in America. We've paid our dues for star-gazing at the ant-hill gods."

"Mom said it's because you're lazy."

Pablo laughed, "You're getting quite skilled at playing sides off of each other. Don't get too good at it or relish being an instigator or you'll find yourself eventually blamed for trouble you might not have even started, or done so long ago you can't remember it and wonder why you're being scapegoated."

"Will you come to church with us? It'd make mom happy."

Pablo smiled. "Now you're a peacemaker, eh? I'll skip the show. Jesus taught to mock and ridicule the wealthy and powerful, but I don't like making enemies of them, especially if they're in church: they may start imitating the Pharisees. One good thing about America is there are plenty of battles to choose from, though there's probably too much recruiting going on for all the factions. Perhaps that's part of working towards a kinder, gentler fascism to unite us under a bully who promises a singular vision thing."

"Dad," Hector asked, "didn't they make human sacrifices on those buildings in Guatemala?"

"It'd be like constructing an abortion clinic in a college town," Pablo said; then inspired added, "built for the progress of conveniently getting rid of an inconvenience that stands in the way of buying a piece of paper that qualifies a person to sit in front of a screen and communicate with shades in shady business deals. Sounds like a good idea for a paranormal movie: contacting one's aborted fetus via telecommunication."

"Aren't the Mayan cities deserted?"

"Maybe they got atomized by a neutron bomb: left the buildings standing and turned all the people to shadowy ashes. Probably done by astronaut deities because the Mayans were unraveling the secrets of the universe. Here's a little modern version: when I walked the two blocks to turn in the modem after we had to cancel our computer subscription, two smokers going into the eight-story building after their cigarette break asked what I needed. I said I wanted to talk with someone and return the modem. They said the building was empty and to telephone instead to get the right order number for the modem to be returned by their designated parcel service- which, by the way, was very expensive- and I realized they didn't want to deal with humans in the third-dimension. Maybe they're scared of a disgruntled customer going on a shooting-spree."

Hector thought a moment, then asked, "Does God really need that much blood?"

"That's how some people think It lives through us. Any service can be bought and used as a spy agency. Some might think it's a non-physical, white-collar crime, so it's victimless; but when it actualizes on earth, people like us are sent to do the fighting. The people in towers we built control us with a few buttons and we render unto them blood- preferably somebody else's, of course- and if we're lucky a messenger will arrive from them. Maybe we'll listen to his or hers advice about wars and how to deal with the folks in the towers; or if the messenger goes native with us, be encouraged by tower-commands to kill him or her."

"And make hero stories and shows about them."

"Form perfect messengers in our own messed-up images," Pablo said; "which is what I'm trying to teach so I don't end up living through you or you through me."

"Does that mean you'll quit writing about me and making up those songs?"

"Oh, you mean like the one I just invented. The little bumblebee, known as Hector, soars through the grace of soda pop nectar, which like the pollen of a rosy flower, spreads images and emboldens his power."

"Dad, do we sometimes hate God because we love It more than we do ourselves?"

Pablo laughed, "We're supposed to love It more, anyway, even if It might go against what we think we are. If we knew what we truly are, we probably wouldn't like ourselves very much in our present states, which easily leads to abstract resentments aimed at God. Why do you ask? Do you like hate me for singing odes to you and rigging a way to have your mom take you to church?"

"Kind of."

"Once more unto The Void." Pablo paused, then added, "I don't want to fight with you about it, Hector, but sometimes giving up a few of your desires can lead to better things."

"Oh, I don't feel crucified. I just don't like being used in struggles of character-building."

"We live in a world where everything is in motion, son," Pablo said. "I'll use even worse words: at work. The older generations use the younger to be trained consumers of the latest fashions, then wonder why the young have no honor or respect for the old. The young eventually learn being directed by a cause to an effect doesn't mean they'll always share in rewards. Even the best people and biggest heroes can have trophies taken away from them. One of the evils I've taught you, and probably inadvertently still am, which I hope you don't pass along, is how to betray trust."

"Even memories are better than nothing."

"What memories will you have from watching television? Do you want to live through actors and try to direct their lives or have them direct you?"

Hector smiled up at his papa and replied, "It's easier than thinking for myself. And we'll have shared memories."

Pablo rubbed Hector's head, "That's true, you little drone, you'll have it memorized from all the reruns."

"Just like Antony at the top-level of his video games." Which Hector diplomatically didn't mention was his personal ambition to achieve during summer afternoons at Antony's air-conditioned house.

Pablo was not beguiled, and said, "He's going to be so good at them he'll get bored and buy new games and you'll never catch up."

"He lets me practice on the TV while he's at the computer, then, when I'm at top-levels, we play against each other."

"Sort of like the gods of Olympus competing through humans. Well, I hope you'll find more depth in the characters of the *Iliad* than in cartoons randomly blowing things up."

"Oh, it's not random, dad. It takes a lot of practice to go up levels."

"Do your duty by it, I suppose, and chase after those imaginary power-token rewards." Pablo shrugged, "The king-maker, Karl Rove, would be proud of you. One of the lessons in a book we got is how to slash through never at peace or rest illusions. Which your generation will escape from because you'll all be blind from staring at screens, deaf from ear plug-in noise, won't be able to speak because languages have been mangled, and of course your hands will be numb from the button-pushing control panels of your insular worlds. Then you'll be as easy to manipulate as a cartoon figure in a video-game because you'll follow anyone who makes any sense whatsoever. Have you studied photosynthesis in school yet?"

"No. I don't think so."

"Even vegetables go to the light with the help of turd."

ACT II

Girl of My Rapid Eye Movement

He [Hermes] caught up the staff, with which he mazes the eyes of those mortals whose eyes he would maze or wakes again the sleepers. Holding this in his hands, strong Argeiphontes winged his way onward. He stood on Piera and launched himself from the bright air across the sea and sped the wave tops, like a shearwater who along the deadly deep ways of the barren salt sea goes hunting fish and sprays quick-beating wings in the salt brine. In such a likeness Hermes rode over much tossing water. But after he had made his way to the far-lying island, he stepped then out of the dark blue sea, and walked over the dry land, till he came to the great cave, where the lovely-haired nymph was at home, and he found that she was inside. There was a great fire blazing on the hearth, and the smell of cedar split in billets, and sweetwood burning, spread all over the island. She was singing inside the cave with a sweet voice as she went up and down the loom and wove a golden shuttle. There was a growth of grove around the cave, flourishing, alder was there, and the black poplar, and fragrant cypress, and there were birds with spreading wings who made their nests in it, little owls, and hawks, and birds of the sea with long beaks who are like ravens, but all their work is on the sea water; and right about the hollow cavern extended a flourishing growth of vine that ripened with grape clusters. Next to it there were four fountains, and each of them ran shining water, each next each, but turned to run in sundry directions; and round about there were meadows growing soft with parsley and violets, and even a god who came into that place would have admired what he saw, the heart delighted within him. There the courier Argeiphontes stood and admired it. But after he had admired all in his heart, he went in to the wide cave, nor did the shining Kalypso fail to recognize him when she saw him come into her presence; for the immortal are not such as to go unrecognized by one another, not even if one lives in a far home. But Hermes did not find great-hearted Odysseus indoors, but he was sitting on the beach, crying as before now he had done, breaking his heart in tears, lamentation, sorrow, as weeping tears he looked out over the barren water...

...she set before him a table which she had filled with ambrosia, and mixed red nectar for him. The courier, Hermes Argeiphontes, ate and drank then, but when he had dined and satisfied his hunger with eating, then he began to speak, answering what she had asked him: "You, a goddess, ask me, a god, why I came, and therefore I will tell you the whole truth of the tale. It is you who ask me. It was Zeus who told me to come here. I did not wish to. Who would willingly make the run across this endless salt water? And there is no city of men nearby, nor people who offer choice hecatombs to the gods, and perform in sacrifice... Now Zeus tells you to send him [Odysseus] on his way with all speed. It is not appointed for him to die here, away from his people. It is still his fate that he shall see his people and come back to his house with the high roof and to the land of his fathers."

...long-suffering great Odysseus shuddered to hear, and spoke again in turn and addressed her: "Here is some other thing you devise, O goddess; it is not conveyance when you tell me to cross the sea's great open space on a raft. That is dangerous and hard. Not even balanced ships rejoicing in a wind from Zeus cross over. I will not go aboard any raft without your good will, nor unless, goddess, you can bring yourself to swear me a great oath that this is not some painful trial you are planning against me." So he spoke, and Kalypso, shining among divinities smiled and stroked him with her hand and spoke to him and named him: "You are so naughty, and you will have your own way in all things. See how you have spoken and reason with me. Earth be my witness in this, and the wide heaven above us, and the dripping water of the Styx, which oath is the biggest and most formidable oath among the blessed immortals, that this is no other painful trial I am planning against you, but I am thinking and planning for you just as I would do it for my own self, if such needs as yours were to come upon me; for the mind in me is reasonable, and I have no spirit of iron inside my heart. Rather, it is compassionate."

-Homer *Odyssey* 5: 47-84; 92-102; 112-115; 171-191

Who hasn't heard a story of a bad journey, even if it's as mundane as a drive to the corner convenience store? After Hermes finishes complaining about his voyage, and not being able to stop in somewhere for a sacrifice-feast (pre-franchise fast-food restaurants), the bargaining begins for Odysseus's fate. Kalypso says the deities are jealous of the affair, and the Olympians shouldn't judge because they also cavort and consort with humans. As passionate as she feels on the subject, she stays civil to Hermes, recognizing in his guise the authority of the sandal-winged staff-bearer. The Greeks believed strongly in the chain-of-command; it was a means of forming order out of nature that was still dangerous and had to be propitiated via even more dangerous deities headed by Zeus, the all-father, and a great-great grandpa to Odysseus. Athena, a goddess of civilization, the loom, and wisdom, pled to Zeus on behalf of Odysseus stranded with Kalypso; Zeus wasn't gulled by Athena's intrigue, but he did give direct orders to Hermes to pass along to Kalypso, whose order was a balance between nature and civilization, domesticating Odysseus to be her sex-slave. Since that wasn't going over too well with him, and probably didn't enhance their love-play, she considers making him a god.

Kalypso's cave is hospitable, but her temptation to Odysseus to make him a god and rule with her on a remote island that even the gods' messenger doesn't enjoy the trek to is rejected by Odysseus, with pointed slick flattery to the power of Kalypso. He wanted his own civilization, the king of a culture made in his image. All the lady of nature made him do was weep and mourn his absence from those of his kind because all his fellow shipmates had been killed. In a way, we are all like that: wanting oneness with what we recognize, and a high-technology society makes it easier to shop for what we think should be ours to help identify us.

Estella doesn't think too highly of me passing along such stories to Hector. When I mentioned taking him camping on weekends instead, she gave me a rather nasty look and said we don't have a tent, and she didn't want him missing Saturday or Sunday church service, as if that had been my secret scheme. Okay, maybe it was on a subconscious level. Anyway, he's quickly losing interest in our read-athons, and I don't speak very well to an inattentive audience, so maybe I'll cancel reading to him every night after dinner. What's the point of being unappreciated and having the fearful sensation that my family wants to kill a messenger of literature? I'm leading him away from civilization as he knows it to a more primordial era when humans closely identified with and fought against animals and nature. What's done is done: like my somewhat wicked past, which Estella may forgive but not wholly trust me not to repeat. I don't like everything in my life but it's better than being lost in a world of "might have beens".

I'm more pragmatic now about solemn oaths and blessings, having done my share of eternal "never again" vows during hangovers and strung-out recuperations. Odysseus is reasonably paranoid, considering his travails, so he asks for a vow from Kalypso and she gives him a 'I'll do unto you as I would do unto myself' quasi-blessing (fortunately for him, she liked herself). As civilization progressed, and considering the Greeks retained their piratical tendencies, they probably viewed oath-breaking as valid excuses for revenge looting and rapine more than as something holy and binding to the chain-of-command that would bring down the wrath of deities.

* *   * * *   * * *   * * *   * * *

When Isaac was so old that his eyesight had failed him, he called his older son Esau... Rebekah had been listening while Isaac was speaking to his son Esau. So when Esau went out into the country to hunt some game for his father, Rebekah said to her son Jacob, "Listen! I overheard your father tell your brother Esau, 'Bring me some game and with it prepare an appetizing dish for me to eat, that I may give you my blessing with the Lord's approval before I die.' Now, son, listen carefully to what I tell you. Go to the flock and get me two choice kids. With these I will prepare an appetizing dish for your father such as he likes. Then bring it to your father to eat, that he may bless you before he dies." "But my brother Esau is a hairy man," said Jacob to his mother Rebekah, "and I am smooth-skinned! Suppose my father feels me? He will think I am making sport of him, and I shall bring on myself a curse instead of a blessing."... Rebekah then took the best clothes of her older son Esau that she had in the house, and gave them to her son Jacob to wear; and with the skin of the kids she covered his hands and the hairless parts of his neck. Then she handed her son Jacob the appetizing dish and the bread she had prepared. Bringing them to his father, Jacob said, "Father!" "Yes?" replied Isaac. "Which of my sons are you?" Jacob answered his father: "I am Esau, your first-born..."

Jacob served it to him, and Isaac ate; he brought him wine, and he drank. Finally, his father Isaac said to him, "Come closer, son, and kiss me." As Jacob went up and kissed him, Isaac smelled the fragrance of his clothes. With that, he blessed him, saying, "Ah, the fragrance of my son is like the fragrance of a field that the Lord has blessed! May God give to you of the dew of the heavens and of the fertility of the earth abundance of grain and wine. Let peoples serve you, and nations pay you homage; be master of your brothers, and may your mother's sons bow down to you. Cursed be those who curse you, and blessed be those that bless you..."

Jacob had scarcely left his father, just after Isaac had finished blessing him, when his brother Esau came back from his hunt... "Who are you?" his father Isaac asked him. "I am Esau," he replied, "your first-born son." With that Isaac was seized with a fit of uncontrollable trembling. "Who was it then," he asked, "that hunted game and brought it to me? I finished eating it just before you came, and I blessed him. Now he must remain blessed!" On hearing his father's words, Esau burst into loud bitter sobbing... But Esau urged his father, "Have you only that one blessing, father? Bless me too!" Isaac, however, made no reply; and Esau wept aloud. Finally Isaac spoke again and said to him: "Ah, far from the fertile earth shall be your dwelling; far from the dew of the heavens above! By your sword you shall live, and your brother you shall serve; but when you become restive, you shall throw off his yoke from your neck."

-Genesis 27: 1; 5-12; 14-19; 25-30; 32-34; 38-40

Jacob probably had a serious unresolved Oedipal-complex, and his father went blind like Oedipus did, and both had warring sons; one of Oedipus's asked for a blessing, or at least a lifting of the curse his father had sworn. The ancient Greeks also loved a good violent hunt. Autolycus took his grandson, Odysseus, hunting and the latter received a recognizable wound's scar from a tusk of a wild boar. The Jews had a later civilization, and with domestication of herd animals, Esau was an archaic anomaly for loving a hunt in the country; but he was proud of it and had his father's greatest approval. When I lived in the urban jungles of a California inner-city we sometimes went looking for prey, but on my part that was an infrequent excursion. Simon was wilder and has the stitch-up scars of a few knife-wounds on his torso to impress anyone who is impressed by such things, like the sergeants in our Tsar's forces.

After I moved to the Midwest, the cities' rural surroundings weren't explored much by me. I had some friends who went hunting but they didn't invite me because of their disbelief in drunk-safaris with weapons, which is probably just as well because I wouldn't want to pass that tradition to Hector. He and Antony might sneak one of his father's beers to share while murdering animated creatures in screen-entertainments, which is something I can say I didn't teach my son. The closest he comes to nature hunting is occasionally killing a bug with a fly-swatter. Estella dotes on him, and the few times I mentioned having more children she was evasive until I hit all her buttons and she exploded in a fury that was respectable in size and portents of things to come when angered about who was in control of what.

* * *   * * *   * * *   * * *

Mercutio: You are a lover; borrow Cupid's wings
And soar with them above a common bound.
Romeo: I am too sore enpierced with his shaft
To soar with his light feathers, and so bound
I cannot bound a pitch above dull woe.
Under love's burden do I sink.
Mercutio: And, to sink in it, should you burden love-
Too great oppression for a tender thing.
Romeo: Is love a tender thing? It is too rough,
Too rude, too boisterous, and it pricks like a thorn.
Mercutio: If love be rough with you, be rough with love;

Prick love for pricking and you beat love down.
Give me a case to put my visage in.
[He puts on a mask]
A visor for a visor! What care I
What curious eye doth quote deformities?
Here are the beetle brows shall blush for me...
Romeo: I dreamt a dream tonight.
Mercutio: And so did I.
Romeo: Well, what was yours?
Mercutio: That dreamers often lie.
Romeo: In bed asleep, while they dream things true.
Mercutio: O, then, I see Queen Mab hath been with you.
She is the fairies' midwife, and she comes
In shape no bigger than an agate stone
On the forefinger of an alderman,
Drawn with a team of little atomi
Over men's noses as they lie asleep.
Her chariot is an empty hazelnut
Made by the joiner squirrel or old grub,
Time out o' mind the fairies' coachmakers.
Her wagon spokes made of the wings of grasshoppers,
Her traces of the smallest spider web,
Her collars of the moonshine's watery beams,
Her whip of cricket's bone, the lash of film,
Her wagoner a small gray-coated gnat,
Not half so big as a round little worm
Pricked from the lazy finger of a maid.
And in this state she gallops night by night
Through lovers' brains, and then they dream of love;
O'er courtiers' knees, that dream on curtsies straight;
O'er lawyers' fingers, who straight dream on fees;
O'er ladies' lips, who straight on kisses dream,
Which oft the angry Mab with blisters plagues
Because their breaths with sweetmeats tainted are.
Sometimes she gallops o'er a courtier's nose,

And then dreams he of smelling out a suit.
And sometimes comes she with a tithe-pig's tail
Tickling a parson's nose as 'a lies asleep;
Then dreams he of another benefice.
Sometimes she driveth o'er a soldier's neck,
And then dreams he of cutting foreign throats,
Of breaches, ambuscadoes, Spanish blades,
Of healths five fathoms deep, and then anon
Drums in his ear, at which he starts and wakes,
And being thus frighted swears a prayer or two
And sleeps again. This is that very Mab
That plats the manes of horses in the night,
And bakes the elflocks in foul sluttish hairs,
Which once untangled much misfortune bodes.
This is the hag, when maids lie on their backs,
That presses them and learns them first to bear,
Making them women of good carriage.
This is she-
Romeo: Peace, peace, Mercutio, peace!
Thou talk'st of nothing.
Mercutio: True, I talk of dreams,
Which are the children of an idle brain...

-Shakespeare *Romeo and Juliet* I, 4: 17-32; 50-97

Civilization has changed our dreams and our pursuits of the best bargains (including sacrifices to a parson's deity and ideal sex-mates); the folks running the biggest deals don't do it in the third-dimension but in satellite space- as wispy but controlling as Queen Mab or her predecessors- and the results are birthed onto screen-worlds, which people dream of engaging with while asleep because they don't know what nature is except temperamental and beyond their control. Bad breath doesn't matter in video sex, and an automobile is easier to manage than a horse and chariot. How can a dreamer avoid the constant barrage of commercials for a better life and the progress of society without being an outcast? What are humans becoming with accouterments and disguises? A false name in an artificial system? Some of us may not really know who we are, just role-players with no set image, like Jacob and his faceless deity, except what was reflected in Adam. Since then, whether via fig-leaves, looms, assembly-line sweat-shop apparel, or expensive celebrity demigod brand clothes, humans have been in costumes. No wonder the ancient Greeks believed human fate was unspooled on a loom, and no matter how many different clothes they wore or their wives or slaves spun, life's masquerade was done when Fate's thread ran out. Nature can be harsh, yet now we dress for artificial environments. I wonder about the supposedly educated college students walking in twenty-degree weather to get to the taverns with no coats, no hats, no gloves, no brains.

We aren't an interesting enough of a species to have cameras in everyone's hands and on each street corner, whether for money, entertainment, or safety; it may bring out the exhibitionist in people but there's always a sense of unrealistic phoniness because they desperately want momentary fame, even if it lands them in jail, where there are more cameras to perform for, which just makes the whole thing boring. When the film runs out, The Show is over, and the children of an idle brain are no longer stars in their own programming but an audience to their descendants' reruns.

Perhaps, like the Hindus' belief in Brahma- who dreams the worlds into existence until awakened- we get swept into our leaders' visions and play their scripts with whatever mantras are popular at the time. To paraphrase Gerald Ford when he granted Nixon a pardon despite never being convicted, 'It's time to end this national nightmare.' During Reagan's heavily medicated inept reign, we dreamt we went back to Vietnam, won the war and then watched the victory onscreen. On and on it went, and now Obama has us dream we're in covert agencies, calling down drone airplane strikes with cell-phones, sending our foes into phantom zones so we can dream some more of how we control the universe with buttons or a simple word.

The Hebrews' *Bible* standardized their language and customs, akin to how the *Iliad* and *Odyssey* were instrumental for the ancient Greeks' culture. Shakespeare's 16th-17th century English has much of his era's slang, and may not have aged well for contemporary time because the modern lingos, with global communications, alter so quickly. The modern etymology trade goes with corporate business, like something from Orwell's *1984* newspeak. Some are blessed by the new languages and some don't know what it's all about, depending on knowledge of the magic words. Love, like a hoodwinked Cupid, can be blind; another popular proverb is, 'A blessing in disguise.' Combine the two and one can have a real mess that breeds discord for some and harmony for others. Perhaps love itself has changed with all the altering of guises, though our primordial instincts remain. It's curious the things we believe can save us or further us along to a decent, if not great, destiny. Even as the world around us becomes barren, we still receive and transmit messages that we're aiming for a right- and perhaps righteous- fate, blessed by our high-tech oracles. I know after I'd been sober for several months it was tempting to play a wish-fulfiller to Estella and Hector, but circumstances and my natural miserliness didn't allow for it. It's difficult to use the chain-of-command "deniability factor", which the leading politicians of the 1980's admitted to crafting whenever a devious scheme might go bad, in a small family.

Whatever I read I become a living hieroglyph of, and I've read a lot the past few months to escape my personal pit in Hades, where I've seen Tantalus tantalized by food and drink just out of his grasp. Different characters bound from me like Hamlet assumed various personalities to preserve himself from court-intrigues while devising revenge at the commands of someone from another dimension. Perhaps a Mayan astronaut deity is guiding me for a purpose more obscure than the ghost of Hamlet's father's mission. It's difficult for me to objectively judge my history from this juncture because my composite person now has altered from what composed my former perspectives. I know, however, that it was weakness which compelled me to marry Estella when there were so many other options. She studied my weak-spots and used them against me.

Perhaps it's wrong to judge the fulfillment of temptations that others have; maybe it's best to simply shrug and say, 'It's not my style.' Maybe the various gods and goddesses are evolving their believers to cull the herds. Is stealing or tempting away believers or smiting those of a different system a crime? If nothing else, Vespasian and Jesus helped rid the Jews of corrupt Pharisees and Sadducees, who may have been reincarnated as Roman Catholic Summoners and Pardoners, whose jobs were terminated during the Protestant Reformation; and new life awaited them as modern creditors in high-tech finance institutions: we get taught to build good credit by deficit spending, hoping to be absolved through faith in work.

Recruiting for lifestyles has become a major industry and it's difficult to stay indifferent to the constant barrage; the recruiters, having learned some techniques from history, want trainees to be either hot and eager to join or cold and opposing so they can be pointed out as divisive foes. Some folks image it as a struggle between good and evil, though mostly it seems a matter of taste according to the personality-shopper. Black people were excluded for so long that now they want their fingerprints everywhere, being taught if it's black it's better, which just isn't true. There are plenty of entertainments about blacks winning in sports, spelling bees, what next? Checkers? Rhyming stitches with bitches doesn't make them poets. They learn overconfidence based on color just as they were once subjugated for the same reason.

During India's struggle to be free of England's colonial rule, Mohandas Gandhi observed to some orthodox Hindus that they wanted English rule without the English. American blacks should have been in the white education system by at least 1920, instead of the Ku Klux Klan becoming popular then; blacks could have had some familiarity with subject matters they now summarily dismiss (for plausible vengeful reasons); education has become so high-tech it's a process of training consumers into being screen-world indentured sharecroppers to student loans so they have to choose between having children or chase the fantasies promised to them by corporations, which want stupid little consumers buying every gizmo that's updated annually.

People like Odysseus, Romeo, and Esau aren't any fun when they sit about weeping, especially if they're so mournful they ruin a good feast and party; best to leave them out in the country somewhere until they get it out of their systems. Hermes doesn't even bother with his great-grandson on Kalypso's island. Mercutio gets tired of Romeo being a kill-joy and tries to elevate his mood, though Romeo ends up predicting a bad outcome for attending a rival House's masquerade party (where he's destined to meet Juliet). And Esau. What a mook. Some blessing his father passes on to him. In a manner, I'm all three characters: searching for home, love, and to be the dominant male. I suppose we've all been adrift at one time or other, hoping someone will steer a course for us, even if it's a blind dream-world induced by some greater power offering a Soma-elixir. Perhaps Americans have become used to living in perpetual fear that their manufactured appetites will never be sated.

Food has probably changed more in the past three decades than for centuries or millenniums, and with it so have humans and their eating, which has become a habit rather than a necessity to pursue a way of life (unless one works in the ever-burgeoning restaurant business). It's still a cut-throat commerce that the Cyclops would fit in well with: like the slash-burn-grow farming tactics in the rain forests. I suppose corporate-farmers were happy to take the land in Guatemala after Efrain Rios Montt sent death-troops into our towns and villages. Does it matter that the Cyclops was a distant uncle of his menu plan, who escaped by hiding himself under a ram? That Polyphemos's blind curse on Odysseus would only work if the proper name was used?

It's hard to believe people once fought for food. Now they fight for trophies that, if not serviceable like women, armor, and slaves in the *Iliad*, are actually destructive such as the use of fossil fuels. Inventing platitudes is a fulltime job: 'We fight to preserve our way of life' but existence changes so quickly that many spend most of their lives in front of screens where they feel they have some control, even if they're being spied on.

A cave, tents, and the street outside a city mansion were where Odysseus, Jacob, and Romeo respectively left for what they hoped were better places, with all the endearments of love promising them they'll put their past problematical relationships behind them. With the means of mass-global transportation, the modern refugees' plight is becoming akin to the ancient wars when the losers were enslaved; currently, the business of human-trafficking, including sexual, is considered a wise investment and lucrative trade: if people get hungry enough, they'll do anything for a crust of week-old bread, until some sort of savior arrives. After the 2007 world financial disaster, tent-towns popped up in thicket areas around cities, populated by those less fortunate than myself. Greece still hasn't recovered and doesn't seem thrilled about taking draconian economic measures on its citizens. I can't say as I blame them for digging in against drastic cutting of social programs such as the European Union conglomerate demands as part of a cash deal to Greek politicians who might end up penniless vagabonds like Odysseus if they make their populace angry, unless they craftily invest in Swiss bank accounts. It's more probable that powerful countries like Germany and France will throw some money at Greece to take in Mideast refugees. It's not that refugees are undesirable to the Germans and French, they just want the ones with money and powerful connections; other nations can have the riff-raff, and deal with the problems when the money disappears. However, bad publicity in such obvious cases of extortion for a humanitarian cause might inspire wealthier nations to accept tent-people.

✳ ✳ ✳   ✳ ✳ ✳   ✳ ✳ ✳   ✳ ✳ ✳

"You are my master and my author, you-
the only one from whom my writing drew
the noble style for which I have been honored.
You see the beast that made me turn aside;
help me o famous sage, to stand against her,
for she has made my blood and pulses shudder."
"It is another path that you must take,"
he answered when he saw my tearfulness,
"if you would leave this savage wilderness;
the beast that is the cause of your outcry
allows no man to pass along her track,
but blocks him even to the point of death;
her nature is so squalid, so malicious
that she can never sate her greedy will;
when she has fed, she's hungrier than ever.
She mates with many living souls and shall
yet mate with many more..."

-Dante *Inferno* canto I: 85-101

Depictions of evil have changed throughout millenniums, both male and female. The intolerant are now considered by some to be a source of rot and corruption, and their villainous extremism is crafted for mass-consumption. Passing life's lessons along to the next generation can be a terrible thing when the new overthrows too quickly for a truly stable pattern to emerge. Dante wanted a highly-structured environment of bliss, but to get it he had to pass through the savagery of war between Houses and the aftermath of reconstruction. The Jews paid their dues, and their young civilization took from other cultures what the Hebrew elite considered the most useful to adopt to pass along in tomes, rituals, and blessings to the next generation, wherein anyone not of a particular lineage was an outsider and dangerous.

A survivor isn't always someone to admire; like most people, he or she has a mix of good and bad traits, but the trends of good and bad change so fast that a survivor can be considered obtuse and stubborn, holding onto the past with both hands and a headful of resentments. After the civil wars in Florence, Italy were resolved, Dante took his side's defeat ungraciously, and despite being offered a return to his native city by the victors, he chose exile, staying at various houses as he penned his opponents into hell. He was probably more sophisticated than the modern couch-surfers, those who travel from one acquaintances' place to the next, camping-out on living room sofas, lives in limbo. While *The Divine Comedy* is intolerant, it's also a great work of art, especially for anyone who's been outside of a society one had wished to form in his or her image.

6

Instincts Replaced by Superstitions

Pablo was irritable when he went to his job at *Mood Food* bakery and café. It was approximately a week later, May 2013. He walked behind the front-counter and grabbed a semi-clean apron. As he was donning it, Vernon appeared from the backrooms and asked, "Hey, Pablo, how you doing?"

Pablo sighed and said, "I feel like a frustrated character from a Thomas Hardy novel. Just call me Pablo, The Obscure."

Vernon replied, "Well, the way you said that, I'll take it you ain't so hot."

Pablo was a bit happy his boss didn't catch Pablo's allusion to the misery his English counterpart went through doing menial labor at a college city where he dreamed of knowledge, opportunities, and success.

Vernon watched Pablo knot the apron at his belly, then said, "I got more good news for you: it's your day to do dishes."

"What happened to Fala, The Outer-Space Knight-Errant?"

"Haven't seen him for three days," Vernon said. "Oh, yes I have: take a look at this."

Vernon handed Pablo a folded piece of paper from an apron-pocket and Pablo uncreased it to see a well-done cell-phone photograph of Fala passed out behind a dumpster, with the caption '*Mood Food's* Employee of the Month.' Pablo laughed, "Where'd you get this?"

"Off our computer web-site. Someone put it out in satellite space a few nights ago." Vernon tried to sound stern despite his twitching grin. "It must've been Crolley. Only management has our computer passwords and I didn't change them after he quit last week."

"Is that the alley behind the bakery?"

"Yeah. I had to take it off our computer site, of course. The owners would've blown their lids if they'd seen it. I can hear them now, complaining about the sort of people I hire."

Pablo grunted, "I hope you changed the passwords. A picture like this spreads like a virus and can mean lawsuits." Pablo studied it and pronounced his art criticism, "Whoever took it did a good job with the nuances: cigarette butts, a stray moldy napkin, a crust of bread; and look, he's got drool coming out of his mouth. Public humiliations have become performance art; Hester Prynne's scarlet letter would be worn with pride." Pablo laughed. "It's beautiful. Well, now you know what became of him."

Vernon took the picture and said, "He'll show up for his paycheck. The last I heard, he flunked his first-year Spanish class."

"Didn't he brag about knowing ancient Greek and Latin?"

"One of the beautiful and the damned," Vernon commented.

"Oh, yeah. He trumpeted about living longer than F. Scott Fitzgerald, who probably could've had more years of life if he hadn't put so much energy into maintaining his shallow image. If he'd been passed out in an alley next to a garbage dumpster, Fitzgerald would've had more stories to write," Pablo said cheerfully; bashing Fala The Outer-Space Knight-Errant was frequently a satisfying, if pointless, exercise.

Vernon said, "Fala's writing them through you, Pablo."

Pablo grabbed a few crusty towels and said, "He thinks he can do everything by telepathic osmosis, like read books and whatnot. Maybe he was reincarnated from earth's first amoeba."

"What do you expect from a guy who watches all those movies of characters learning Kung-Fu from computer programs and thinks he can do the same?" Vernon shook his head and added, "Ol' Fala is wired into perpetual reinvention."

"I can't say I'll miss him," Pablo said, and went to the dishwashing station. A moment later he returned to the front-counter and asked Vernon, "I still get my share of the tips, don't I?"

Vernon nodded, then said, "You can work a full eight-hour shift if you want. You're the only one who doesn't mind doing dishes."

"I'll do it," Pablo said; "at least until you find someone else. Preferably a worker who doesn't think he's a cosmic soldier."

Vernon turned on the music machine to a song that plagiarized a John Keats' poem: "Tender is the night..."

Pablo laughed, "Listening to that tune is probably the closest ol' Fala ever got to reading Fitzgerald. Oh well, at least now he has time to tend to his squire-duties under Ralph Nader to save the universe and free the world to be made in one diversified image."

They walked to the backrooms and Vernon went into the freezer while Pablo began setting up the dishwashing station. When Vernon emerged from the walk-in freezer, Pablo asked, "Did whoever take that picture call the cops?"

"I don't know," Vernon replied. "It must've happened after we closed but the sun was still up. This city loves a drunk with money, which excludes ol' Fala from every place except jail or detox. Or being transported unaware into satellite space to be on our web-site."

"That's what's ruining America: can't get away with the smallest misdemeanor because someone's always there with a camera; only the criminals who sponsor all the media forums can make off with fortunes. We've become our own Big Brother. Why," Pablo said, "it's getting so the town-drunk can't even pass out in private behind a dumpster without a citizen interfering. Hey, tune the radio to the station that does police news and see if our outer-space knight-errant scholar got thrown in the can."

Vernon replied, "Hasn't he been publicly humiliated enough? Do you want him on a chain-gang going around town picking up garbage and cigarette butts?"

"He'd probably smoke them. That guy must have a thousand potential diseases in him and here he was washing dishes."

"He didn't have potential to be anything else," Vernon said, "except a serial-killer. Fortunately, he's usually too drunk to do much damage." "His idea of fate is to feel destined to watch a blow 'em up movie about destiny, where terrible actors and actresses shadow-box or swordfight with themselves until the special effects' crews can add the computerized details."

Vernon walked away as Pablo continued, "Fala's philosophy is to live hard, die old, and leave behind a medical school autopsy cadaver. Can you imagine the things the students will find? It'd be like cutting into a Black Hole, which may be where he came from as an outer-space knight-errant who was seduced by the life of mole- tunneling."

Vernon returned from the front-counter and asked, "What's wrong with you today, Pablo? Is there something I can help you with or is it just that whoever washes dishes gets goofy?"

"You don't think it's funny to associate a bit of light with a bottle of alcohol and resort to it until pickled in formaldehyde?"

Vernon said quietly, "You're too much of a presence, Pablo; you're a lot of things but not obscure, so tone it down before customers start coming in."

When Vernon left, Pablo murmured, "We all act and react differently in the present. Your idea of helping me is to tell me to shut-up. Can't you make yourself more useful than that? Nothing like having screen doctors, sponsored by pharmaceutical companies, running the psychiatric-trade and inspiring imitators."

What did you expect, Pablo queried himself: emotional catharsis for years of blind rage at Efrain Rios Montt? I doubt Vernon's ever heard the name, and why should've he? I'm trying to forget it myself. It's been thirty years since Montt was overthrown as dictator of Guatemala, and the recent guilty verdict, tossed out by the Constitutional Court, for genocide against Mayans might be the closest thing there can be fabricated for justice. Now Vernon begrudges me the use of Fala to craft a scapegoat. Jesus even took on the sins of crucifying god, one of the worst sins ever invented; and his believers have to forgive him for wanting them to be nailed-up as well.

Pablo felt an uprising of abstract resentments, which he knew from experience would lead to grudges as distant as an abandonment-issue with his parents from decades ago. No, he thought: there are plenty of current episodes that need to be as peacefully resolved as possible.

Pablo's mother in California had written him a letter full of hope that Montt would receive a more severe punishment than a lecture about being naughty. Several weeks later, her heart broken, she telephoned Pablo and wept at the guilty verdict being vacated. He insisted to his half-brother, Angelo, that he take better care of their mother; but Angelo was resigned to leaving things as they played out, and if she didn't want to eat or sleep, then it was her decision.

"You're going to let her commit slow suicide in your house?" Pablo asked.

"Hey, Pablo, you're not here. You don't know what it's been like. She's getting to Carol. I mean, she's my wife, Pablo, and I don't want to come home from work and find my wife a nervous wreck and the kids half-crazy because our mom is calling down curses in some Mayan dialect."

"What's she been saying?"

"Hell, I don't know. And that's what it is, Pablo: she's trying to bring hell itself here into my house. I can't have it, Pablo. If she wants to die, I'm going to let her. If you want to come and get her, you have my blessing and can take all her curses."

"I can't do that, Angelo, and you know that. Is there some place you can put her?"

"You'd rather her doped and institutionalized than dead?" Angelo asked. "It's time to close the book on her, which is what she wants. She won't let anyone use the computer or TV because she's afraid she'll miss news on that goddamn trial. Hell, Pablo, she's so strung-out she barely understands Spanish, let alone English. She thinks it'll automatically translate into Mayan in her mind. It's a goddamn nightmare: even worse than when Carol was glued to the TV for the trial about that nanny killing her charge. I'll need an exorcist to get rid of all the curses she's calling down or up or wherever the dark spirits are hiding from her. They'll show up sooner or later and if she's not here to send them to terrorize Montt and that scumbag, President Molina, I'll have to sell my house and move; and it's a buyers' market now, Pablo; you know that from your own experience."

"Are you done now, Angelo?"

"Christ!" Angelo said; then aside to Carol, "Oh, I'm sorry. She doesn't like me using that kind of language, but I'm pissed-off right now, Pablo, so start making travel plans if you want to come to the funeral because I intend to let her die."

"Using cuss words is bad, but wanting your mother to die in your living room is okay, eh?" Pablo said. "Get her some treatment, Angelo, or I'll come out there and I know you won't like what I'll do." They were quiet a moment, then Pablo told his younger brother, "You're infringing on my role as the psychopath of the family, so I'm going to infringe on yours as the respectable one."

Angelo forced a bitter laugh, "That's a sure sign society is falling apart; and you may enjoy a cause to crusade for but you'll probably try to avoid the bad effects."

"Don't bail-out on me now, Angelo. Family is about the only thing I have left."

"Whose fault is that? You were an idiot when you had money and fried-out too many brain synapses. We can't all be nursemaids to your chosen people."

Pablo quietly said, "There's more to people than just utilitarian purposes. I can't believe you think the only reason they exist is for your pleasure."

"You put us through a lot of pain," Angelo replied, "while thinking you were superman. I don't want to cut my losses and run, but why should I suffer? All that succeeds in doing is making me resentful, then I take it out on my wife and children. How much innocence has to be ruined to make you happy? Some of these geriatrics want to live forever, draining resources and trying to get us to live like they did seven decades ago. Mom won't be happy until we're all in a small rural village working as dirt-farmers. But I can't get her away from the computer and TV where she can relish her vengeance on the bastards who destroyed her village. So I'll tell you what I'll do, Pablo: I'll get her to a hospital and if they can save her without too much work-"

"What do you mean, too much work?"

"It's measured by money, Pablo, and how much it'll effect my insurance premiums."

"That's bogus," Pablo said.

"It's the only standard I can go by, and it's not my fault you never learned that. Dick Cheney has the taxpayers settle his reckoning whenever he needs a new heart. I don't have that luxury, and can't afford a pound of flesh. Anyway, I think she's mostly dehydrated so they'll probably just stick a few tubes in her arm."

Pablo allowed himself to release his wrath; becoming philosophical, he said, "I suppose things are the way they're meant to be but that doesn't mean it's perfect."

Angelo said, "Welcome back to the third-dimension, Pablo. God forgives but karma doesn't."

"Neither do cameras," Pablo replied, "unless they're rigged."

Pablo tried to find further consolation in a philosophy, so he went to the college library, which was generous in allowing non-students to check-out books. He was carefully polite to the campus security guard who stopped Pablo along the sidewalk and checked his identification cards and asked where Pablo was going; to him, the guard was just another unranked general infantry soldier for America's idiosyncratic militarization, which spanned from the covert and sublime operatives to uniformed thugs, and amateur, self-appointed Cerberuses. At Pablo's insincere, though well-acted, humility, the security officer expressed satisfaction in being the Alpha-male with a hint of scorn, and allowed his suspect to move along. It had been a Friday night, near the end of the spring semester; except for a few white women as worker-students, and a dozen or so foreign exchange students doing some group-studies, the library was empty. Everyone else was at the taverns, getting smashed and complaining about jobs going overseas. At least so Pablo thought, as he browsed through the library's computer catalogues.

Having read some of Thomas Aquinas's *Summa Theologica*, Pablo decided to investigate one of the major influences on Aquinas, and found Aristotle's *Nicomachean Ethics*. It was a sixty-year-old hardcover book which also contained *Metaphysics*. The young lady at the check-out post put a rubber-band around the volume to keep it from falling apart before it left the library.

According to Aristotle, Pablo found out, Nature is substance, and the ancient Greek philosopher attempted to track it to the first cause. The global conglomerates that sponsor scientists and media forums prefer crafted illusions of Nature by Number: Form is only a being in potency and not actualized, though whether Form is eternal is anyone's guess.

Percy Shelley's *Prometheus Unbound* had the universe formed in Jupiter's tyrannical image, which was reformed into harmonious Nature after he was dragged to hell by Demogorgon, a misbegotten son of Jupiter. Aristotle, however, was quite careful with his imaginary god-imaging so as to leave no room for doubt among any potential accusers who might have found him an annoyance and sent him the way of Socrates unto Zeus to find out personally what the afterlife was really like.

It occurred to Pablo that one god might begrudge humans the use of fire, while another promises- and does not lie- that the knowledge of godhood is attainable. Destiny's fortune can be purchased with invested fortunes that humans hope will pay in the ways the high-finance speculators have estimated; that the professional speculators also bet against a good destiny is something people around the globe have learned to accept as a common, albeit abstract, business practice. Like the interpreters of the archaic Sibylline books of prophecy, modern speculators profit by keeping their work as arcane as possible.

"Those whom the gods would destroy, they first make proud," Pablo murmured as he turned on the dishwashing machine. And yet, he thought: it's characteristic for humans to blame gods for creating pride. John Milton's Lucifer had Sin leap from his brain, which was based on Athena, a virgin warrior goddess of wisdom, emerge in full conception from Zeus's head. We certainly can think much of ourselves- even if we don't know anything- which is part of our biological equipment that is targeted for temptations crafted by speculators investing in new and future products to be actualized or spin in eternal Forms of potency. To Aristotle, god is a thinker who thinks of thinking; or, as Fala would put it of his favorite popular-cult ballad, 'I was jeanyushing with the jeanyushes when they jeanyushed that song.' Pure genius.

Vernon appeared from the front and asked, "What's wrong with the dishwasher? It sounds sick."

"I don't know. I just turned it on."

"Well, turn it off a sec." When the clanking stopped, Vernon opened the door-panel and said, "Jesus Christ! Whoever worked last night hid a tub of dirty dishes in there just so's they could get out of here quicker."

Pablo laughed, "Not even Fala would do that. The least they could've done is put them on a rack. I'm going to have to soak those dishes for an hour just to get the crud softened up."

Vernon was irate and glared at Pablo, "It ain't funny."

"Did you have a bad weekend at the farm or something, Vernon? You seem upset over a minor technical difficulty."

"Mop the floor, Pablo, and mind your own business."

"Okay." When Vernon was out of range, Pablo muttered, "God, it's not like we're in Afghanistan being point-men searching for booby-traps. It's ironic that our troops' biggest fear now is the weapons we give our allies. They graduated from the box-cutter razor-blades of the 9-11-1 air attacks to some heavy firepower. It's almost as illogical as the Romantics' poetry, though at least the latter has better form."

Why do we try to live out illogical myths? Aristotle bashed his predecessors' beliefs in Numbers equaling Ideals and other assorted numbskull philosophy. It's curious, though, what people invest in, and as the tolerance for pleasure increases, we need more to achieve the desired results. Perhaps that's why mixing Numbers with Ideals is so tempting for a nation that hasn't yet accepted the logic of the metric system of measurement. Numbers are merely measure, yet in a Capitalistic society big numbers mean greater rewards and pleasures, even if going the wrong way; as Ronald Reagan said, "Deficit spending is good for the economy." Directly after the 9-11-1 air attacks on America, Georgie Junior and Cheney told Americans to go out and spend money, which they did, using credit cards to buy mortgages on houses they couldn't afford.

Now when I want illogical myths, I read poetry. Shelley's *Adonais* eulogy for John Keats has an eerie prediction of Shelley's death by drowning, which actualized the next year. I doubt Nature mourns her dead poets any more than dead mathematicians, nor does Nature look out for the formers' best interests despite their lauding Nature as beneficent. Nature and Actualization are subject to changes, which can appear capricious; but potency at least seems eternal, its fluidity like the Samsara of life's deathly ocean leaving one system to be realized in another.

The ancient Mayans believed the various Forms lived in Nature through the blood of sacrificed victims, and also had an extremely logical measurement of space. They were crushed by people who drank their god's blood and thought the world was flat. The poorly-constructed Gregorian Calendar is still used, complete with long dead deities' names.

It can be difficult to represent oneself in a society fixated on role-playing under the guise of democracy. Collecting identities for a profit is a major industry, and the global markets encourage it, calling it diversity. The numbers' rackets promise Ideals, like 666, the mark of the Beast, or the mark of gods'; and all we have to do is invest in the bad math so as to gain 72 virgins, or the 7 horsemen spreading world destruction like

71

global conglomerates: a sort of moveable feast. They are the true American expatriates. Yet as humans, our systems cannot help but to have corruptions. Thus, in a Capitalistic society we tend to throw money at problems as a sacrifice to keep things running as smoothly as possible.

Pablo thought of Fala's infatuation with Ralph Nader, and how Fala insisted he didn't waste his vote on the erstwhile presidential candidate in the 2000 election. Al Gore won the majority, yet lost through the Supreme Court's voted verdict which appointed Georgie Junior, like Samuel the judge anointed another king of Israel to replace one who didn't heed Samuel's god-inspired orders. The public's votes didn't matter, and no one that Pablo noticed was vociferous about changing the system to one person, one vote to decide the matter. The structure, though it had obviously failed, would stay entrenched because of the dogma that candidates would not campaign in less-populated states, despite modern convenient transportation; and Pablo knew that presidential wannabes rarely, if ever, made even a token appearance in South Dakota, which had only 3 electoral votes: the standard 2 senators and 1 member of the House of Representatives. The media forums shied away from any mentions of altering the election system because they made mucho dinero from over-extended political campaigns, and didn't want the major political parties' sponsors getting revenge by interfering with media profits.

Yet people want to invest in others' problems, which are usually based on the utter inability to cope with the third-dimension: be it the wars in the Mid-East, which would terrify any reasonable person; or addicted to escaping into screen-worlds; or the use of dope; or all three: bombing civilians through drone aircraft via screens while goofed-up on pharmaceuticals.

Vernon walked up to Pablo and said, "I apologize for being short with you. It's been hell trying to get my parents to sell the farm."

"It's okay," Pablo replied. "Is Cookie working today?"

"She'll be in in a few hours. I'll tell her to leave you alone."

"I appreciate that, Vernon."

"Everyone wonders why I promoted her but you wouldn't take the job."

Something which Pablo did not want his wife to know. Despite his convictions in sacrificing towards the general good of future generations, he was not willing to surrender his work as a poet and historian for the managerial torments of *Mood Food* for his family: instead of working on an hourly-wage, management was on a steady salary, sometimes on the job for more than fifty hours a week and liable to be called in to work at any time, which meant earning less than minimum-wage when the percentage was averaged. He said indifferently, "Well, Cookie is adept at bullying the teenagers. Just don't have me open the store with her because she doesn't know what she's doing."

"Her insurance package got processed so she can afford her medication now."

"I don't care," Pablo said. "I'm not going to be alone with her because only one of us will survive and I have the better punch."

"Let's not get into that. I'll schedule you to wash dishes around her."

"Sounds fair. She can try to instill the fear of god into someone else. I got to admit, though, she does a thorough job of getting her minions to scrub the place clean. I'm surprised they don't tell her, 'I love you, Cookie Dearest.'"

"Jesus, Pablo, do you have that whole show memorized?" Vernon laughed, and said, "When she called me up all hysterical from you breaking her will, I could hear you in the background reciting lines. I tried to keep from laughing but it was so damn funny." Vernon sighed. "I hope you understand that I have to side with her against you."

Pablo shrugged. His philosophy towards *Mood Food* had changed during his tenure to a belief that hybrid hierarchies have been around since people painted walls with animal parts on humans. Some folks find it amusing, like the Hindus. Other times, lambs of god get sacrificed, especially if they try to lead the flock away from organized, powerful hierarchies, which have been mechanized. "I don't like making enemies," Pablo said, "but perfectionists in an imperfect world can get in the way."

"She is sort of a wrathful goddess, ain't she?" Vernon said, shaking his head and walking away.

"I've done my time in the Bardo of Cookie. What's her major, anyway?"

"I think it's Business Personnel."

"She seems more the type to take out a huge student loan to get a degree in Women's Studies, the modern day equivalent to a girls' finishing school."

Vernon said, "At least back in the 1800s they learned something useful like how to sew and play the piano."

Communion and Arenas

Pablo tried to work as quietly as possible. There were so many voices, mechanical and human, that he felt part of a poorly conducted orchestra. No wonder Fala consumed alcohol into a black-out state of turpitude where a god without attributes and no pre-formulaic systems awaited beyond consciousness.

Ginny was at the self-propelled slicer on the far side of the back-room from the dishwasher. She added to the vociferous battering by plugging in the radio on a shelf while some semi-frozen tomatoes were sliced at a pre-designated width by the cutter. She swayed with the noise of an echo-chamber voice which was backed by an arrangement that had no instruments. Was it any worse than shrieking cat-being-gutted guitars? Pablo didn't know or care. Like a banshee from an operatic underworld Wagner might compose, the sounds haunted Pablo, who had no interests or investments in hell breaking loose on earth.

He searched his consciousness for an authoritative figure he felt he could trust to deliver peace and serenity. Choosing leaders was an ancient tradition and what civilized nation, in their right minds, would select Jesus Christ instead of Vespasian? The Jews tried to do away with both and had their collective asses kicked all over the Mideast and Europe. Who wouldn't rather have a seat in Vespasian's Colosseum than be the main entertainment fed to lions? A month after employees of a fast-food restaurant franchise walked off their jobs due to poverty, Obama cut Food Stamps on the nation's unemployed. So much for cheering-on an American workers' rebellion; it's every person for him or herself: no work, no bread.

Estella had been correct more than a decade ago when she told Pablo his ambitions were fruitless dreams; that there was not a single professor who would give Pablo the necessary great recommendations to move on to the next collegiate level. Still, he thought, she didn't need to pour salt and curry into my open wounds by saying the only people I worked with well were the folks from my dope-dealing occupation. He'd saved those profits to attend college and become legitimate, and all he succeeded in doing was making enemies of the professionals who could have furthered Pablo's career as a historian; now he was doing the same with Vernon and Cookie: the former resented Pablo for refusing a promotion, and Cookie because he'd been offered it first.

Pablo looked at Ginny without scorn, realizing she was padding her high school resume in plans of not being a 35-year-old semi-frozen tomato slicer. Above her head, on the wall, was a poster with a cartoon drawing of several happy faces in a circle and one frowning cry-baby face outside the joyful ring; a slogan read: There is no *I in Teamwork*. Pablo smiled at the slowly revolving camera at its post above the door leading to the front-counter.

George Bush Junior, with his vision thing for a global democracy he would supervise, truly lacked superior vision. In a complete context, perhaps it was right that America was led by men who resented and wanted to out-perform their fathers from whom they inherited supervision issues, which makes for good stories. Few people could justly accuse Obama of being soft against Muslims, despite having a father of that faith. Vespasian credited the previous ruling heir-line of the Roman Empire, then set about establishing his own after squashing rebellion in Judea.

What portents did Pablo have for his son, Hector? They didn't seem auspicious, to be sure, however Pablo might not be reading them correctly. Hector might become a patriot; as rebellious as an oppressed Syrian; or a pirate like a profiteering member of Al-Queda stirring-up unrest in hopes of then presenting a peace made in his own image; perhaps, with so many job opportunities in various militias, he could join something like the Secret Service and be a king-maker in the manner of the Praetorian Guard who found various ways of protecting or assassinating Roman Emperors (like Caligula on his way to the Palatine games) and their foes according to ambition, pay, and even, absurdly, honor. No doubt Obama felt more secure in bolstering covert agencies' roles while reducing the military's, which could stir bad-blood; but Pablo didn't share those sentiments of safety because none of them were working for him: new presidents routinely built their own secret networks because those already in place had questionable loyalties. Hector was many things, but camera-shy wasn't one of them. He scurried about to expand his audience even more than Bob Gates, the retired Minister of War, who ambitiously hustled for jobs as media forums' military analyst, or as a lobbyist for weapons' manufacturers and dealerships to make sales' pitches to his cronies in Washington D.C.: a true patriotic Capitalist who spreads the wealth by hiring ghostwriters to bash Obama's purported defeatism while American soldiers are still in the fields of Afghanistan, telling them their commander-in-chief is a moral coward.

Reliable sources, Pablo thought, are rare these days because everyone wants to be the first to cover whatever story will garner wealth and fame. A person can tell one truth, be deemed reliable, then spew packages of insane lies. At least Suetonius can be credited with double-checking his sources while penning *The Lives of the Caesars*.

Roy Webster brought a tub of dirty dishes to Pablo, who had difficulty gauging the young man's sincerity, especially regarding race and gender issues. Roy said, "I hear a black street-gang is trying to muscle into Sioux Falls."

"Ah, the military use of highway interstates."

Roy looked at Pablo with a querying gaze and asked, "Whattya mean?"

"Eisenhower encouraged multi-state road connections for military purposes, which makes things easier for gangs to colonize territories."

"Sioux Falls won't put up with that," Roy grimly affirmed.

"I don't know, Roy," Pablo said; "corporations against colonists. My money is on the colonizers because the only thing corporations breed is franchises. A street-gang can easily out-number them."

"Yeah," Roy said bitterly; "then all their children will be on welfare and the homies will take even that and the Food Stamps from their bitches and whores."

"Everyone wants to be subsidized, Roy. It's no reason to get upset."

"You're a defeatist, Pablo."

Pablo shrugged, "Just like Obama, eh? Can't decide whether to democratize, colonize, or incorporate Afghanistan. But you don't be like Bob Gates and spread gossip about me being indifferent to the fate of Sioux Falls."

"You're not that wishy-washy. You just don't conform to group efforts."

"Are you gathering psychic energy or something, Roy?"

"You make it sound superstitious."

Pablo laughed, "There are no atheists in foxholes, Roy, and I don't mean to discourage you as the auxiliary defense against a street-gang moving in forty miles away."

"Well, you know my girlfriend lives there and I don't want her neighborhood being colonized into a slum like what happened in Iowa."

"Shouldn't you get back to work?"

"Nah, it's slow right now," Roy said. "But you heard Vern talk about Demosberg and how the city managers took federal money to bring in blacks who were career criminals or permanently unemployable. They turned his college area into a hell."

"Kind of like the Black-Hole of Calcutta, eh? Well, what do you expect from colonists? They didn't know the native ways of computers and cable television so they got their amusements making homie-babies."

"Doesn't that make you mad?"

"You know what," Pablo said, "they took the city hostage for a few years and all of them ended up in prison; and the college made the problem in the first place by forcing the students to live in dormitories. It was sheer, unmitigated greed. Then the landlords in that area were stuck with tenantless houses and apartments so took whoever had money: federal funds for homies replaced federal grants for students. It's our own fault the government sells us out so we need loans from other nations. Besides, Sioux Falls jailed the Lakota and it created a power-vacuum for black folks to fill."

Roy made a slight grinding of his teeth and walked away.

Ginny began stacking the sliced tomatoes into plastic containers. Pablo said, "Those are going to taste like mush."

"Well, mostly they're just for color anyway. Dab them with some ketchup and no one will know the difference." What would Americans be without their condiments? The French have sauces and Americans their

Tabasco-flavored pickle relish. Ginny wrote the day's date on a strip of masking tape and stuck it on the container. "Say, Pablo, you like to read. What do you think of *Sense and Sensibility*?"

"I used to try to escape it, Virginia."

"No, I mean the book by Jane Austen. We're reading it now in class."

"Oh," Pablo said. "It's not a bad escape route from Fala: you won't find him in a Jane Austen novel; even if her characters made it to London, there wouldn't be Fala passed out in a gutter by a pub." He saw Ginny crease her brow, but continued, "He'd fit in well with Pistol or Falstaff, though: a truly Shakespearean degenerate. He'd probably make it to Russia, too, for a part in a Dostoevsky story."

"I don't let him into my mind like that," Ginny commented. "We may fit roles to people with our sensibilities but I always use pride and prejudice for character fill-outs."

"That's an interesting thing about ol' Fala: as he goes about franchising his identity, he tries to collect everyone's buddhis for his shows."

"What's a buddhi? Or dare I not ask?"

"It's where we distinguish sense objects in our consciousness. Some folks try to connect them all together so everyone has the same enlightenment or destruction. Or, I suppose, both at the same time. For instance, the Buddhists in South Vietnam got tired of the buddha buddha buddha call from American helicopter rotor-blades spreading death from above; so, naturally, the Buddhist monks got some gasoline and torched themselves in photo-opportunities for the American audience. It didn't make much sense, but religious wars rarely do; and it all worked out because the Roman Catholic president was betrayed and sacrificed as a scapegoat."

"I just asked about a book, Pablo, not for a history lesson."

"Does that mean you won't find a character to fit me with in *Sense and Sensibility*?"

"There aren't a whole lot of over-educated dishwashers in Jane Austen."

Pablo laughed, "Or in Henry James, for that matter."

"I haven't read any of his stuff," Ginny said.

"You might like it. The characters digest each other into their consciousness, using metaphors to place them in scenes like on a boat or at a park."

"Is that all they do?"

"Yeah, pretty much," Pablo said. "If a fellow doesn't have to worry about making a living, he can spend a lot of time collecting minds. In fact, that's what some people do for careers. It usually isn't very interesting, but Henry James made money from it."

"It always comes down to that, doesn't it?"

"Well, yeah; and women are doing it now more commercially too. Why do all that work just to be poor?"

"Jesus was poor."

"And he made powerful enemies by condemning folks to hell. A story-teller should be open-ended and give the audience escape-routes other than adhering to roles in a fable. A few jeers from the peanut gallery as art criticism and up he went on a cross."

"They were parables, Pablo, not fables."

"Oh," he said; "I didn't mean to offend you." He laughed, "Kind of like Jesus offended the Pharisees: he sure learned the meaning of 'judge not lest ye be judged.'"

"Leave me alone or I'll tell Vern."

"Right on. Time to shut-up."

I suppose that sounded like nonsensical blasphemy to her, Pablo thought: I better be careful or she'll fit me with a role I don't want to play and I want to stay more popular than Jesus. The average teenage consciousness wants only prefabricated systems to be adapted for expansions of their own patterns; if they think it doesn't apply to them, they aren't interested. Currently, the older folks call it entitlement, and wonder at the greed of their spawn in demanding instant gratification; the very media forums used to bash that selfish mentality keep offering faster access to more enhanced screen-worlds at quickly rising prices and commercialize words like 'empowerment' as if life is a video-game one has to power-up through by collecting identities and tokens. If a screen-world takes longer than a second to appear at commands, people are impatient; yet, ironically, they have nothing better to do than sit in front of screens for eight hours at a time. We are so inundated and heavily invested in politics and entertainment that people often feel they've paid for the right to sneer and jeer at the performances, or to hire someone to do it for them.

Ginny finished her chore and left without turning off the radio. Pablo went to it and violently yanked on the cord to unplug it.

Yes, he thought: I'd better be careful because there are forces at work that'd rejoice to see me lose my job. Americans are always celebrating something- like the former importance of Feast Days in the Roman Catholic Church- usually an entertainment: sports, a TV show's season being available on video, a music award ceremony, a new movie, or- even worse- a promotional announcement for a movie to start filming in three years. Our homes and job sites have become auxiliary arenas. We celebrate everything except our wars in the Mideast, which people seem to not want to know about because of the logistical nightmares of the geography, which few people have the patience to study. Americans' big rewards, which are going global, are watching someone else win an award.

Vern appeared from the front-counter and said, "What've you been saying to Ginny?"

"Oh," Pablo said, "we were talking about the ancient Greeks' victory over Persia."

"And that made her call you a pain in the ass?"

"Well," Pablo replied, "some of the Greeks were notoriously kooky about that kind of stuff."

"What does Cookie have to do with it? She isn't even here."

"I know she isn't, Vernon. I said kooky, not Cookie." Pablo paused over a coffee mug with green lipstick on the rim and put it in the rack of cups. "To be honest, I don't know what upset her. I just mentioned after their triumph there was a fantastic plethora of Greek art, science, and philosophy. I was going to compare it to some of the Allied nations after World War II but she left."

"You were arguing over that?" Vern asked, his face becoming incredulous.

"I didn't think it was an argument. She asked if I'd read any of Sophocles' plays, and I said I was reading Herodotus' *Histories*, then it went from there. A great war can really impact a society and an ugly one can do the reverse."

"Don't you think you were talking over her head, Pablo? I mean, she's in high school for god's sake. Ancient cultures aren't her program except watered-down Oedipal Complexes."

"Well, I thought everyone here is cultivated. Someone even told me I should get cable TV to expand my horizons."

"I'm the one who said that, Pablo." Vern said, irritated. "You don't know how to play to your audience. Just leave them alone, especially the high school kids, and after work I'll buy you a soda."

Pablo nodded, "Thanks, Vernon. I guess you're right. I shouldn't be taking hostages. I don't like being responsible for them."

"It's one way to make the world in your image. What do they call it? The Stockholm Syndrome? Something like that. Oh, and leave the radio alone. I don't want World War III breaking out here in the kitchen so I'm drawing a demarcation line around the radio: consider it the 38th- parallel. Some group-study proved people work better with background music."

What kind of work is it, though? Who funded the research, and how was the information relayed to the public? Pablo asked Vern none of those questions.

Vernon smirked, "I know you don't like being a prefabricated rebel asking for the spotlight, munitions, and money, but you got to change your show. You ain't the only individual here: we're all fighting for some things and against some things. But don't try to expand your empire like Cyrus or Darius."

"How do you know those names?"

"Bible-study, Pablo. Some of us need more focus than you on world views. It's like you're trying to get us all to be Sophocles or Plato. But you said yourself that ugly wars retard culture."

"Oh. I did say that, didn't I?"

"Yes, you did." Vern wagged a finger, saying, "So let us enjoy our music, TV shows, movies, and computer playtimes. If you want to believe we're only fooling ourselves, what do you care? Just don't take a superior attitude about it. It ain't your job to bring us to the light while you're supposed to be doing dishes."

"Thanks, Vernon. That kind of puts things in perspective: corporate wars produce corporate art."

"Whatever. Just keep in mind we're audiences to a lot of different things, and if you feel overwhelmed by us trying to get you to consume them too, remember everyone does that to everyone else."

"We're all hostages of Babylon, eh?"

8

War Rituals

It was a mid-October evening in 2014 and the weather deities were beneficent in bestowing warm and sunny weather. Pablo walked home, occasionally whistling a cheerful, though tone deaf, version of a tune which was part of a movie's soundtrack Hector had watched the previous night while Pablo prepared the family supper. He saw someone approaching a half-block away and recognized the shuffling limp. "Oh, geez," Pablo murmured, "still paying for my sins." Maybe if he's drunk, Pablo thought, I won't register in his mind.

It was a vain hope because Fala's cavernous face lit up with joy and his own hope. He was the reason Pablo had quit carrying spare change and one-dollar bills, for he disliked lying to people such as Fala, who could easily scent a quarry's trail. Fala had missed his calling as a big-game scout; then again, with so many species nearing extinction, Fala would have to be a poacher, which was even more illegal than whatever shenanigans he performed since failing in his dishwashing career. Some favor humans are doing endangered species by putting them behind barbed-wire fences and cages, Pablo thought: I'd rather be killed than be the pet-project of some moron who has the misguided belief I belong in a prison for my own good.

They exchanged greetings and Pablo watched as Fala scanned the perimeter for cigarette butts and aluminum trash. He had a newspaper folded under his left arm and Pablo asked, "Where'd you steal that?"

"It was in front of a restaurant that must be closed for the day, so it wasn't really stealing. I need to look in the want-ads for a job."

"Do they even advertise in papers for jobs anymore?"

"I don't know. I just looked at the headlines." Fala swung the rattling garbage bag he had over his shoulder to the pavement. "Looks like Iran might play ball with us about denying them their wannabe nuclear power."

Pablo smiled, "I remember in the mid-1990s when France extorted civilized nations for better trade agreements by threatening to do nuclear bomb tests if the French didn't get more money. I mean, Jesus, they made the Mafia look like schoolgirls in comparison. I wonder what we'll have to give Israel not to bomb Iran until we give the go-ahead; probably more weapons and money, half of which they'll spend on our politicians."

"Ah, we ought to do the whole world anyway. At least France is Catholic and hates the Muslim invasion draining welfare programs while recruiting for their wars, like what's going on here."

Pablo nodded, "How're you paying rent now, Fala?"

"I got a voucher from the county but it's only good for a month." A dim bulb seemed to light Fala's face and he quickly changed the subject. "Are you still working at *Mood Food?*"

"Yeah. I'm doing your old job."

"Are you working a full-shift?"

Pablo could foresee the angler fishing and replied, "I don't have any money for you. Sorry, Fala."

"Do you get any of the tips?"

"I cashed in the change for bills and only have a few fives." Pablo added, "I need to get some groceries." He didn't bother saying he left the extra change hidden at *Mood Food* until there was enough for a five-dollar bill.

"Oh. I've been sniping all day but two weeks of rain ruined all the butts."

Pablo gave him a cigarette Pablo had pre-rolled, and said, "I gotta get going, Fala. Watch out for the Morlocks."

"What're those?"

"Underground predators, like the Manson Family, from H.G. Wells."

"Never heard of them. Are you making it up?"

"It was on TV last night after the news. *The Time Machine.*"

"Oh, I saw part of it but I blacked-out. Can you help me get well? I'm a little sick right now and need to clear the cobwebs."

"You seem in good spirits."

"I'm not though," Fala pled: "my shin hurts and my eye is bothering me. I can't even breathe through my nose and my ear is ringing."

"I'm sure that cigarette will improve your health," Pablo mercilessly said; "and that's all I can recommend because I can't cure you."

Pablo could tell Fala was weighing the situation, and that he'd decided he might be able to use Pablo in the future if he wasn't too irritated now; so Fala said, "All right," trying not to sound bitter, yet found it difficult to surrender the notion that his tale of woes had only gotten him a roll-your-own cigarette. "Gee, I wish I had bus fare."

"The bus-line doesn't run this late." Pablo looked at Fala curiously and asked, "What's your big reward for fighting the fight? A piece of snatch?"

Fala shrugged, "And they usually try to make me feel grateful for getting that. I'll show them what's what, though. Ol' Fala isn't done for yet."

"You sound like you have a messiah-complex."

"Everyone collects identities, why shouldn't I? And I'm a real person," Fala said, a bit of spittle flying from his mouth, "not like all these college students and business suits. Empty vessels, that's what they are."

"Waiting for you to fill them, eh? When did you dye your hair?"

"Last night. I was drunk and didn't wash it all out so there's some streaks in it." Fala's laughter sounded unconvincing.

"Maybe that makes you more of a real person, Fala. Oh, I see you're wearing fingernail polish, too."

"My friend, Patty, did that. She said she wanted to see how it looked before trying it on herself."

"Wasn't that your excuse the last time I saw you with fingernail polish? That some other broad, Sheila- I think- wanted to see how it looked?" Pablo noticed Fala's agitation at being caught in a lie, but pressed further for the fun of it. "I don't know about adapting the attributes of the current females in your life." Fala squirmed and looked around. "You're supposed to be a real person, Fala, not the duplicate image of someone else."

"I have a lot of different sides to me, like collecting people. Jesus said there's power in group prayer."

"Didn't you hear? God's an atheist and doesn't believe in any of the versions we built of It in our systems."

"But that's only in fake systems. I'm not artificial."

"So is this vision you have telling you you're real as real as the dream that told Xerxes to wage war against the Greeks? I mean, are you like an oracle we should consult that's better than being guided by screen-images?"

"I don't lie and I don't steal," Fala insisted passionately.

"Well, that's odd, Fala, because the police-blotter two days ago said you were thrown in jail for shoplifting."

"That was different. I was sick and needed a drink."

"You just fibbed about not stealing so that makes you a liar and a thief."

Fala was upset. He worked his toothless bottom jaw and spluttered with exasperated futility. He'd have bared fangs if he had them. He couldn't believe Pablo would frustrate Fala's hopes for booze money with the insulting truth. He knew now that Pablo owed Fala even more than when their meeting first occurred. Like many Americans, Fala thought he was special and the rest of the world should recognize that by pleasantly granting him whatever he might want at any given moment; and if they did not acquiesce then all available means to gain his goal were fair-game. Though he had faith in the Capitalist system when it served his demands, he did not believe in fair-trade: people should pay for his company no matter how insane he was; for the fee, he would unveil enlightened oblivion. His wrath, however, overcame his hustler instincts. "You're such a goddamn Jew."

"No," Pablo replied, "I don't believe in making sure rigged diplomacy fails by sending settlers into other people's territories."

"You're an immigrant, aren't you?"

"That was part of the diplomacy for America to get cheap labor." Pablo smiled at the insight, "With refugees scattering around the world, you can safely bet the global conglomerates will relocate to follow the herds. They won't even need to poach because they'll have bought favors from national governments."

"Maybe that's why so many people are picking up guns," Fala said, wiping his eyes.

"Perhaps we've lost the ability to make peace," Pablo said, patting Fala on the shoulder. "More than ever, people feel the need to fight for identities and whatever objects they think helps define them."

"All I have is a bag full of empty aluminum cans to sell at the recycling plant."

"Then you can afford some alcohol, get drunk and forget how miserable you were while canning, but have a few empty cans to start the routine again tomorrow. Plus, you'll be able to further your personal, though repetitive, tales of the apocalypse."

"And you won't help me do that?"

"I've got my own family's quests to tend to," Pablo said. "Besides, I have to consider the community, which you'll probably judge and condemn during your self-induced madness."

"But I'm a lot of fun," Fala said desperately, figuring he'd invested enough in Pablo to deserve a twenty-four ounce can of high-octane embalming fluid disguised as beer.

"No you're not," Pablo replied, shaking his head. "The few times I've seen you lit, you wept like a baby and talked gibberish as if a possessed born-again Christer. Every trail you follow leads to alcohol and bad craziness. You're sort of like those folks who believe their leader ripped a fabric surrounding earth and channeled in space for alien monsters."

"Sounds like science fiction."

"It all depends on perspective and the things that shape our perspectives," Pablo said. "Americans have a wide variety of fantasies to choose from. Krishna said: 'Whatever you believe in, you'll go to.'"

"I don't believe in fantasies," Fala affirmed.

"You shouldn't offend the lord of alcohol, Fala. He- or she- might be on Mount Olympus or Sinai right now judging your faith in him. Or her."

"It must be a female," Fala said; "and a fickle bitch at that."

"No, it only seems that way after you've taken one of your many vows of eternal sobriety; then, of course, you have to be punished before forming a new covenant with her."

Fala sighed, saying, "And make an act of contrition."

"Which may involve helping a fellow-traveler get drunk to serve your Lady."

Fala looked helplessly at the sky and said, "You're an apostate now, aren't you?"

"I don't like having responsibilities I can't control, but I like even less being someone else's responsibility."

"Do you still believe in charity?"

He is clever, Pablo thought; and said, "Well, Fala, I have mixed feelings about it. Georgie Bush Junior wanted to turn over the federal government's welfare programs to organized religions to dole forth as they saw fit to their adherents; and heretics- if not burned at the stake- would either have to proclaim false piety or be denied access to programs, which would succeed in making them meaner as they watched religions not only not pay taxes but get money from the government despite their supposedly being separate. It's a curious thing to trust a government more than the sundry religions America has to offer. I guess, in a way, secularism won; at least for now."

"You didn't answer my question."

"Well, here's one for you, Fala: the king and the land are one."

"Oh, just what we need: an all-powerful secular government."

Pablo grinned, "It's better than investing faith, munitions, and money in Abraham's three religions just for the rigged self-fulfillment of some insane prophets' hallucinations. People are willing to be censored, spied on, and told what to buy in a constant barrage of media forums so long as they can call themselves open-minded and diversified."

"Yeah, I saw fags getting married made the front-page headlines again. Nothing like real news." He said in a falsetto voice, "'It all depends on your perspective.' Yeah, well in my perspective those two boozed-up cowboys in Montana fulfilled their perspective by kicking that AIDS-ridden faggot around and hanging him up in the boondocks as a scarecrow. A better performance art than those stupid staged candle-vigils people had for the homo."

Fala vacillated in social and political perspectives according to his mood and the company he thought as his audience: he might be a Ralph Nader fanatic one moment, then a beer later defend Georgie Bush Junior's policies because the latter had sobered from alcohol and cocaine binges. Pablo didn't care for pigeon-holing personalities, but he did think of Fala as being akin the narrator of Dostoevsky's *Notes from Underground* who said: 'They won't let me…I can't be good!' So Pablo ignored his own people-pleasing attributes, played along with Fala's homosexual-bashing and said, "I came of age during the 1980's full-blown AIDS epidemic scare, when homos were dropping like diseased flies; nowadays, when they die, it's standard operating procedure to avoid all references to AIDS or HIV so I was surprised the media reported that that homo had it. Maybe it was because he got hung-up on barbed wire during a chilly night, caught a head-cold that turned into pneumonia, and since he had no immune system he was destined by the gods to become a martyr for everyone having casual unsafe sex."

"If there's no danger of pregnancy, there's no fun, but that's a chance of bringing new life into the world, not catching some death-sentence disease." When Pablo laughed, Fala sighed and continued, "I watched the past few decades as parts of society packaged the fashion of it being hip to be queer; they call it a lifestyle when it's just a sex-act, and if all they have to offer as culture is a drag-show contest and queer versions of everything heterosexual, count me out. It's not as if they invented it."

"The Persians learned to stylize it from the Greeks, right before various oracles set them at war with each other. The unbelievers were quickly overruled by the state religions."

Fala shook his head, "Don't you think it was more greed than their gods' wills that set them to war?"

"Of course it was, but they had to sell it to the public, just like the sponsors of our news. Anyone who won't buy into the incestuous wars of Islam, Judaism, and Christianity is a heathen; and, like in Herodotus, people switch sides all the time. It's nothing new except the firepower to blast the earth to smithereens and our collective consciousness being happy or sad at once again being suckered into a losing game."

"Right now I'm very sad," Fala said, "that you won't invest in my game."

"Your quest for the grail has succeeded." Pablo said, and took the wallet from his front pocket. "I don't suppose you can break a five."

They paused a few minutes while a squad of Air Force jet-fighters flew overhead. When the awful noise had diminished, Fala said, "They must be on maneuvers from Sioux Falls. They probably have a simulated bombing-pattern for my apartment."

"Just how paranoid are you?"

"They know where everyone lives and have fixed targets for practice."

"You're not an enemy of the state, are you, Fala? I sometimes think of you as an ambassador for the lords and ladies you serve."

"Why wouldn't they target my embassy?" Fala asked, with a nasty gleam in his eyes. "They know I'm gathering disciples for my own maneuvers."

Pablo laughed, "So much for the sanctity of diplomatic immunity. The same can be said for America's ambassador to Iraq, running our military show there. God help him if the Sunni rebels get hold of the embassy: just like what happened in Libya a few years ago. Money and diplomacy don't always fix a stirring of bad-blood. You don't seem the militia-type, though."

"I'm not. I let others do it for me. All they care about nowadays is running up a body-count; like that punk who was planning a shooting-spree and thought three casualties at the Boston Marathon's bombing was lame and had no style. It's too easy of a pickings these days and too simple to locate a herd of humanity at some kind of show. And nowadays it's all about the number of dead. Hell, anyone can go out and do that."

"The Persians thought twice about invading Greece after being massacred at Marathon." Pablo said. "And that was General Ridgway's main directive in the Korean War, not to fight to win but to tally a huge body-count of Chinese so they'd want a cease-fire."

"That's the proper diplomacy for a nation obsessed with actors and actresses: kill off anyone who wants to hog the stage."

Pablo nodded, "You're my stand-in for my rebellious college years. I'd rather send you to represent me, and fill the gaps my absence would make, than do the acting myself in revising history from different perspectives."

"Casting me as a villain, eh?"

"Applying street-smarts to our long, tumultuous relationship with Iraq might be of some value, or at least something new in the memories that thread through our collective minds."

"I say we let them kill each other, then take the oil-fields for ourselves. That's really defending America's interests."

"True," Pablo said; "we never cared about humanitarian interests in Iraq before, so why start now? Unless we have to gild it for public consumption. It's a good thing Obama didn't supply weapons to Syria's rebels because that may have armed Iraq's militias, which trained and practiced in Syria before going home to set their own land in order."

"Like Timothy McVeigh, huh?"

"Or Guy Fawkes." Pablo laughed at Fala's quizzical blink of his eyes. "Well, we can involve Iran's Shiites with Iraqi Shiites and toss them in the ring against the Sunni rebels. Maybe even barter munitions to both sides like we did in the 1980s. If Iran rejects that deal, then we'll just blame Iraqi Shiites for not sharing power with Sunnis."

"What's the difference between them Sunnis and that other group?"

"Shiites? It's a bit like Roman Catholics and Protestants and apostolic succession: one Muslim group believes in Mohammad's heir-line (like the Pope), and the other formed their own pedigree lineage. So they kill each other to find out whose side Allah is on."

"Right on," Fala said; "and if Allah is playing them off each other, why shouldn't America?"

"Good point; and not too hard to sell that attitude to the American public since I've noticed gasoline has gotten less expensive, so the price might be right to at least get benign ambivalence from us. Well, you squint-eyed, gimpy herald, where shall we go to get change for the five? A petrol station is just down the street. I don't know what its name is because so many different conglomerates buy and sell the franchise. Almost like the banks in the 1970s and 80s before high-financial computerized corporate take-overs; it was a lot easier for gangsters to buy banks back then, until the government muscled in on the rackets and set up their own money-laundering." Pablo didn't mention his former troubles of managing wads of undeclared cash.

"How about *Reynaldo's*? They have the cheapest beer in town."

"That's a mile away in the opposite direction from my home."

Fala said, "And the recycler is way on the other side of town from *Reynaldo's*. They couldn't have made it more inconvenient for me."

"Quite a conspiracy against you. And what do you save per beer? Twenty-cents?"

"Thirty-six. Besides, I've been banned from all the *Quickee Shoppy* stores."

"Why?"

"I don't know. I went in there to get a beer last week because my leg hurt and I didn't think I could hump it up that hill to *Reynaldo's* and the manager said I was banned from all the franchises. I must've done something in a black-out. We don't want to go there anyway because you have to buy something to get change."

"It's just down the street though. I'll buy you a beer, then you can cash in your cans and go to *Reynaldo's*."

"Yeah, but the beer at *Quickee Shoppy* is expensive."

Pablo shook his head, "I'm not going to worry about thirty-six-cents, Fala. Do you want a beer or not?"

"You bet I do," Fala said with jubilant exuberance as if professing an article of faith. "I knew you were my friend."

Pablo smiled. How quickly loyalties change. I bashed him, he reacted, and now we're best buddies. "We've normalized our relations, as a professional politico might say. Sorry if it felt like I was slapping on an economic sanction, keeping you from your blissful state."

Fala made a burring sound with his lips, "There's no normalcy in the world anymore. Everyone's too busy looking for a performance to invest in. Things change so fast that anyone who hangs onto a set standard is ostracized or used by an opportunist proclaiming to be the embodiment of their ideals."

"At least alcohol is still cheap, legal, and convenient."

"That'll probably change, too. Say, have you read any of Gogol's works?"

"I've heard of him, but no."

"He wrote a short story about a sorcerer in the Ukraine who partied with Russian Orthodox Christians and then went to orgies with their religious enemies, right before a war broke out between them."

"Nothing like making a sober decision to take someone's life. The Hindus called it Soma Wars. It makes one wonder how much to trust the computer wizards fooling with global finances; I have a hard time believing they don't skim from the top whilst levying out economic sanctions against nations with the push of a button."

"Great," Fala said. "We got a lot of mongoloids with no foresight running things in America: stirred up a revolution in the Ukraine knowing it would piss-off Russia who sent in troops and arms their own brand of rebels, so we slap money-embargoes on them; and desperate for cash and oil, Putin sells munitions to our enemies in the Mideast and elsewhere. Who the hell did Obama's planning or did that crack/cocaine he did when younger fry too many synapses?"

"Oh, well, it's more convenient than blockading a seaport or laying siege against a walled-city. Twenty-million Russians died during World War II, so they're not likely to take a fall as a patsy. I suppose screen-game warfare was bound to evolve. At least alcohol is reliable in escaping the third-dimension." Pablo sang:

"This is what Fala believes
when the porcelain god calls for dry-heaves:
Please, lord, all of last night I forget,
but accept my sacrifice to the toilet."

Fala laughed, "My ribs still hurt from three mornings ago. But you're not going to start making fun of me again, are you?"

"Ah, Fala, we're a nation that tends to over-do rewards and punishments, but if we don't enforce some kind of order, even an artificial one, then the rot sets in and people get too bitter and cynical towards the chain-of-command. Not everyone wants to be revolutionary, and if the media forums overplay unmasking cowards and lechers, which of us can honestly throw the first stone?"

"There's always street justice."

"Yeah," Pablo said, "if you want to put faith in homicidal gangsters crazy on steroids and cocaine; a lot of whom are government informers to wipe-out competition. Or would you rather have your hand chopped-off for stealing?"

"No, but it's more real than the delusions of justice we get from the court system."

Pablo laughed, thinking of Samsara, the illusion of life's deathly ocean, and said, "The human body is ninety-percent water and our personalities are ninety-percent fantasies. We go to war to preserve our way of life, which is based on escaping the third-dimension, and we're willing to blow it all to pieces so that we don't have to escape it anymore."

"Did they ever decide on building that shale oil refinery near town?"

"They're waiting on federal funds to finish the water pipeline from the Missouri River."

Fala nodded, "Oh, yeah. They'll need a steady supply of water for the refinery, where we can all have jobs; and twenty years from now, when the corporation moves to a better water supply, we can all have jobs cleaning up the mess. Well, here we are. Thanks for helping me get polluted."

"What's your flavor?" Pablo asked as they stood on the street corner across from the convenience store.

"A can of *Twasted*. They ain't exactly subtle in their packaging but you won't be paying for the marketing or a celebrity hired to shill it against an enemy celebrity shilling a different brand."

"I must've been out of the drinking-game too long. I never heard of it."

Fala grinned, "A true advertisement genius invented the name: a combination of twisted and wasted."

"I guess that's an honest business maneuver. I'll be right back."

ACT III

9

Sensitivity Training

"Alkinoos made her [Arete] his wife, and gave her such pride of place as no other woman on earth is given of such women as are now alive and keep house for husbands. So she was held high in the heart and still she is so, by her beloved children, by Alkinoos himself, and by the people, who look toward her as to a god when they see her, and speak in salutation as she walks about in her city. For there is no good intelligence that she herself lacks. She dissolves quarrels, even among men, when she favors them. So if she has thoughts in her mind that are friendly to you, then there is hope that you can see your own people, and come back to your house with the high roof and to the land of your fathers."...

But now Odysseus came to the famous house of Alkinoos, but the heart pondered much in him as he stood before coming to the bronze threshold. For as from the sun the light goes or from the moon, such was the glory on the high-roofed house of great-hearted Alkinoos. Brazen were the walls run about it in either direction from the inner room to the door, with a cobalt frieze encircling, and golden were the doors that guarded the close of the palace, and silver were the pillars set in the brazen threshold, and there was a silver lintel above, and a golden handle, and dogs made out of gold and silver were on each side of it, fashioned by Hephaistos in his craftsmanship and cunning, to watch over the palace of great-hearted Alkinoos, being themselves immortal and all their days they were ageless...

On the outside of the courtyard and next the doors is his orchard, a great one, four land measures, with a fence driven all around it, and there is the place where his fruit trees are grown tall and flourishing, pear trees and pomegranate trees and apple trees with their shining fruit, and the sweet fig trees and the flourishing olive...

Then in turn Alkinoos spoke to him and answered: "Stranger, the inward heart in my breast is not of such a kind as to be recklessly angry. Always moderation is better. O father Zeus, Athene and Apollo, how I wish that, being the man you are and thinking the way that I do, you could have my daughter and be called my son-in-law, staying here with me. I would dower you with a house and properties, if you stayed by your own good will. Against that, no Phaiakian shall detain you. Never may such be to Zeus father's liking. As for conveyance, so that you may be sure, I appoint it for tomorrow..."

-Homer *Odyssey* 7: 66-77; 81-94; 112-116; 308-318

...Ares entered the house. Then he took her [Aphrodite] by the hand and spoke to her and named her, saying: 'Come, my dear, let us take our way to the bed, and lie there, for Hephaistos is no longer hereabouts, but by this time he must have come to Lemnos and the wild-spoken Sintians.' So he spoke, and she was well pleased to sleep with him. These two went to bed, and slept there, and all about them were bending the artful bonds that had been forged by subtle Hephaistos, so neither of them could stir a limb or get up, and now they saw the truth, and there was no longer a way out for them. The glorious smith of the strong arms came and stood near. He had turned back on his way, before ever reaching the Lemnian country, for Helios had kept watch for him, and told him the story. He took his way back to his own house, heart grieved within him, and stood there in the forecourt, with the savage anger upon him, and gave out a terrible cry and called to all the immortals: 'Father Zeus and all you other blessed immortal gods, come here, to see a ridiculous sight, no seemly matter, how Aphrodite daughter of Zeus forever holds me in little favor, but she loves ruinous Ares because he is handsome, and goes sound on his feet, while I am misshapen from birth, and for this I hold no other responsible but my own father and mother, and I wish they never had got me. Now look and see, where these two have gone to bed and lie there in love together. I am sickened when I look at them.'....So he spoke, and the gods gathered to the house with the brazen floor. Poseidon came, the shaker of the earth, and the kindly Hermes came, and the lord who works from afar, Apollo, but the female gods remained each at her home, for modesty. The gods, the givers of good things, stood there in the forecourt, and among the blessed immortals uncontrollable laughter went up as they saw the handiwork of Hephaistos...lord Apollo son of Zeus said a word to Hermes: 'Hermes, son of Zeus, guide and giver of good things, tell me, would you, caught tight in these strong fastenings, be willing to sleep in bed by the side of Aphrodite the golden?' Then in turn the courier Argeiphontes answered: 'Lord who strikes from afar, Apollo, I wish it could only be, and there could be thrice this number of endless fastenings, and all you gods could be looking on and all the goddesses, and still I would sleep by the side of Aphrodite the golden.'

-Homer *Odyssey* 8: 290-314; 321-327; 334-342

Aphrodite didn't sign a prenuptial marriage contract, but the only way her humiliated husband would release her from the snare was for Poseidon to promise to pay any debt Ares might renege on after gaining freedom and deciding he'd paid enough dues by being a public display for gods to laugh at. Baal Clinton felt he didn't owe any lawsuit money for accusations of sexual harassment by a woman who did nude photographs that surfaced in a girly-mag when she got famous for taking Clinton to court. Ah, the jokes heard round the world; rather like the bard singing for his supper in Alkinoos's court with a ditty about philandering deities.

The gossip that soars through the airwaves, like Helios (the sun, as a kind of surveillance helicopter) telling Hephaistos about his wife and the god of war, cuts both ways: it can make me enlightened and sick, and may not be reliable. It comes in various forms, like the shapes Athena and Hermes assume to guide Odysseus. Unlike him, I don't trust anyone that crafty because nature is dual and it's difficult for mortals to fathom the gods' motives, especially when they're notoriously fickle, moving from one chosen group to the next, like Yaweh's moveable feast from Jews to Christians to Muslims. A deity can give all the orders it wants to, in an orchard or through the *deus ex machina*, but I'll make my own choices. The one time I was old enough to choose to follow another's directions implicitly, of my own will I became a dope-dealer, which convinced me I lack the skill to select worthy guides. Suggestions...well, maybe. However, I have realized that since I rebel against following strict advice or commands then I shouldn't issue any of my own, though that doesn't keep me from doing it.

High-technology surveillance has had a major impact on marriage, sort of evolved from Hephaistos's magic watch-dogs at Alkinoos's palace, and Odysseus wisely knows he's being watched and analyzed, and follows Athena's advice to supplicate the women. I'm not as much of an outsider as I used to be, but Estella has deeper roots in the community. A sewing-circle from her church is teaching her to knit while I stay home and read and Hector hangs out with his buddies. The truth is, I don't trust anyone, not even Estella. Since I got her pregnant, I had the fear of god put into me.

I considered moving us to another region, but it would be imperative to have false identities and in running away to keep from being prey to my old illegalities, we would have to commit more crimes; and with entire lives in computer systems, fake identities could bring down the hammer of American justice. Besides which, I don't want to tell Estella or Hector about the Tsar cleaning house, Hugo, or the district attorney's investigation; even if they agreed to flee with me, I'm uncertain they could stay in assumed personalities.

When I first met Estella's family, who moved to this region from New Mexico in the late 1960s, they were dismayed that I'm not Hispanic, or even a bit mestizo. Maybe I should've tried harder to win them over instead of putting forth a parallel coldness. Now they're indifferent to me, and when I go to their family gatherings I pretend to watch whatever's on television, which is usually sporting events, especially soccer; a pastime that, counting all the stratums and business generated such as hotels, gambling, and restaurants, has become a multi-trillion-dollar industry. Its big news now is a global tournament being played in the middle of a hundred-degree temperature desert, with accusations of chicanery and bribes to have it played there. Of course the headquarters are in Switzerland where people are so heavily invested in secret funds that no one dares audit accounts. My only surprise was that thus far it hasn't involved Dubai, but Estella's family is watching the scandal with all the potent enraptured attention of detached hooligans.

They were disappointed I didn't encourage Hector to play soccer, and football doesn't interest him much, which is a good thing because severe brain trauma is so rampant in that game it's like decapitating players as sacrifices according to aptitude after contests in the ancient ball-sports; or even referees who take the chance of a high school coach sending players out to gang-tackle the ref for making a disagreeable ruling, and the ensuing thuggery becomes a popular show on international computer sites. There's also nothing quite like observing an audience watch an audience go berserk and tear down a coliseum or fanatically attack a fan wearing the wrong team colors; and oh! the lamenting the professional members of sports' shows do, even as they try to whip-up a frenzy for the next game their sponsors have chosen to broadcast.

When Hector's buddies joined a pee-wee baseball league, he enlisted too, and I practiced with him. All the players tried each position, but his first coach made Hector the permanent short-stop, which- I must admit- made me proud. I coached for a season, when the children were about ten-years-old. As they got older, parents began taking it very seriously so I didn't argue when Hector followed his friends and quit last year. If they'd gone another season, through 8th grade, they'd have had a good team and maybe ended their careers with a league championship, before high school started and even more pressure was put on local heroes, who can easily become the tag-line of countless jokes and gossip with one flaw.

Infidelity among deities was a laughing matter, but between humans it was cause for bloodshed, like the war at Troy, ostensibly over Helen. Odysseus knew that his affairs with goddesses would be forgiven, however he wisely declined to practice bigamy because passions would flare and the deities might've punished him, being- as they were- in charge of human breeding through vows and blessings, including marriage. Athena and Hermes, the latter telling Odysseus how to bed Circe, were his guides homeward and could've turned mean or refused to help Odysseus had he wed or seduced Nausikaa, the daughter of Arete and Alkinoos. Nothing like being harshly judged by unchaste deities; and how could a pure god or goddess understand the faults and foibles of humanity?

You never know what you'll get when you side with a rebel angel who is in the market for prestige and power and doesn't want to just switch to a new brand of oppression. We could have a rerun of the Korean War, only in the Mideast, with Russia backing Syrian royalty and us supporting the rebels. Or Ukraine and Crimea being partitioned, each going with whatever nations offers the best bribes. Vladimir Putin, Russia's chief, made a lot of oligarchical buddies from American loans- while our social programs were dismantled, which only succeeded in filling prisons- who are willing to throw some money (not their own, of course) at the civil wars. Part of the historians' inheritance is the urge to correct all the fallacies and set the world straight from their ancestors' flaws. Herodotus, who felt compelled to make his history bigger than Homer's *Iliad*, wrote of Greek and Persian colonists having confrontations in the Ukraine-area that was background for the wars staged between a monarchy and a partly democratized confederacy.

In a way, I don't blame Russia for protecting its borders; and they needed a strong-man after Yeltsin, who drunkenly squandered their satellite states, empowered the mobsters' black markets, and got Russia deep into debt. Putin was the head of the Soviet Union's main spy-ring, and has so much dirt on so many people that their safest choice, though perhaps not honorable, is to toe-the-line and hope to make some profit while at it. It's easy enough to demonize Putin, or hope he's like the reincarnation of Darius and fails miserably in his attempt to quell Ukraine.

* * *　* * *　* * *　* * *

Rebekah said to Isaac: "I am disgusted with life because of the Hittite women. If Jacob also should marry a Hittite woman, a native of the land, like these women, what good would life be to me?"...Esau noted that Isaac had blessed Jacob when he sent him to Paddan-aram to get himself a wife there, charging him, as he gave him his blessing, not to marry a Canaanite woman, and that Jacob had obeyed his father and mother and gone to Paddan-aram. Esau realized how displeasing the Canaanite women were to his father Isaac, so he went to Ishmael, and in addition to the wives he had, married Mahalath, the daughter of Abraham's son Ishmael and sister of Nebaloth.

-Genesis 27: 46; 28: 6-9

Compared to Arete, the wife of Alkinoos and propositioned mother-in-law of Odysseus, Rebekah was a snob of the first-caliber; she would be disgusted by Nausikaa doing laundry at the river: that's what slaves are for. Yet native women often have the reputation of wanting to expand gene-pools. Esau wanted something different in a woman, maybe because he wasn't too keen on his mother; but when he realized his revenge on Jacob was delayed and Rebekah had manipulated Isaac for further in-breeding between her favorite son and a first-cousin (of course from the mother's side), Esau quickly also found a cousin to marry. So much for diversity. The early North and South American colonists had their belly-warmer native women but didn't keep records of their off-spring. One good thing about not being Hispanic is I don't have to worry about Estella being some kind of distant relation. Choosing wives and mates is a tricky business, especially while on the run. Ah, the gods can control harsh breeding-programs; and there's something to be said for a native woman who seems exotic to an outlander. We tend to reflect that which most captivates us, but in-breeding slows nature down enough to domesticate, though too much of it makes mongos.

Consistency has never been a strong point for humans, as we are an imitative species that changes according to the necessities of adaptation; as the pace becomes frenetic through machinery, we change to suit alternate dimensions. America is now training and arming Syrian rebels; we fight beside the Shiites against the Sunni in Iraq, and fight the Shiites in Yemen to aid the Sunni. The common American misconception seems to be: "Sure, we were shooting at them, but that was twenty days ago. Haven't they gotten over that yet? I mean, now we're arming and training them. Don't they owe us some loyalty?" Blind desires with no clear objective may be the appropriate wars for a complex, heavily-medicated nation that has lost touch with nature, like the Hindu war-god who was unaware he wanted to mate with his mother. America's enemies don't believe our fabricated myths and propaganda that center around our military and spy agencies, and our foes probably aren't interested in learning to all lace their combat-boots the same way as a means of instilling instant obedience to orders; however, they will take the weapons and munitions' training we give them to use against us when we try to adopt them as pawns in the wars, which probably inspires belief in our stupid gullibility rather than fear and respect. If I were in the general infantry and was given instructions to arm and train someone I'd been shooting at the previous day, my conceptive impulse would be to frag the idiot commander issuing the order, then blast the person I was supposed to help kill me. Yet during this madness of arming foreign foes, there is a growing call among Americans to rein in the domestic free-wheeling gun industry.

The first thing my mom did after landing in America was learn the currency rate, not the language, and applied for social programs; with gold and domesticated animals (including slaves) no longer being the standard exchange, she did the wise thing. Will refugees become future cannon-fodder with the proper munitions' training, or angry outsiders in the nations that adopt them to multiply and be fruitful and use old tales to create their own stories? Perhaps pursue the latest American art-form of being paid to complain that they made money from an audience that forced them to say derogatory things about themselves and what they think they represent; that others should pay for making believers feel guilty through criticism of their fantasies. No matter what you do or who you are, it's someone else's fault if you feel bad, and by god, they should pay for it. As the common motto goes, reaching beyond all boundaries: 'I only want to empower people I agree with, who can bring about the fulfillments of my wish-list.' It's to be expected that immigrants will herd to people much like Odysseus went to Arete for sponsorship, only not all such community leaders have her mythic qualities of beneficence. It would be tempting to manipulate new-arrivals for one's own purposes.

A person could probably delineate the exact sequence of modern feminists deciding they should teach student girls to empower themselves via sex, as if that takes some sort of skill or talent that trained courtesans lack as an institution and which have existed since the earliest civilizations. I tend to the belief that power comes with a price, and if women are willing to run the risks of getting raped to further their careers, then announce thirty years later that their celebrity daddy-figure did them dirt, and they went back for more to have him help prod their careers, well there's not much I can do for them. Perhaps in his next life he'll do something like that on the streets, get imprisoned and repeatedly raped himself. Yet to try to get men to bow to women for their empowerment as a sterile figure of sex in classrooms or onscreen is a certain way to excite those who demand to sow seeds in

Harlots of A Fruitful Harvest; so, ladies, good luck with your role-playing towards empowerment. If they want their own stuff, third-dimensional and otherwise, they'll have to protect it themselves; I won't do it for them: I'm not a hired gun. I can only control where I put my sperm, and haven't done the best at that; it's not the females' fault I want them that way, and if it's used to create something that tethers us together in genetic strands or formed to protect women from me, then I have to discern which battles are worth engaging and what to walk away from without resenting part of my essence being used against me. Perhaps that's why I don't want to invest in Estella's desire for more machinery because it'll just be another means for her to wage combat and get revenge.

The advocates of self-responsibility want the world made in their image. They don't understand that I can't be self-responsible if they dictate what I think, say, and do to achieve it. I know I'll fail at teaching self-responsibility to Hector because no one is truly capable of understanding anyone else's full responsibilities, including that to an ever-changing community. However, many of them are good at blaming those of us who don't accept their formatted means of self-responsibility, a rejection that causes the woes of the universe. We are the disobedient Adam and Eve in their Garden of Eden, and we too blame something else because we do not exist in a vacuous void: better to be under the influence of free will than ignorant; and using free will to deny responsibility for being tempted into our own creation via Original Sin is like being a Yaweh who smote the serpent. That Yaweh sent a son to take on a godly punishment shows Yaweh reflected on where self-responsibility ultimately belongs.

It's human to take credit for someone else's work and blame others when things go bad. I certainly felt I deserved the zenith I had several years ago when I owned a house, two cars, a motorcycle, and all the technological paraphernalia that Hector and I learned together how to use. When the bottom could no longer support the system and fell out, I was quick to scapegoat the people who I thought had tempted me into investing in their illusions; like so many others around the world, I believed I had been misled, not by Lucifer, but by a born-again Christian president and his motley horde of Platonists promising something more solid than shades.

Two sides of the same coin in money-changing America: "Conform to our institutionalized diversity of laws protecting people's feelings from being hurt, or you'll be labeled an outsider." Or: "Believe in our scripture as god's script or we will smite thee." Invest according to pay-offs in fantasies, not for clean air, water, food, and land. Homer knew it was safer to make fun of the deities' faults and foibles than the ruling humans, who were frequently considered descendants of gods. The Roman Catholic Church and the pope's *deus ex cathedra* (from the throne, and thus commanded by God) have become something that are no longer dangerous to openly bash and ridicule. Yet even though everyone wants to be first with the joke, it's not totally safe to publically humiliate anyone for a laugh because there're too many weapons lying around, including screen forums to display any indiscretions from the joker's own past. The *deus ex machina* gives and takes away and knowing some Muslims are notoriously humorless about their religion, it's best to jibe a god the believers feel comfortable laughing at, though there are always a few spoilsports in the arena.

* * *   * * *   * * *   * * *

Romeo: Can I go forward when my heart is here?
Turn back, dull earth, and find thy center out.
Benvolio: Romeo! My cousin Romeo! Romeo!
Mercutio: He is wise
And, on my life, hath stolen him home to bed.
Benvolio: He ran this way and leapt this orchard wall.
Call, good Mercutio.
Mercutio: Nay, I'll conjure too.
Romeo! Humours! Madman! Passion! Lover!
Appear thou in the likeness of a sigh.
Speak but one rhyme, and I am satisfied;
Cry but "Ay me!" Pronounce but "love" and "dove".
Speak to my gossip Venus one fair word,
One nickname for her purblind son and heir,
Young Abraham Cupid, he that shot so trim
When King Cophetua loved the beggar maid.-

He heareth not, he stirreth not, he moveth not;
The ape is dead, and I must conjure him.-
I conjure thee by Rosaline's bright eyes,
By her fine foot, straight leg, and quivering thigh,
And the demesnes that there adjacent lie,
That in thy likeness thou appear to us!
Benvolio: An if he hear thee, thou wilt anger him.
Mercutuio: This cannot anger him. 'Twould anger him
To raise a spirit in his mistress' circle
Of some strange nature, letting it there stand
Till she had laid it and conjured it down;
That were some spite. My invocation
Is fair and honest; in his mistress' name
I conjure only but to raise up him.
Benvolio: Come, he that hid himself among these trees
To be consorted with the humorous night.
Blind is his love and best befits the dark.
Mercutio: If love be blind, love cannot hit the mark.
Now will he sit under a medlar tree
And wish his mistress were that kind of fruit
As maids call medlars when they laugh alone.
O, Romeo, that she were, O, that she were
An open-arse, and thou a poppering pear!
Romeo, good night. I'll to my truckle-bed;
This field bed is too cold for me to sleep.

-Shakespeare *Romeo and Juliet 2*, I: 1-41

    Mercutio wears himself out from all the sex-jokes directed at Romeo and his constant craving for romance, which Mercutio thinks should be energized by Aphrodisiac fruit that even women laugh about when men aren't present (like a banana has certain phallic connotations). So Mercutio goes to bed, not standing vigilance- even getting the wrong name in his incantation of Romeo's current love- unlike Hermes/Mercury, whose epithet, Argeiphontes, was earned after putting to sleep, then killing Argus, the beast with myriad eyes and Hera's watchdog to make sure her brother-husband Zeus didn't get some snatch on the side. We watch each other with devices similar to Hermes winged shoes and staff of slumber, waiting for a lapse of reason to be put on video and spread across the globe. Romeo is left alone to blunder into a disastrous relationship, and Odysseus goes free.

Cookie is getting more assertive at *Mood Food*, which conjures forth my natural aggressiveness like some dark spell from an ancient incantation. I doubt Vern will veto my co-employees' petition votes to rid them of me. He tried to promote me because I know how to get around on computers and place orders, which he intensely dislikes doing; and he personalized it when I refused. He's been the manager there almost as long as Putin's been in power. Vern's proud of his motto: 'God, Guns, and Guts Made America Great.' He asked me to have coffee with him after work and I thought about what we might talk of, and mentioned to him the hatchet-man of the Jews, Sampson, was based on the Greeks' Hercules. He got rabid, raised his voice and said the *Bible* was true in every aspect; so I decided not to have coffee with him. I hurt his feelings even more when I- as politely as I could- turned down an offer to attend his Bible-study group. I wouldn't be entertained, let alone interested, in some goof's soliloquy on *The Book of Revelation* being currently fulfilled. We tend to want such things to be arranged behind the sets so we can recognize the signs and have something to believe in other than a world-wide video of a moron farting on a cracker then eating it and saying, "Everything tastes better on a Butter-maker." I get the feeling many Americans subconsciously believe their assumed culture isn't worth fighting for, and at least with the *Bible* they have ready-made propaganda offering better lives for sale.

I don't want to invest faith in fantasies just to escape the third-dimension. In a way, I've just returned to it, and it's not as bad as I thought it was; and I've recovered from being a refugee from another dimension. There really is no shame in being poor. I have sympathy for Hector not having the funds to compete with most of his peers. Maybe it'll build his character in a good way or build resentments so he'll get a career putting the shaft to people and when he feels guilty about it, he'll blame me. All guides have flaws. I'm fatalistic that we must face destiny alone and it can be far removed from previous plans: if wearing the crown at a stadium, one is entirely alone, surrounded by sycophants and regicidal intrigues; if wearing tattered rags in the ring of an arena, facing a starving leopard, one is also alone. I wonder how the *Gospel* writers knew what Jesus said while in the Garden of Gethsemane; maybe his fellows heard it in their sleep. Jesus died with two criminals, and I like to think that Fala was the kind thief.

Reputations seem to be actualized in America by images. Arete would be summarily dismissed by modern women for her morals and good standing in the community because she's not onstage doing a monologue about her vagina. A command performance for Bubba Bill Clinton: throw some snatch his way and be rewarded with a high-status job, benefits, and health-care; at least so considered many feminists during Baal's impeachment process. Arete's only good because she has a reputation to maintain and knows she's being watched, but given the opportunity would be a corrupt slut like Aphrodite, and may already have been only no one knows about it except readers of Lucius Apuleius's *Transformations* which does varied humorous versions on the story that Mercutio would've approved of, including the wronged husband catching his wife and her lover, the latter being corn holed and beaten by the vengeance-greedy husband, witnessed not by a deity but a man who was altered into a donkey and thrashed along to destiny. That was back when people believed their deities' eyes were everywhere; now they're global conglomerate surveillance auctioned to nations and other corporations. Apuleius's versions of that section of the *Odyssey* later inspired Boccaccio who influenced Chaucer, and he became the grandfather of the English language. I suppose we all get the kind of guides we deserve on life's pilgrimage, though it's so easy to change identities and stories that it's difficult doing background checks to make certain we're not following a disreputable gazoonie unless one trusts a corrupt computer system that can purchase a new, improved reputation with sacrifices. One can wipe out or invent an identity with a few conjuring buttons as quickly as Hermes mercurialized into new shapes.

* *   * * *   * * *   * * *

I was among those souls who are suspended;
a lady called to me, so blessed, so lovely

that I implored to serve at her command.
Her eyes surpassed the splendor of the star's;
and she began to speak to me- so gently
and softly- with angelic voice.

-Dante *Inferno* canto 2: 52-57

King: So is it, if thou knew'st our purposes.
Hamlet: I see a cherub that sees them. But come, for England! Farewell, dear mother.
King: Thy loving father, Hamlet.
Hamlet: My mother. Father and mother is man and wife, man and wife is one flesh, and so, my mother.

-Shakespeare *Hamlet* 4, 3: 51-56

Hamlet didn't have much of a guide when setting out on his mission for revenge, which included a side journey to England. Getting advice from a ghost to murder an uncle is another reason for Hamlet to act insane; yet the problem with pretending to go crazy is one might step over the boundary and actually go there. He was under close scrutiny and had to use his own questionable wits to out-maneuver intrigues, and for that he is likeable and despicable, and even more diplomatic with head-hunters than I am with my employer and co-workers who seem to want to broadcast themselves through me like the ghost of Hamlet's father. They team-up against each other, switch alliances, and resent that I have no loyalty to any of them nor partake in flying gossip. I did enough of that when I was young, and it seems to happen if one associates one's self with the Word of a *deus ex machina* god and feels compelled to spread the news, mostly bad: a few saved, the rest damned. The only person I like to talk about at work is Fala, and that's mainly because he's a true survivor: he's seen almost as many horrors as I have and I respect him for it. He drives everyone away with his induced insanity, so those horrors are all he has to keep him company, which makes him one of the loneliest people I've met.

10

Antiseptics versus Plagues

Pablo's first thoughts upon unlocking the family's apartment door was to beeline for his smoking table-tray for a puff of can'sa'sa from his peace-pipe. After greeting Estella, who was boiling eggs, and Hector, who barely glanced from his comic-book, Pablo took off his coat, and the t-shirt with the *Mood Food* logo, and inhaled a deep draught of smoke. He got a glass of cold water from the jug in the refrigerator, tossed the shirt into a laundry basket in the closet and put on a sweater.

"Are you going to shower before we eat?" Estella asked, gazing at the stop-watch in her hand timing the eggs.

"Well, I don't smell as bad as Philoctetes but I do feel exiled. And have some bad resentments."

"Am I supposed to know who that is?"

"Take an educated guess; maybe you'll surprise us both."

"The name sounds too strange to be in *The Scarlet Letter*." Estella looked at Pablo and smiled, saying, "I can usually follow your literary allusions according to the books you're currently reading." Pablo grunted, not liking to be so transparent. "What made you read that anyway?"

"Something someone said a few years ago. And it was on sale."

"You need to use your library card more, Pablo. We can't afford or have the space for a bunch of books."

Pablo did not want to be drawn into an argument over books disappearing into the cyberspace of electronic hand-held devices which made them easier to censor- oops, there goes the 13th-Century- so he said, "Are you going to guess who Philoctetes was or is the reference going to go unappreciated?"

"Tell me, if you feel so compelled."

"A diseased weapon's dealer during the Trojan War. There. Now you'll be able to sleep tonight."

"No I won't," Estella replied; "I'll be too worried about the guy who came looking for you today. And these eggs: they're so small since chickens aren't shot-up with hormones anymore."

Pablo was quiet, then stepped closer to her as she ran cold faucet water over the pot of eggs. He murmured, "Who was it?"

"I don't know. He was here about an hour ago, waiting at the door for us. Said he needed to talk to you."

"Was he a cop or from Simon or what?"

"I just told you, Pablo, I don't know. He looked like hell, though. He said he'd try back later tonight."

"What color was he?"

"Like you," Estella said: "Indian-Mayan."

"I want you to take Hector and go to Sioux Falls," Pablo said, taking out his wallet.

"What're you talking about? Is it about something when you met with Simon?"

"Don't ask. Just take the money and get a hotel room for the night. Call tomorrow about eleven. Oh, and while you're at it, get me some kinnick kinnick and can'sa'sa from the Native American art gallery. And don't spend it all on gambling machines."

She laughed shrilly and said, "I'll have Hector so I won't be able to go into a casino." She closed her eyes tightly and shook her head, "We don't have money for this. How'll we pay rent?"

"I have some money squirreled away I didn't tell you about. Right now we don't have much choice: just get a cheap room and don't tell me where."

"What kind of deviltry are you into now?" She started crying but Pablo refused to reflect on shame until she and Hector were safely gone.

"It's something from the past. That's all I can say." He wouldn't hug or console her; his mind was focused on survival, a trait he'd hoped he would never again have to utilize. "Get going and I'll walk you to the car. Come on, Hector. You're going to spend the night in Sioux Falls, rotting your brain with cable television."

Hector didn't appear very excited at the prospect of spending the night with his nervous-wrecked mother. He stood up, eyes wide and face concerned, "Why don't you come with us, dad?"

"I'll be all right," Pablo replied, keeping his tone calm. Since he had sobered, his son had expressed a deep empathetic desire to look after his father. It didn't weary Pablo, but it was disturbing that he was perceived as more immature than his child.

"Hector, go wait in the hall," Estella said, her voice shaky but stern with no hysteria.

"We don't have time for this," Pablo said. "You both have to leave now."

"Not until we get a few things straight: like why I can't stay at my brother's tonight."

"Don't go to Eduardo's."

"Why not? I mean- get out in the hall, Hector, now!"

"Abu Ghraib," Pablo sighed.

"What?"

"There are ways of finding things out which may be unreliable but can give a certain satisfaction."

"Are you talking about torture?"

"Come on. I'll walk you out."

She grabbed her purse from the kitchen counter and said, "I expect a full confession tomorrow, Pablo, or Hector and I are gone permanently."

Pablo ran his fingers through his hair and replied, "You'll get one, you'll get one." He stared hard at his wife and said, "I'll tell you everything as if you were my priest. I'd hoped it'd all blown by but if it's what I think it is, you need to know."

"Mom," Hector asked, "can I have a soda for the ride?"

"I don't want you getting all caffeined-up. How many have you already had?"

"Two," Hector lied.

"Okay, go ahead and get one. But only one."

Pablo said, "That reminds me: get his medications and your bathroom stuff before you go. Toothbrushes and whatnot."

"I'll get them, mom," Hector said, grabbing an empty plastic grocery bag from under the sink and charging to the bathroom. Hector hadn't been in full survival mode for several years either, but if he couldn't save his parents, he would at least try to function good in the crisis.

While he was busy in the bathroom there was a lull, then Estella said, "Is it always going to be like this with us?"

Pablo shook his head. He realized his terror of being alone had prevented him from informing his wife and son about Pablo's former Tsar wiping clear any trace that could be linked to him; nor had Pablo mentioned Hugo, who might be more reasonable than an assassin for the Tsar. The latter would probably only surface for a quick kill and not have revealed himself to Estella. It seemed to Pablo his fate was to deny and fight his destiny.

"This is something from the past, isn't it?"

Pablo didn't answer, but thought: Maybe studying history's repetitions is like an incantation that summons resurrections. He kissed her on the forehead, not daring to look into her eyes, and said, "Clean up a bit and get rid of the shakes. You have to be able to drive safely. Hell, it'd be a bitter irony if you had a car-wreck driving away from potential danger."

Estella sobbed a laugh and wiped her face with a paper towel. "I'm glad I didn't put make-up on today."

"You don't need it. You may've slowed down a bit but you've kept your looks, for which I'm grateful."

"You can be so shallow sometimes," she replied, shaking her head. "Was that supposed to comfort me?"

Pablo smiled, "I don't want to part on bad terms." Hector emerged from the hall and his father asked, "Got everything?"

"Yeah. I think so."

"Let me see," Estella said. She pawed through the bag quickly, observing the contents. "Okay. Let's go."

"Can I bring some extra soda for tomorrow?" Hector pled, playing their distraction for all it was worth; despite the immediacy of the situation it was a temptation Hector could not resist.

Estella's voice was a near snarl, "Just bring the whole goddamn twelve-pack."

Hector ignored her tone and gleefully went to the refrigerator; but Pablo said, "Try to take it easy on him and yourself. This is my doing and we'll clear the air later."

Estella glanced about for a moment, trying to focus yet not desiring to roil in ire towards her husband. She sighed and said, "Okay. All right. Walk us down to the car and the innocent bystanders will be out of the way."

Pablo nodded, "We're all looking for a purity that isn't there, but there are gradations of corrupt alloys. Or as a priest might say, 'Something drives me to skip venal sins and graduate straight to cardinal vices.'"

"You're going right back to your alchemy-speak, Pablo. I guess that's something in you that'll always be there." She kissed him on the cheek. "Too many years of trying to find the right mixture. Don't forget to pour cold water on the eggs."

"I have enough roles to play right now; I think I'll skip the house-husband routine after you're gone."

Though Estella and Hector did not notice, Pablo was carefully watching the hallway and two flights of steps they descended to the small entrance foyer. He allowed Hector to precede them because Pablo didn't want to stir more anxiety by forcefully calling his son back; nor did Pablo trust his own nerves to not be angry with Hector if he blithely ignored his father and went on swinging the soda in his hand, humming a cheerful tune. However, at the front door, Pablo told Hector to walk with his mother, and they proceeded to the dimly lit parking lot.

The weather was crisp with chill but not windy. Pablo felt a moment of sympathy for his wife and son, driving an hour in the aged car with no heat, most of which exited through the exhaust system. It took a few confusing minutes to convince Estella to take off the mittens she had darned the previous autumn and to wear gloves while driving. When their car had gone a block, Pablo sighed relief and trudged to the apartment.

After clearing space in the refrigerator, he put the pot of eggs on a shelf. He showered and finished reading Ben Jonson's *Bartholomew Fair*, staged in England a few years before Shakespeare's death in 1616. At a less strenuous time, Pablo would have wrote a brief dissertation on the Puritan character, Zeal of the Land Busy, comparing him to Nathaniel Hawthorne's zealous Dimesdale who, except as a sperm donor, was worthless.

For several years, Pablo had made his living by mixing cocaine with baby food powder then selling it. Perhaps he had helped destroy many lives; he certainly sold a means by which to do it. Now, if his supposition was correct, a vengeful wraith named Hugo was out for Pablo's blood, despite being kin. After all the drug and alcohol safaris upon which Pablo had embarked, the monsters- potential or actual- he had dealings with had finally tracked him down and he was cornered. There was nothing he could do but laugh at it.

"Every man to his humour," he murmured, picking up the peace-pipe; "I'd rather be sanguine than choleric."

A tapping at the door ended his soliloquy. He got up from the padded chair and opened the door. "Hugo?"

"Yeah. It's me."

"I can't let you in if you're drunk."

Hugo grinned, showing yellow teeth, "Nope, just a bad hangover which won't keep me from killing you."

Pablo laughed nervously and let Hugo step inside. He looked around then moved into the living-room.

"It must be a helluva hangover. I haven't seen you in years and I must say I'm not happy you showing up like this." He was convinced his unsteady cousin would drop onto the sofa for a nap, but instead Hugo circled the room, then stopped in front of the bookshelves.

"All these yours?"

"Most of them, yeah."

Hugo glanced at the titles, cocking his head to read them sideways. He looked at Pablo and said, "This is all white stuff. Where's the pride in your own culture?"

"This is my culture now. And I take pride in knowing more about it than most white folks."

"Some consolation booby-prize for a dishwasher."

"How long have you been watching me?"

"So do you feel great about out-smarting everyone at work while you scrub-a-dub pots and pans?"

Pablo tried to use a malfunctioning plastic butane lighter manufactured in Vietnam to start a cigarette. He offered one to Hugo who declined it.

"If it makes you feel any better, my intellect has become suspect due to the drugs and alcohol, but I've got a wife and son to support."

"I saw them leave. A wise policy on your part. Did you learn that in a book or while you were selling dope with Simon and Rico?"

"What do you want? You see how I live. It's not much but it's my life."

"Have you heard of Hunapu?"

"No. It sounds Mayan and I haven't had any connection with that in years."

"You should read some of those stories," Hugo said; "show some interest in your heritage."

"Have you read them in hieroglyphs?"

"What?"

"Hieroglyphs," Pablo said. "A lot of the oral tradition was lost but some stories were put down in pictures."

"I know what hieroglyphs are. I read them in English."

"Well how do you know they were accurate? I taught myself Egyptian hieroglyphs to read their *Book of the Dead* because the published translation was done by a half-wit."

"What're you getting at?" Hugo said sharply.

"Maybe our devils were just part of a necessary show for those scared by a great light of oneness."

"Dim is the heart that casts only one shadow."

"Something like that, yeah."

Hugo snorted a laugh of disdain, "Ah, Pablo, you're such a fool for poetry. You're the kind of person who puts the Romance into Roman Catholicism. Still a believer?"

Pablo shrugged, "I like the continuity of the Church: the Father passing onto the Son and Holy Ghost."

Hugo smirked, "A son of dubious birth inheriting the universe. Have all the pedigreed people become inbred mutants?"

"No," Pablo said, "they're just overly concerned with the material heirlooms."

"Some of our mothers got around when they landed in America, though I doubt they were looking for romance as much as stability in the third-dimension. Maybe Henrietta had to pay for their sins."

"I don't want to invest in your particular brand of psychosis. In America, we have a wide variety of craziness to buy into."

Hugo sneered, "Women are our first communion but you seem to think only a man can bear the sins of the world."

"I didn't say that; but if one tried, he'd want some vengeance against whoever or whatever he felt had compelled him to do it. The very sins he took on to bear would force him towards revenge."

"So what would've you done at Christ's trial?"

Pablo squirmed a moment, then said, "Well, I can understand humans wanting revenge on the Almighty for making a world of predators and prey, but part of the duty of being a protective predator is knowing how to punish and reward, corruption notwithstanding; so if I'd had authority then I'd have had him nailed-up, just to teach him a lesson, and taken down before he was dead. Let him be nursed back to health, then sent on his way, maybe into exile, to help compose *The New Testament*."

"You think his death would've caused too much bad-blood?"

"Yeah," Pablo nodded. "I mean, he earned a punishment of wicked hallucinations through loss of blood because he hurt business as usual. But he didn't really deserve to be executed. Who knows? Maybe the visions he had up on the cross were fabricated into *The Book of Revelation*."

"So his death and resurrection are all lies on his own part."

Pablo shrugged, "Or crafted illusions to serve the greater purpose of teaching life is fragile and no one escapes from it with their material goods. That was probably a hard lesson for Jesus to learn; maybe that's why he's reported to have ascended bodily into heaven. I imagine once he'd recovered from his punishments, he realized he had nothing to show for all his work except some wishy-washy apostles, a scarred beat-to-hell body, and vicious visions." Pablo emitted a forced laugh, "I hope he didn't earn too many worldly rewards while shaping the stories of his resurrection."

"Do you hallucinate?"

"Not anymore. Hector did for a while but we got him on a low dosage of meds."

"Ah, the sins of the father strikes again."

"Estella is a lot of things but innocent isn't one of them."

"Hmmm," Hugo thought a moment. "Is that what you'll say as a character witness at her Last Judgment?"

"There was a time she could've only said of me- to quote Shakespeare- 'Drunkenness is his best virtue'."

"Bearing false witness against yourself?"

"No," Pablo replied; "I don't need to make myself any worse than I was or still am."

"I get the feeling you're laughing at me, like in one of those books of yours: *The Atheist's Comedy* or something. You don't know how truly bent my nature is right now: it's like being possessed by a rebel angel whose superiors are dealing in dope and murder," Hugo nodded; "and like the wrath of God, clears out the dreck, whether proud and idle Seraphim hooked on Holy Ambrosia or fallen ones who infect everything they touch."

Pablo chewed a corner of his lip, then said, "Dostoevsky wrote a novel about something like that set in Tsarist Russia."

"What happened to the characters?"

"Plunged to their deaths like a herd of swine off a cliff."

"Do you think that's where we're heading? I mean, sometimes I can almost feel a physical presence taking away any good qualities I might have." When Pablo didn't reply, Hugo said, "Well, you don't need to worry about me having a coronary here in your living-room."

Pablo forced an edgy laugh and said, "I wish you would."

Hugo shook his head then said, "You had a Tsar once."

"I'm not even a satellite-state anymore, Hugo."

"Not much of a Promised Land you won here."

Pablo shrugged, "It took me a few decades to learn to respect money."

"Do you respect guns?"

"Enough not to have one. And in the state Hector's in, I wouldn't want him finding it to shoot at ghosts."

"I thought you said he was medicated."

Pablo said, "I insisted on low doses. Sometimes, like if he watches too much television, he starts bringing them into his dimension. Mostly he just imitates some of their less than endearing traits, but once in a while he talks to them."

"We've all learned stupid monkey-tricks, but it keeps the global economy going," Hugo said. "Maybe our ancestors were right about channeling in aliens or spirits."

"Well, I don't know if Hector needs an exorcist or if he's just too lazy to read a good book."

"Maybe it's spirits making him not want to read. Maybe they're competing with all these books you have for possession of him." Pablo drew on his cigarette and released smoke. Hugo continued, "In the old days, the Mayan people wrote on a piece of paper, put blood on it and burned it on their lips to summon deities."

"Kind of like Biblical prophets had hot coals put to their mouths."

"That's just it, Pablo: I have a dope-dealing family with gore on their mouths, insane and needing to be purged."

Pablo said quietly, "I've been out of the business a long time, Hugo."

"That's a curious thing to say, Pablo. I mean, I was trained- lost my freedom, really- to kill to protect liberty."

"I've pulled more than one structure down on my head and on those I was supposed to love and protect. All I got out of it was wreckage, Hugo, even when I succeeded, or thought I did, in getting revenge on offenders. It usually ended up like something from the last scene of *Moby- Dick*."

"What in heaven's name are you talking about?"

"Revenge," Pablo said; "revenge on Afghanis or Iraqis or a whale. You're plunging into deep territory. You have to remember we're human, not just instruments for you to get vengeance. No matter how bleak our consciousness is, there's usually a more accurate explanation than the struggle between good and evil."

"Like money?"

"Even money's changed now. Mostly it's just numbers on screens or Isaac Newton calculus codes drifting around satellites waiting to be plundered by an up-for-sale computer-hacker."

"Maybe aliens or spirits want it that way."

"Well so do humans," Pablo said, throwing up his arms. "We may be disengaging from the third-dimension but we're still human. Or is your ambition to be an avenging angel?"

"I was a good soldier, Pablo, so don't talk to me of war and revenge. You don't know anything about it."

"You're putting me in a position where I have to relearn all the stuff I want to write-off as history."

"Ever kill anyone?"

Pablo replied, "I'm not going to answer that."

"Here's one you may be compelled to answer: where's Simon?"

Pablo hesitated, then said, "He's somewhere on the East Coast. He stopped by last year and said you were on the prowl. I knew it was you at the door because I looked you up at the library on a computer and saw some pictures. That's all I know."

"Who was with him?"

"I don't know," Pablo said, shaking his head. "I didn't meet him."

"Well I did. He showed up in California with a fresh supply of dope and word reached me he'd been with Simon." When Pablo stayed quiet, Hugo asked, "Aren't you interested?"

"No."

"How many cops have ties to the military? Just guess."

"With the blanketing of Homeland Security, I suppose at least one you know who wants to help."

"Ah, good guess," Hugo said. "The district attorney's special squad went after this buddy of Simon's but I found him first. Do you know what he told me?"

"That they stopped by here."

"You're getting good at this. Unfortunately, he wasn't as talkative about where Simon is and time was running out. Did you know this pal of Simon's was a half-brother to Rico?"

"No," Pablo said.

"I did. Seems Simon thought this fellow would be enthusiastic about protecting Simon, considering the debt our family owes me, especially Rico's clan."

"Is your idea of freedom being free from all foreign influences?"

"Except good things," Hugo replied after a moment of consideration.

"Then you want purity, not freedom." Pablo nodded, "There're a lot of people who feel that way about Hispanics coming to America."

"She was my daughter."

"And this is my home," Pablo snapped, trying to sound vicious. "It may not be pure but you're invading it."

"Purity; freedom," Hugo exclaimed with an angry dismissive gesture. "That's all fine talk coming from a gangster. I served my country, Pablo, and all you've done is dealt dope and read books. Who the hell do you think you are, judging my right for pure revenge?"

"It's not pure if you're running up a casualty-list because you can't get to Enrico."

"You know, he testified against some low-level thugs and they put him in protective custody. They wouldn't even let me attend his trial! Said I was too wrathful and they couldn't press charges for selling Henrietta as a sex-slave because there wasn't enough evidence. And he'll be in witness-protection in another three years: new name, new house, money. I can't get disability benefits from the military and they're going to reward Rico with taxpayer funds for being a criminal. So who's more pure, Pablo? Who's more free? We've got half our society watching the other half perform insane exhibitions, paying the audiences to choose sides, weeding-out the worst, who somehow get rewarded anyway."

Pablo realized his cousin was becoming dangerously excited, while Pablo's own inner-fuel could not stoke whatever fury would be required to react; so he mildly said, "That's part of the reason why I've chose to live quietly."

"And you don't know where Simon is?"

"No. I don't want to know where any of them are anymore. Let me return to my pathetic but peaceful existence, eh, Hugo?"

"Let me check your cell-phone."

"I don't have one; Estella took hers with her. I don't have any records you can check. No address book, no computer accounts, nothing. If you kill Simon, I don't want to know about it."

"Because you'd feel obligated to snitch?"

"No," Pablo said. "Because all the family I have is hiding from you, and if you leave me, my wife, and son alone to live our own way, that's enough for our family's insane attempts at purity to last another generation."

"What about your brother, Angelo?"

"He was born in America. He doesn't really understand us." Pablo shrugged. "Hector...well, he got some of my demented gene-tags. He'll never really know freedom: always feeling hunted, oppressed; gleeful about thinking he's escaped something like a pointless genocidal massacre."

Hugo pondered a moment, then said, "I did things in Iraqi and Afghani villages...I mean, we almost always killed the right people- whatever that means- but I hadn't really thought about what happened in Guatemala when we were children."

"It was a long time ago. We have different masters now."

"I'm going to leave, Pablo. I suggest we stay out of each other's paths. I function better under commands, but I know you'd only rebel against orders."

11

Deregulating Order

Pablo was at his writing-tray, copying an excerpt from a book. He liked to handwrite passages because it seemed to help get his mind around whatever he thought was significant enough to put on paper and carry with him for several days. He was copying a paragraph from Tacitus's *Histories* covering a civil war in the Roman Empire, when mutiny among the rank-and-file soldiers was to be expected, for if their leaders switched allegiances, so eventually would the lower-echelons doing the combats. Roman generals and emperor-wannabes were surprised that a forced march through Italy's mountains did not instill loyalty into conscripted foreign troops.

"If we attack under cover of darkness, we shall at least be as bold, and shall enjoy more licence in plunder. If we wait for the light, we shall be met with entreaties for peace, and in return for our toil and our wounds shall receive only the empty satisfaction of clemency and praise, but the wealth of Cremona will go into the purses of the legates and the prefects. The soldiers have the plunder of a city that is stormed, the generals of one which capitulates."

Pablo was familiar with the siege of Cremona: the Romans turned their foreign troops loose to raze a Roman city to rubble…something Iraqi Shiite leaders might do to their own civilization, allowing Iranian Shiite fighters to plunder Sunni-areas.

Pablo knew he was a poor general in not permitting Hector great profits the past few years while expecting him to follow his father's lead. Pay-offs were due, and Pablo was uncertain how to proceed. He thought of Hugo and his multiple tours of duty in the Mideast; at least when the Tsar had set Pablo to dope-dealing, the trade was lucrative for both of them. That Pablo had spent the money on things which were terrible or embarrassing memories was something he found difficult to accept: so much money and time gone to waste. He had been a kingpin in colonizing the town for the Tsar and now was nothing but a target if Caesar decided Enrico's betrayal deserved punishment on his family members since Enrico himself was out of reach.

Estella was wiping the kitchen-counters clean from supper specks. She said, "I'm returning the library books tomorrow."

Pablo glanced at her and said, "They're not due for another two weeks."

"Hector's going to start doing dishes again."

He stared at her, "Oh great: another male dishwasher in the family." She ignored his irate tone and he said, "You have to consult me with things like this. I read those books to him for a reason, one of which is so he doesn't grow up to be a dishwasher."

"What else can he do with the education you're giving him? You say we should pay our dues to earn protection and well-being in this community, then you read him stuff that no one his age has anything to do with. You don't even know what books are popular among his friends."

Pablo shrugged, "Probably something to do with magic, just dumbed-down versions of what we read without the gods and goddesses."

"No, not what we read, what you read to him. And-"

"You know, Estella, I do know what I'm doing. The Hindu god of war was born through his father's blindness, and it's a metaphor of how we're all born blind into this world, in perpetual battles with choices. I should have some input to my son when it comes to decision-making."

"You don't make any sense, Pablo. You talk a good game but this isn't one of your drug wars."

"Oh, and you know who blinded the father of the war-god? The mother. Think about that. Hector's not a pawn between us."

"Good, then you won't mind me still taking him to church." She rinsed the dishcloth under the faucet, then wrung it and draped it over the spout, while saying, "Since your cousin showed up here I've been thinking it's time for you to retire as Hector's general in whatever private war you're waging. If the Muslims or whoever want to think their god is a general in life's battle, then that's their affair. Hector's going to be Catholic."

"I think he should have other options than as a sacrifice. Dick Cheney believes there are evil little Dick Cheney's in every one's heart and before they multiply and go after their genitive, they should all be crucified."

Estella snorted in disdain, "What do you think Hector does while you read those books to him? You want him as a sacrifice to you. It's torture for him to sit and try to pay attention."

"Did he say that to you?"

She shook her head, "You know how to read books but not how to read people." Pablo sat stunned. "He needs something bigger to give himself to for direction. You can't cut-it, Pablo; and while I respect you for trying to be a...general, you don't have what it takes, let's face it. You didn't rise very far in the Kaiser's army either: all you did was hurt people, and I'm not going to let you drill Hector with some instructions that just confuse him and make me angry."

Pablo flatly said, "That's infringing on my space."

"You mean you're going to defend the caves you build in our son's head?"

Pablo felt like Polyphemos cannibalizing guests. He said, "I'm not recruiting him for a lifestyle."

"And this isn't like the massacre of your village for land estate developers," she replied. "You want Hector to be all these different things and he's only fourteen. You want him to be a peasant and a king; you want him to be a patriot and a non-conformist; you want-"

"Stop it, Estella."

"You think he should be a smart-mouth liar and honest, stoic, and tactful."

"I think I've been fair."

"You consume all that stuff, but does it have to be so we're unhappy?"

He morosely said, "I just want to share it."

"Your fortune might change as you think destiny plans it, but Hector deserves stability. Did you ever think your fate changes because you read those storylines and make bad decisions? If they're such profound works then they must have some effect."

"Are you trying to get me to be a wrathful Achilles now?"

"This isn't about revenge," she replied. "We're not property or trophies."

"Then what's it about? I hate to break it to you, Estella, but being Roman Catholic isn't popular anymore; in fact, there're more unaffiliated Americans than American-Catholics. And when your church gets taken to court to be forced to wed homosexuals, that'll just be added bad imaging in the media, though they should be used to that by now, and probably can no longer afford the best lawyers."

"Don't start on my church. I'm warning you."

Pablo said, "You're the one who began the what's popular. Even the former defenders and cover-uppers are scramming away from pedophile priests, or at least so far as we know. Do you really think a culture that breeds such sin is better than learning some ancient stories from me?"

"Why are you trying to drag everything down?" she asked. "Because I won't let you have your own way? When someone else takes stuff apart and reforms it to his image, you get mad. But when you do it, you're convinced it's just and fair. Do we really need to pull down the structure of our lives right now?"

Despite her sound reasoning, Pablo felt rebellious: he was a zealot fighting against Roman occupation or a Palestinian defending his region from Israelite invaders. Pablo resisted business as usual because his pride would not let him sell his soul. It had taken him this far and he owed it to himself and whoever was unfortunate enough to follow him to carry on nay-saying, which seemed an addictive thrill. There was a look of crushing angst in people's eyes when he didn't invest in the latest trend, be it a catch-phrase or computer-site votes on a video, that he enjoyed more than if he had taken part in the most recent fad. In a way, he rather resented Estella for revealing that particular cynical pleasure while in his current consciousness: it distracted him from manufacturing an argument. He puffed furiously on a cigarette and finally said, "I'm not going to compete with you on whose delusions are better and should be taught to Hector. Maybe that's why we have to medicate him, because between the two of us he doesn't know what's what."

"I'm glad you feel that way because it shows deep in you you know I'm right."

Pablo near exploded; it was one thing to agree to an armistice and come to terms, quite another to acquiesce to righteousness. "No, I don't think that. That's what it's all about in this country: being right and having civil rights that prove you're never wrong because you won a lawsuit with money."

"Freedom isn't free, Pablo."

"Yes it is, and I'm tired of hearing that damn mantra. If it isn't free, then what is it? You're talking about empowerment, and that isn't free because it always comes at someone else's expense. Do you really believe we should empower, especially by munitions and training, people in the Mideast who were our enemies ten days ago?"

"They're jealous of our freedom," she replied.

"Another tired old mantra. We're losing civil rights, selling them to the highest bidder. A South Dakota Democrat senator was voted out because he was considered a wealthy elitist and was replaced by a guy who had seven-million-dollars in campaign funds and ran unopposed, and somehow that's okay because he's Republican. You know, this state is actually taxing food-pantry charities now. And legislators want to lower the basic minimum wage one dollar an hour for everyone under eighteen-years-old. Poor people can't afford lobbyists and lawyers like special interest groups can, with briefcases full of writs and money: that's how they decide there's no such thing as global warming, or-"

"You're losing focus here, and I don't want to hear a homophobic rant," she said, throwing up her hands.

"I'm talking about my responsibilities as a father; and if I can't afford for him to invest in every screen-trend, then I should at least show why stories from the past have a mixture of light and dark: that imagination isn't just one-dimensional or something to be manipulated into money-making."

Estella smirked, "Characters in those stories cared about material goods."

"Yeah, and they suffered for it and maybe learned they couldn't take it with them. Odysseus lost all the loot he'd plundered and when he washed up on the Phoenicians' shore all he had was his body, soul, and memories. Hector should appreciate what he has."

"I'm tired of being poor and you saying all is right to live like this. The best way for us to continue is for you to give on this: it's a Christian nation and he'll accept that as his system."

"With Roman Catholicism as the brand name."

"Shut-up, Pablo." They glared at each other in a moment of intense dislike. Pablo sighed and looked at the ceiling: the religion of Montt was winning again. She said, "The world is changing, and Hector can only have a good effect- which we both want- if he's part of the system. You can rediscover Homer on your own. Lord knows you don't trust academia as a guide."

"Okay," Pablo shrugged. "You won my ambivalence, and like other people heavily invested in their lifestyles you'll probably try to get my approval to have some fantasy psyche-energy to fulfill your perfect wish."

"I'm not someone you can just unleash your sarcasm on," she replied. "Treat me with respect."

He took a deep breath and said, "You're right. I apologize."

She nodded, "Maybe it's time for us to move to the next level. We've proved we can be poor and live on top of each other. We need to branch-out more instead of bottling grievances until they explode."

"We have been tense," Pablo agreed. "I figured it would blow over once we got Hugo out of our systems."

"Maybe he was a catalyst. Maybe it brought to the surface things we'd buried. Looking at our future now, I don't like what I see, not for any of us. We could at least try to be middle-class: save some money, and I can take a few courses at the University. It won't cost too much if I keep working there."

Pablo unenthusiastically asked, "What do you want to major in?"

"I was thinking about marketing management."

Pablo hid his scorn, "You want to do commercials?"

"There's a whole booming market for Hispanics now and I could get degrees in language and marketing."

Targeting her own people, Pablo thought: but at least it's legitimate. He felt a bit of bitter disappointment that she was taking the lead in their relationship to a different destiny. He had gone along with her for several years and was comfortable as she made major family decisions. So long as he had his time to read and write, he didn't mind her assertiveness because she knew how to temper her dominance by seeking his input on matters she controlled. She was proficient at planning and executing, and Pablo enjoyed the nuances of just going along and being pleasant: it suited his unambitious career. She would not allow him to stay a dishwasher, living paycheck to paycheck, unbothered by their financial straits because he was lost in tomes of other people's even worse despair. Unlike his wife, Pablo had no recurring nightmares of counting coins in order to wash three loads of laundry or whether a four-pound bag of flour was a better investment than a two-pound sack. He considered himself as domesticated as he cared to be for the civilized system in which he resided: his thoughts were his own and he could walk away from troubles not of his making. If Hector and Estella aspired to more, then it was their desires, not Pablo's. How, though, could he explain that without seeming selfish?

At that moment the landline telephone rang and Pablo answered it. "Hello?"

"May I please speak with Pablo Nuri?"

"You are."

"Good evening, sir. This is Alison from Rennings and Colton Estates. How are you tonight?"

"What do you want?"

"Sir, we're offering a free tour of our new estates to you and your friends with no purchase necessary. We have some beautiful lots that I know-"

It was too tempting for Pablo to resist. "Hold on a minute and you can talk with my financial guru. It's for you, Estella." He handed her the phone, grabbed a Balzac novel from a stack of books, and walked to their room to read in bed.

Seconds later, Estella called out, "That wasn't funny, Pablo. I'm enrolling in classes next autumn so you better not hide any more money from me."

12

Heckler for Hire

Hector was in the Dreaming City of Melnibone watching the courtiers and elite celebrate an ancient festival which no longer served any purpose except to give people something to anticipate and dream of before and after the actual fete. Hector sat on Elric's throne, ruling with dispassionate interest. Hector's realm had become one which consumed foreign trade and only produced entertainments, and the drugs to enhance them, for his nation and other countries' appetites. Hector, however, tried not to be scornful of what he had inherited; his duty was continuance, and perhaps he could format a new network with deeper meaning for future generations and secure the kingdom as a place of culture and strength.

A distant voice said to Hector/Elric, "This isn't worthy of your attention." Hector thought of following that call into another realm, but he might not be the ruler there and Hector enjoyed his place of eminence. He looked at his albino white skin and decided it was a price he was willing to pay for ruling, despite the intrigues. The rare drugs, culled from plants in a great forest, kept him mentally and physically alert to the dangers posed by his ambitious cousin and followers.

The scene abruptly focused on a teenaged girl with glossy black hair, who looked remarkably similar to the Lakota girl who once lived in an apartment house three blocks from the Nuris. Leslie had been Hector's first love two years previous, and their awkward physical relationship was a memory treasure held tight by Hector. They were in a cave by the ocean, fulfilling the desires which had been unconsummated. Hector was disappointed and frustrated when a shattering invasion took the love-play's place.

He was on a mountainous battleship, feeling weak and discombobulated. He had no war-cry, only a sighing rent of love for Leslie as naval combat exploded around him. Hector tried to collect his faculties to wreak havoc in the fray, but he was strung-out and felt lost because he'd neglected to take his dose of dope. He succeeded in killing a few enemies with an awesome frenzy of swordplay, while somewhere in his consciousness was a mantra, "But I took my medications last night...I took them..."

Hector fell limp on the deck and his leering cousin, whom Hector could not place a familiar face to, pushed him overboard. Hector sank among leviathans, drifting with the tides' ebbs and eddies. As he sank into darkness, a voice from below said, "The Fisher King must understand the need for sacrifice." Whatever that meant, Hector didn't care because he aimed for a dreamless zone with a sense of vague vengeance toward the Dreaming City.

Bodies were piling up along the corridor which led to dark forgetfulness; and Pablo was there, sorely wrathful and saying, "Every system, natural or artificial, has sacrifices for the means of what is called progress; whether the standard propaganda proclaims to make things equitable or encourages greed among everyone or only certain groups, people learn power by targeting others."

"That's old stuff, dad," Hector said, trying to explain as quickly as possible so he could rush into the dreamless void before it closed.

"I want to know what you'll willingly sacrifice," Pablo demanded, "before one, or many, are forced on you. The medications you take are important but won't fix or cure you. You're a visionary and that entails obligations and misunderstandings. Eventually, we'll have a president who'll be a famous satellite star for projectile-vomiting on his, or hers, friend's best coat at the age of fifteen, channeled throughout the world on screens. But before then, there'll be sacrifices: like the Supreme Court nominee who admitted to smoking marijuana and was sent into limbo; learn the hypocrisies of eras' without being bitterly cynical because, in turn, Bill Clinton said of marijuana-smoking, 'I didn't inhale'. Then we had party-boy cokehead Georgie Bush Junior and now Barak Obama who said he smoked crack/cocaine. Don't be a sacrifice but learn to make your own sacrifices without destroying people.

Being able to tell lies consistently may meet with approval in society, but that doesn't make it right. Learn that you have little or no control over what's been promised will empower you."

A fat old white man appeared from the dreamless void and said, "That's bad for the economy."

"Shut-up!" Pablo snarled. "I don't want my son performing pointless consumerism tricks for you to build a paradise on him."

"But we're diversified," the now pasty-white fat man replied, "and if he'll conform to that the world will be at his fingertips."

"Diversity?" Pablo bellowed. "The more you deregulate government guidelines for the world conglomerates running the show, the more you regulate the consumers. Shouldn't you be guarding against another global catastrophe by overlooking the corporations instead of spying on us?"

"But," the albino man said, "look at how the economy improves and all the great things on the market."

"Like what? A goddamn rediscovery of a 1980's popular-cult song? You think I should encourage my son to invest in that?" Pablo took a moment to relax and regain control; the incident with Hugo had interested Pablo in Mayan stories and he'd done some research on them. He placed a hand on Hector's shoulder and leaned down to look his son in the eyes. "All he offers you is a stadium seat in Xibalba, the hall of the dead, cheering on demigods playing a pointless, violent game while using their audiences as sacrifices to keep power. And when not at the coliseum, you'll be working at one of their plantations or factories churning out apparel with their names on the logos. If you're lucky, you may be able to afford screen-networks owned by entertainment conglomerates that also relay news, and own casinos and sports' channels and control gambling by computer. It's rigged for you to lose, Hector, and he's tempting you into willful ignorance; which I can understand because it's attractive, but to be retarded and call it brilliance is about as goofy as goofed-up gets."

The albino man had changed into a glowing spirit, and his voice resonated as it said, "He can bring about a change with his energy: to make things more fair and equitable."

"Go to hell," Pablo said. "Do you think I'm an idiot? You drain us of all good will and replace an evil cycle with one wherein everybody is equally stupid. Now beat it, world-controller, trying to tempt us into a brave new world of useless distractions, training generations to perform monkey-tricks for cell-phone and security cameras and covert agencies."

"A bitter man who has been his worst enemy all his life and wants to make everyone as disturbed as himself. His proud vanity will not allow him to accept that about himself. We offer peace and he spurns it out of self-pity, clinging so fiercely to his misery that he wishes to pass it on to you as a gift and heirloom. There are new ways of doing things, but he holds fast to ideals he both loves and hates because he believes the past inevitably returns and everything else is folly. He will even deny his inner-essence the resources to flourish."

"And what if I do?" Pablo sneered. "At least I'm not running-up a body-count then denying any responsibility for it. I'll pay the price for selling dope to unstable minds, or helping to cause the instability. You just want to use them to form a blank consciousness you can scribble your will onto, instilling in them the beliefs that whatever system they're in can solve all the problems with what you train them to invest: be it education, social programs, legislation, religion, sexual relations, covert and overt military, and so on."

Hector saw the stacks of corpses lining the corridor begin to move. He watched the deadly wounds heal and the trails of dry darkened blood turn white and liquefy to stream down the hall toward a magnificent city where humans and beasts of the land and air roamed peacefully: nature and civilization in harmony, with a cool breeze seeming to walk among the denizens.

"Why keep him in the past?" the glow said to Hector's irate father. "Shouldn't he be given free will toward his own future?"

"I will not barter with you for my son," Pablo replied. "It's human to want oneness but creation demands duality, and all you're doing is head-hunting for tokens. I recognize you as an agent of Xibalba, playing games with lives and souls. It's no honor for me to be sacrificed for it, or to win and then have a superior or revolutionary take away all my trophies."

"Look, dad, the dead are free," Hector said, eager to move forward. "You don't want to end up like Achilles, do you, dad? Believe in resurrection and come with us."

"It's not a city worth protecting. Go ahead and take your dead: they're as useless a trophy as the dead body of Troy's hero was to Achilles," Pablo said, as Leslie sparklingly appeared, waving a hand and smiling at Hector. He stepped onward to a clear dawn of bright colors, where prairie grass gently swayed from a soothing breeze. Hector looked back a moment and saw his father sitting cross-legged with ghosts who had little or nothing to say.

Estella rushed in and stopped before Pablo who gazed at his wife as if he didn't recognize her. She looked at him pityingly but her voice was merciless and seemed to mock, "I thought our goal was to win legitimate protection." When he didn't reply, she briskly walked to the end of the corridor and plunged in after Hector.

A storyteller appeared amid the quiet shades and began an oral recitation which Pablo could not follow, so one of the ghosts handed him a book by Ivan Turgenev, translated from the Russian language into English. Pablo thought: A good thing about globalization is a wider variety of translations. He opened the novel, *Fathers and Sons*, set shortly before the Emancipation of the Serfs. How does an older generation adapt to the frenetic changes of their young? Targeting them as consumers before they know better seemed America's way, but what about foreign influences? It was a calm counterpoint to Dostoevsky's weird and gory ridicule of everything he deemed non-Russian.

As Pablo read, the scenery about him began to change and he was absorbed into an arena, surrounded by an audience of multi-colored people. A wizened Lakota lady sat on a high dais, as though in judgment of the angry groups of white men and women in the gaming-pit, seated in front of computer screens, typing away in vindictive debate; the words could be seen to rise in the air and with a flash of light burst and spill out furious phrases like thunder.

"You have no grasp of history. What would be so great about being a white male serf in Tsarist Russia? Or a soldier in an army perpetually at war, dying from a sword-scratch's gangrene because there're no tetanus vaccinations and no one tends to the wounds of common soldiers? You teach crap that makes white men all through history some kind of King Henry the VIII."

"But men were more able to rise through the hierarchies."

"Most of them couldn't. How would you like to know you'd live and die as a dirt-farmer peon to a feudal lord and be lucky if you could provide your family enough to eat, and be even luckier if a son could inherit your miserable job?"

"Exactly our point: the feudal lords were male."

"Yes, and they oppressed their own race and gender so the ladies of the lords could have salon soirees which have degenerated into our education system of teaching a woman's diary from two-hundred years ago instead of Lord Byron's poetry."

"Perhaps," said a silky white man's voice, "if women were allowed to publish then we would have works of art other than just diaries."

Someone from the audience called, "Soon the big news will be court cases about some dead celebrities' electronic-mail, the great inheritance of cyberspace: some goof's world-view while drinking rum in front of a screen, as if the literary estates from the Twentieth Century aren't bad enough."

That inspired Pablo to comment, "I tried reading George Gordon Byron's journals and letters once and it wasn't crafted material. I'm glad Shakespeare left only his work for you to plunder."

The irate white male was not to be deterred, "Do you think male artists didn't have to deal with censorship under Catherine the Great or Elizabeth I? You teach the latest fads, spending hours before computer screens- the modern ivory tower- searching for opinions you agree with, or criticism so extreme no right-thinking person would go along with it. How would you like to be a coal-miner stuck in the bowels of the earth eighteen hours a day?"

"But men still make more money at the same jobs women do."

"Aha, now we've got to it: that's what it's all about it, isn't it? If you make money at it then you're right."

"That makes me wrong about everything," a Lakota man next to Pablo murmured.

"Money makes righteousness, not what you produce, which is a vain remolding of art and culture into your own narcissistic images, yet ostracize people like me who support equal pay for women. You want me to pay you to bash me, and if I don't invest, I'm pigeon-holed in your diverse world as a misogynist. You want an every man, or woman, for him or herself society of money-making."

"We're not that extreme."

"To me, you are. I'm not going to justify men sitting in front of screens watching professional wrestlers on steroids act a script, or channel-in some fat white male calling you feminazis. Jesus, that ain't a culture worth defending! It's just sub-mediocre laziness. But admit you haven't offered them anything to replace the white male patriarchal structure you make careers out of calling evil. If anything, they dig in their heels because you demonize them. They can't escape to sea on a three-year whaling voyage, and what would be so great about that anyway? Stuck on a ship full of men and under the thumb of rigid control with nothing good to eat."

"Hunting whales to extinction."

"Women sure enjoyed the lights the whale-oil gave provided by massacres."

"What about the white male domination in a tale like *The Nigger of the Narcissus?*"

"You're caught behind the self-image of your race and gender, too. For that matter, all of us here arguing about the sinking ship are, but you don't teach to rise above subjectivity. A modern retelling should be titled *Ronald Reagan of the Media*, except he was a sick commander-in-chief of the fleet, trapped in an image that wasn't just an average sailor's. If you're going to retell everything from a modern feminist view then at least learn history. Not everything learned in one system in one way is applicable to every system a person goes into, though they bring their personality with them, not unless you want to train and condition everyone to be the same. Throughout history, culture centered about royal (messed up) families. It was that way for thousands of years. The provincials had their folklore but if a king and queen embraced a new fad, the court did too; and if it lasted long enough, it would influence the average peon. High-technology improved career positions for white men and women, and made it more convenient to locate the social scapegoat of the hour, yet somehow you make it seem as if all white males were deciding religion, justice, entertainments, and business, which you now want to control."

Pablo was amused by the privileged peoples' arguments, each claiming to be oppressed by the other. It was what they did for a living, and might switch sides as quickly as any of the great men Plutarch wrote about who knew how to opportunistically adapt to the changing eras. The battle of the sexes had moved from the yin-yang physics of Nature into the screen-worlds of machines, proving that high-technology had not guided the world towards a nurturing growth, despite men's worry of that: people were still mean and eager to achieve immortality, even if only in a vacuous image. Pablo yelled, "I'd rather watch a porno than you buffoons!"

He heard a hearty cheer of laughter and cries of despair about trying to have an intelligent debate while being heckled. Pablo hollered, "Shut-up and show us your tits! Not you, you pansy, you're ugly and pass off as a man!"

A mantra began, "We want tits! We want tits!" Then changed to, "Orgy-porgy!"

"You're in the arena now," Pablo called. "Cut out the merde de toro and show us big cow udders because this isn't much of a Hemingway experience of a grand matador performing with finesse."

Someone else jeered, "Make the streets run with people and milk!"

Pablo yahooed, "We want a new life to start the old way!"

"Hey look, there's the Pope. I wonder what he wants; must be slumming."

"Nah, he's practicing for a roadshow tour."

"Go away! We don't want any!"

"Mob rule is an ugly thing," a slick academician said.

A woman with a swaying wig stood up in the back of the arena and yelled, "But that's just it: if every state in the nation has elections and they all vote to ban homosexual marriages and it gets overturned by a few judges, then the vote was held only as a matter of form and not because the form mattered; the homosexuals are just another political action committee that use the same sort of blackmail, bribes, and chicanery that other lobbyists do, which only aggravates the very people who are ambivalent to homosexual civil unions, and makes them turn to reactionaries and extremists who promise-"

"As I said, mob rule is an ugly thing, like Hitler."

"Hitler was appointed chancellor of Germany by the wealthy elite," Pablo called with a sneer. "He wasn't elected. The very system you say should not be ruled by the mob, which is in fact a democracy, is devolving for a demagogue fascist to hijack because people feel they have no input into their government. I'll waste no tears for Al Gore because he believed in and worked for the privileged- trophy system all his life, but to be humiliated by a sub-moron because the system-riggers knew he'd increase their profits isn't that funny when nuclear arsenals are involved."

"We want to build safe environments," a compassionate flat-liner in the arena explained.

"There's no such thing unless your goal is to be an angel overlooking Eden."

"Dumb 'em down to the stone-age!" Pablo yelled cheerfully.

"We teach people to think for themselves."

"How can you teach that when you don't have an original thought in your brain? Everything you think is from a computer. Even your statement 'to teach people to think for themselves' is something you borrowed."

"The world around you is going to hell and your colleges are like minimum-security prisons where people are monitored to make certain they're stainless representatives of schools and the corporations they'll work for. Color and gender is only part of an identity and the way you build them is becoming artificial." Pablo turned his head to see the culprit shouting insults; it was a fat Lakota man who seemed to enjoy the spectacle, and enjoyed even more having some influence with it. "You don't teach what creates perspectives, only that every perspective matters and should be a money-maker. Why should I pay you to show me shadows? Anybody with a bit of light can do that. You make stuff up in your heads and think it's real. I'd get the same thing out of sharing a prison-cell with a mob-boss doing hand-gestures by the ever-glowing light of the cell-block."

"How many mass-murderers have you inspired?" Pablo called to the arena-folks who were writhing with indignation. "Not as many as the *Bible*, I bet, but keep working on it. Underworld chiefs don't do the blood-work themselves either; like you, they have button-men and women. It's probably a good thing Georgie Bush Junior didn't fly any missions over Vietnam because he'd have been crazy on acid and bombed his own troops; most likely had LSD flashbacks when he decided to invade Iraq, and thought it was inspired by god. You think you're smarter than him, though a graduate from a prestigious college, and some puppeteers were pulling his strings; but it was only right that he was anointed by the Supreme Court and hijacked the show, using you like puppets to destroy culture via education by training constant consumption of the trendiest open-minded, diversified, democratic image to keep the global economy going and killing anyone who gets in the way."

"But not be bullies about it," added the fat Lakota man.

"How to Take America Hostage 101: (1. Get all the denizens addicted to screen-worlds. (2. Move manufacturing work for those screen-worlds to China and blame someone else for job-growth consisting of casinos and fast-food restaurants. (3. If threatened by America pulling up stakes from China to settle jobs in another region, sell the codes of the screen-worlds to any nation or faction willing to dare to interfere with Americans' entertainments. (4. Watch with glee as Americans plead for help against the culprits. (5. Laugh even harder when mercenary computer-hackers hired by America's covert agencies wreak havoc on the patsy. (6. Up the ransom price by bribing a computer conglomerate that gets a contract fabricating military hardware for America, funded by their taxpayers'. (7. View the Baal screen-world demigod as he farms the work to China and smile as your customers naively believe you won't insert your own cryptic runes in the weapons to override American authorization. Thank you. You've been a good class. Now go out and buy some entertainment products to keep the economy going."

"Oh," laughed a young Lakota woman, "you mean that computer aristocrat, Bill Gates, whose ambition is to be the next Pluto, reigning in hell over lost shades."

"Most of the early Mesopotamian societies had variations of the god Baal, just like America had Baal Clinton and Baal Gates trying to control all the different dimensions."

A white man with graying long hair who sat in the front-row of the arena said, "When I went back to college, the first thing I learned was everything I knew was wrong, so I figured if I was ignorant I might as well be a drunken jester. I had a white male professor who didn't appreciate me fooling with the order of things as he taught the evils of white male patriarchal authority, and was so dumb he thought a metaphysic's poem by John Donne was about sex. He put the poem on a screen and was taking it apart line-by-line; when I pointed out that there were no female names or pronouns and perhaps it was about a soul, because that was what Donne was famous for writing about, the professor got mad and said I was wrong. I insisted that I was probably right and he became angrier and said he was the authority figure on the subject."

"So what happened?" The fat Lakota man asked.

"I got mad right back, yelled at him, and dropped the class."

"Ah, the sin of pride."

"No, I thought it was disobedience in the desire for knowledge. It was like being re-educated in Pol Pot's Cambodia to form a perfect society. He was going to teach John Milton's *Paradise Lost* that semester, and if the white male authority figure professor couldn't understand a sixteen-line poem, how could he grasp an epic about the emergence of free will in the Garden of Eden? I think the professor, like Adam and Eve in blissful ignorance, would've known death if he ever had an original idea, instead of following the latest screen-site fads. I tried the white patriarch again the next semester when he was teaching Literary Criticism and I needed that to get my degree; so he taught a bunch of short stories by Raymond Carver as literature about the white bad daddies of the Twentieth Century. The professor was like a little Charles Manson with a cult-following of female students interpreting the latest trendy schlock to prove that he was a good white male patriarchal authority figure who could lead them to a great place in a society that would recognize them as well-educated, diverse people who, if they stuck to the scripts he was teaching them, should have the world realize how valuable they were; it had nothing to do with learning to be a better reader. Dropped that class too after a savage confrontation in his office laced, on my part, with all sorts of obscenities, and enrolled in another where a white male professor used his platform to wreck his own race and gender and showed movie versions of Twentieth Century English dramas; and I thought: What can I learn from someone who spent his life in academia and in front of screens, who claims to be teaching diversity? He'd have done better to have studied the works he was supposed to be a professional on because he was such an idiot he didn't know Harold Pinter's play, *The Homecoming*, wherein the main character named Ruth is adopted into a wicked white patriarch family was based on the story in *The Old Testament*. After he realized I was right, he probably squirreled away the idea to do a dissertation on it."

"Did you do a thesis?" Pablo asked, wondering how far the renegade had gone in search of a career in the liberal arts.

"I gave up. I thought about doing a multi-media thesis on an all-natural boobious porn actress whose work I respected, because that's the direction education is going in, but I was too bitter to appreciate her talent. I felt betrayed by white males, who blamed the moral rot of every system on their own race and gender. I'm glad women and black folks were allowed into colleges even though it tended to shape-shift academia with modern versions and bad music called street poetry; I don't care if I do sound like a racist misogynist, because my main enemies were idiot diversified white males, which I suppose verified that white men are greedier."

"And dumber, too," Pablo added.

"What became of you?"

The man with the long graying hair laughed, "Went through a slew of low-paying scut jobs while applying to a state university's prestigious creative writing program; their white male chiefs either gave the go-ahead to pillage and plagiarize my stories or simply turned a blind eye to it. So some books, TV shows, movies, and cartoons came out with neither credit nor money coming my way and, jobless and about to be evicted, I went crazy and tried suicide; fortunately, the American taxpayers adopted me as a ward of the state and I'm on a social program of disability. Most of my support-crew have been white women: kind of nursed me back to the third-dimension and helped immunize me from misogyny."

"No wonder colleges cultivate students nowadays with popular-cult tunes. They're much easier to deconstruct," the wizened Lakota lady passed judgment. "It's not hard to do research on it either by trolling computer sites. Students learn to spew out their images and call people like Georgie Bush Junior greedy: they're two sides of the same coin buying and selling brain-dead lifestyles. Why guise the idiom of idiocy as scholarly studies? We might as well do an orgy-porgy."

The various lights of the multi-colored audience exploded and Pablo stirred in bed. He reached for Estella who was deep in a dreamless void. She responded with sleepy resentment until her passions moved to share in other dimensions.

ACT IV

13 The Art of Colonizing Consumers

I answered again in turn and said to him: "Eurylochos, you may stay here eating and drinking, even where you are and beside the hollow black ship; only I shall go for there is a strong compulsion on me." So I spoke, and started up from the ship and the seashore. But as I went up through the lonely glens, and was coming near to the great house of Circe, skilled in medicines, there as I came up to the house, Hermes, of the golden staff, met me on my way, in the likeness of a young man with beard new grown, which is the most graceful time of young manhood. He took me by the hand and spoke to me and named me, saying: "Where are you going, unhappy man, all alone, through the hilltops, ignorant of the land lay, and your friends are here in Circe's place, in the shape of pigs and holed up in the close pig pens. Do you come here meaning to set them free? I do not think you will get back, but must stay here with the others. But see, I will find you a way out of your troubles, and save you. Here, this is good medicine, take it, and go into Circe's house; it will give you power against the day of trouble. And I will tell you all the malevolent guiles of Circe. She will make you a potion, and put drugs in the food, but she will not even so be able to enchant you, for this good medicine which I give you now will prevent her. I will tell you the details of what to do. As soon as Circe with her long wand strikes you, then drawing from beside your thigh your sharp sword, rush forward against Circe, as if you were raging to kill her, and she will be afraid, and invite you to go to bed with her. Do not then resist and refuse the bed of the goddess, for so she will set free your companions, and care for you also; but bid her swear the great oath of the blessed gods, that she has no other evil hurt that she is devising against you, so she will not make you weak and unmanned, once you are naked." So spoke Argeiphontes, and he gave me the medicine, which he picked out of the ground and he explained the nature of it to me. It was black at the root, but with a milky flower. The gods call it moly. It is hard for mortal men to dig up but the gods have that power to do all things.

-Homer *Odyssey* 10: 270-305

Efrain Rios Montt has been declared mentally unfit to be on trial for genocide. Maybe he did what a gangster in America tried when put before a judge: took pieces of his cold-cut sandwich and draped them on his head; truly a meathead whose only remorse was being caught. A month before Montt was excused his cohort lawyer was publicly gunned-down, but I'm sure his investments in the land they razed after stealing it was passed on to heirs: kill one of them and twenty more swarm in to take the place, developing methods of altering the third-dimension from on-high down to jungle levels so that Lucifer himself would be impressed by the ambitions of their intelligent design.

A good thing about America is the variety of demons people can sell their souls to for due rewards and punishments; Lucifer probably encourages competition among minions like Beelzebub and Mephistopheles. The latter two most likely have departments set up to make shopping more attractive so even if people aren't interested in the deals of, say Mammon, and tend toward knowledge, a sale's representative would be adept at how to wheedle a shopper and query, 'Don't you want to be rewarded for your knowledge by fine things?' and the next thing the person knows is they've sold their soul for a mansion and swimming pool when the original goal was to solve quantum astronomy problems; not only that, but the punishment factor to set balance to the reward is being hit over the head with a stupid-stick and going to palm-reader astrologists to make major life decisions.

It's tempting to play a messiah-messenger in every system a person may find him or herself in, or attempt to alter the nature of others, especially those entering from outside one's system. Sex is a powerful drive and its genitive urge has become more of an entertaining escapism than an act of love to enhance and stabilize personal relationships and communities. Weddings are merely an excuse to celebrate and throw a party; the marriage itself will likely end in divorce, perhaps because so many other systems are available to colonize via magical technology and offer artificial environments where women feel safe, which men might subconsciously resent for unmanning them.

The further a civilization progresses the more artificial their pleasures and entertainments become, including sex, due in part to leisure time, wealth, and recruitment: like the Greeks a few hundred years after Homer had time to develop and groom young men to corn-hole. Nowadays, they insist on marketing it and say God loves them and have messiah messengers in their support systems, proclaiming God loves everyone; and if that's true, God also loves anti-queers: both sides use vitriolic means to bash their opponents, which in media forums is entertainment rather than news. Trying to control a population through sex consumption will eventually breed something uncontrollable. I refuse to go to war to uphold the sexual liberties Americans purchase. The Greeks often postponed wars for their perpetual festivals, even when the urgency for military involvement was immediate; and sometimes respected foes' celebrations, like America's policy with the Islamic season of Ramadan.

We raid each other's systems to patchwork new ones and create hybrids, wherein people are cast as bit-players in staged oracles. Some folks can't accept not being everywhere, perhaps believing that God is everywhere which means It is in them too so they are also everywhere. I've taken enough physics to know atoms move from place to place so there is some science to support the phony metaphysics: to bring it into the third-dimension requires a sorceress like Circe or an adept gene-splicer. Having the alter-ego of a pig and taking that form wouldn't thrill me, but who can blame her for protecting her island? She obviously didn't want some common pirates looting her system, which she had arranged in an order she understood and enjoyed reigning over with her various brands of food and elixirs: eat moly, become holy; drink bad wine, become swine. Sound advice from a staff-bearer who prepares Odysseus (a great-great-great grandson of Lucifer) for an encounter in a godly garden of bliss where savage animals like panthers and wolves are meek and mild: an enlightened Adam with the will not to be ignorant or ashamed about knowing his own and a female's natural anatomy, which they both enjoyed, despite their crafty artifices. That was before artificial laws made those kinds of potion crafts legal or illegal according to control of land, wealth, and legislators, but after cavemen (and women) fought over coca leaves and fermented fruit. I wonder if Hector's tried marijuana yet. The crunch is on for federal and state legalization of pot, and they'll do whatever it takes to control the business by nipping in the bud any present and future competition via prison, rehabilitation treatment, and snitches that make illicit dope-use even more dangerously paranoiac for the average pothead who can't understand why such a great feeling has to entail weapons and cut-throat business maneuvers, so when they get busted, they think 'But it's just pot and I shouldn't have to be imprisoned for it' and rat-out everyone, be coerced into dealing dope, and graduate to harder drugs.

The epitome of equitability, which is what many people desire, is the nullification of sex: no more, 'My baby is better than your baby.' It's not easy to program humans to consciously surrender such animal instincts, though I've noticed the training has stepped-up a few notches. America, at best, is confused by gender-issues and the dope they partake of doesn't enhance clarity. They learn bad anatomy in the education system by playing with numbers and tinker-toys in biology, and classes based on transcending one's genitals by dressing—up as the opposite sex. A person could go to the local thrift stores to do that, or borrow a sibling's clothes instead of taking out student loans. The education business now has colleges and universities settle franchises in cities away from their home-nests as they compete in colonization, which means offering the most recent fads, and classes convened by computers make it even more convenient. No more, 'When I was young we had to walk three miles to school, uphill both ways.' Almost as arduous as what Odysseus had to go through to get lessons from Hermes. Circe, though a daughter of the sun-god, knew the dark arts, and like Parvati could not withstand all of The Great Light, filtering through only enough light into darkness to make their own systems. In Parvati's case, it was children who fought against their ungenitive father, Shiva, because they did not recognize him. Making babies for the wars: keep them stupid and in the dark and they won't ask why or who they're fighting. That flash of a nuclear bomb might provoke pleas for peace and arrange for a system of stable consumerism world-wide with genetic cloning; eventually, though, an ambitious World Controller would do a light-bearer Lucifer and try to run all of it, causing a reaction by other World Controllers who don't want to lose their thrones: like the war between Oedipus's sons.

I used to try to say things, like I've written here, whilst drunk but it usually came out as slurring insults and slurs that became tiresome through repetition; and even using the excuse of being drunk at the time, though plausible, became an outdated catchphrase.

✳ ✳   ✳ ✳ ✳   ✳ ✳ ✳   ✳ ✳ ✳   ✳ ✳

Jacob departed from Beer-sheba and proceeded to Haran. When he came upon a certain shrine, as the sun had already set, he stopped there for the night. Taking one of the stones at the shrine, he put it under his head and lay down at that spot. Then he had a dream: a stairway rested on the ground with its top reaching the heavens; and God's messengers were going up and down on it. And there was the Lord, standing beside him and saying: "I, the Lord, am the God of your forefather Abraham and the God of Isaac; the land on which you are lying I will give to you and your descendants. These shall be as plentiful as the dust of the earth, and through them you shall spread out east and west, north and south. In you and your descendants all the nations of the earth shall find blessing. Know that I am with you; I will protect you wherever you go..."

When Jacob awoke from his sleep, he exclaimed, "Truly the Lord is in this spot, although I did not know it!" In solemn wonder he cried out: "How awesome is this shrine! This is nothing else but an abode of God, and that is the gateway to heaven!" Early the next morning Jacob took the stone that he had put under his head, set it up as a memorial stone, and poured oil on top of it. He called that site Bethel, whereas the former name of the town had been Luz.

Jacob then made this vow: "If God remains with me, to protect me on this journey I am making and to give me enough bread to eat and clothing to wear, and I come back safe to my father's house, the Lord shall be my God. This stone which I have set up as a memorial stone shall be God's abode. Of everything you give me, I will faithfully return a tenth part to you..."

-Genesis 28: 10-14; 15; 16-22

As a daughter of Helios, Circe was a goddess in her own right; the sleep-controlling Hermes met his great-grandson while Odysseus was awake to prepare him for some grub's alteration blessings. Jacob, making a getaway from his twin-brother after bargaining for birth-rites and blessings centered around meals, dreamed of his ancestors' deity and messengers, imaging a deal in land and progeny. Which story is more pragmatic? The later one, of course, begetting a lineage whom inherit real estate, renaming the territories as the Jews so pleased. Odysseus's bargaining was simply to save his skin and men in order to get home, not to claim every place he landed as his own; the later Athenians were more ambitious than the Ithakan. Jacob's mother would find a native woman like Circe loathsome, perhaps frightened that a raw, ripe woman can make a man effeminate or primitive; yet Rebekah was not above changing her favorite son into animal skins to get what she wanted: sort of a non-witchcraft Circe, and kosher enough not to use a pig's hide for the metamorphosis.

Stories alter with passing eras, and it's easy to think one is new when it is an old tale in disguise. Where are we being shepherded to with our scripts and scriptures? Hermes had a staff (or wand) to control levels of consciousness and knew the secret food to energize wish-fulfillments; he was also worshipped in stone phalli pillars that set boundary-markers for landowners, like the one Jacob arranged after his delusional dream of grandeur told him the land was his, marking his territory- which was more civilized than peeing- to pass along to descendants. The roving Odysseus, however, only stayed with Circe for a year, though some legends report she had a child by him who inadvertently killed Odysseus at a discus-throwing contest. The Jews, like their scripture, repeat cycles and that's part of their bargain with Yaweh: passing along the scripts they domesticated and rewrote as an (bastardized) inheritance. There is now a growing popular movement in Israel to make it a pure Jewish state.

Borders are changing rapidly this era and money doesn't necessarily buy a safe place. We got rid of a strong-man in Iraq, Saddam Hussein, who had a network of thieves behind him, and replaced it with puppet-committees. When they finally had elections that Bush Junior and his cohorts couldn't rig, despite all their previous practice and desire to forge a democracy at gunpoint, the Sunni were outvoted and started rampaging through the Mideast; and the irony is, we helped entrench the corrupt Sunni/Ba'athist system with our oil-for-food policy organized by Big Baal Clinton and Hussein. Then we couldn't understand why the profiteering minority Sunni and majority Shi'a of Iraq didn't want enforced equality, religious or otherwise. We ran their petroleum industry so incredibly evilly the Iraqis actually had to buy oil for their own use from foreign sources. Who'd of bet some would look on Hussein's former rule as coherent and sane? Well, maybe Estella. She never met a bet she didn't like. It's akin the allegorical she-bitch Dante met and couldn't get around: we can either take the bad trip we've bred as the fruits of our desires and hope for a better guide than the misleading use of covert agency's reports; or dig-in and wait it out with pointless entertainments guiding us to a stupor in which we are easily manipulated, hoping for a resurrection from Xibalba (land of the dead) by twins like the Mayans' saviors, so new games can start. The lords of the dead land were tricked by the twins through a prank in which one decapitated the other and then brought him back to life; and the Xibalbans, believing such a performance would enhance their shows on the ball-court, asked for it to be done to them, which the twins proceeded to do without bringing them back to life. Ah, the greed that inspires compulsions to learn new monkey-tricks, or at least to pass the time with: from the highest legal court to settle a case in a professional ball-game, down to the lowest strata, the rigged corruption is hard to avoid as it tempts with a promise of resurrecting fulfillment.

✿ ✿ ✿ ✿ ✿ ✿ ✿ ✿ ✿ ✿ ✿ ✿

Mercutuio: The pox of such antic, lisping, affecting phantasimes, these new tuners of accent! "By Jesu, a very good blade! A very tall man! A very good whore!" Why, is not this a lamentable thing, grandsire, that we should be thus afflicted with these strange flies, these fishmongers, these pardon-me's, who stand so much on the new form that they cannot sit at ease on the old bench?...

Mercutio: Come between us, good Benvolio. My wits faints.

Romeo: Switch and spurs, switch and spurs! Or I'll cry a match.

Mercutio: Nay, if our wits run the wild-goose chase, I am done, for thou hast more of the wild goose in one of thy wits than, I am sure, I have in my whole five. Was I with you there for the goose?

Romeo: Thou was never with me for anything when thou wast not there for the goose.

Mercutio: I will bite thee by the ear for that jest.

Romeo: Nay, good goose, bite not.

Mercutio: Thy wit is a very bitter sweeting; it is a most sharp sauce.

Romeo: And is it not, then, well served in to a sweet goose?

Mercutio: O, here's a wit of cheveril, that stretches from an inch narrow to an ell broad!

Romeo: I stretch it out for that word "broad" which, added to the goose, proves thee far and wide a broad goose.

Mercutio: Why, is not this better now than groaning for love? Now art thou sociable, now art thou Romeo; now art thou what thou art, by art as well as by nature. For this driveling love is like a great natural that runs lolling up and down to hide his bauble in a hole...

Nurse: God gi' good morrow, gentlemen.

Mercutio: God gi' good e'en, fair gentlewoman.

Nurse: Is it good e'en?

Mercutio: 'Tis no less, I tell ye, for the bawdy hand of the dial is now upon the prick of noon.

Nurse: Out upon you! What a man are you?

Romeo: One, gentlewoman, that God hath made for himself to mar.

Shakespeare *Romeo and Juliet* 2, 4: 26-35; 66-91; 108-117

Do we ruin ourselves with sex jokes for a beastly laugh, marring the image God so carefully crafted for reflection? Mercutio wants to lead Romeo on a merry hunt toward women as a sort of promised land where saucy seed can be planted. And Romeo, the perpetual romantic spouting love poetry to Juliet, tops his friend in smutty talk. Unfortunately, some of the word-games haven't aged well, but a goose was slang for a prostitute in Shakespeare's era. It was one of the many ways Shakespeare made the *Odyssey* uniquely English, while concurrently having Mercutio denigrate foreign influences and affectations as England struggled with European nations for religious and cultural identities. An irony is the play was set in Verona, Italy. Hermes/Mercury was incarnated by Shakespeare into Mercutio as a human cousin to royalty. To quote the 2012 Republican nominee for president, "Corporations are people." Some political candidates firmly avow their patriotism and antipathy towards foreign influences, which control them anyway via global conglomerates that can limitlessly donate campaign funds which travel faster through satellite space than Hermes. I'll give credit to Obama for having the guts to criticize that particular Supreme Court ruling. Muy bueno for him.

The breeding-game of white folks has changed as they slowly become outnumbered. Hermes advises Odysseus on a potentially violent rendezvous with Circe; Jacob is promised progenies and land as he's guided to Rachel and Leah, whose father Jacob has to vie with to win both; Romeo and Mercutio's sparring of bawdy witticisms changes into arranging a marriage between the rival Houses of Romeo and Juliet. Only Jacob is successful in his against-the-current spawning. Nowadays, there's plenty of advice about how sex should be consumed, handled, performed, avoided, talked about, etcetera, depending on one's personal taste or- god forbid- conscience. Training people to consider sex as they would any other matter that requires time, energy, and probably money has become standard operating procedures. As Mercutio might say, 'Love just gets in the way of a good time.' It's human nature to make fun of sex, no matter how weird it gets; indeed, it can be formed into art yet seem natural, like domesticating goats, pigs, or geese in a pen, bred for a business or wizard prank.

Controlling offspring has become a major industry as well. Before an infant is born, many Americans are already in debt and further investments are almost impossible to avoid, especially if searching for escape-routes. Many people are now getting in touch with their inner-Internet child, and screen-writers, political hacks, covert agencies, predatory religious proselytizers, and corporate fad-makers troll the screen-worlds for inspirations then produce exhibitions for mass-consumption. Put a copyright on your recent brain-child or performance and take the imitative descendants to the highest courts to get your share of the profits.

So the story changed over 2,500 years from survival to inherited real estate to romance and sex jokes. Is there anything to glean from the messages or should I just be entertained? I think Hermes, a god of thieves, may have laid out a path for future scribblers who steal scripts and justify land-grabbing, so he can stay alive in spirit throughout millenniums in pirated works. Jesus was accused of stealing Yaweh's good name to bring new stories to people, and was crucified in the manner of thieves' punishments, which is one of the many reasons he's not worshipped by some people. I suppose I understand that, because there are certain traditions and rituals I'm reactionary against changing; or want to alter them only to suit my desires.

* * *   * * *   * * *   * * *

I mean that when the spirit born to evil
appears before him, it confesses all;
and he, the connoisseur of sin, can tell
the depth in Hell appropriate to it;
as many times as Minos wraps his tail
around himself, that marks the sinner's level.

-Dante *Inferno* canto 5:7-12

Autolycus: How now, rustics, whither are you bound?
Shepherd: To th' palace, an it like your worship.
Autolycus: Your affairs there, what, with whom, the condition of that fardel, the place of your dwelling, your names, your ages, of what having, breeding, and anything that is fitting to be known, discover.
Clown: We are but plain fellows, sir.
Autolycus: A lie: you are rough, and hairy.

-Shakespeare *The Winter's Tale* 4, 4: 710-726

"Gentlemen of the jury, the individual who is on trial here for his life is a mental as well as a moral coward- no more and no less- not a downright, hardened criminal by any means. Not unlike many men in critical situations, he is a victim of a mental and moral fear complex."

-Theodore Dreiser *An American Tragedy*

Despite not being a criminal, I sure spend a lot of time in jail.

-Fala

Autolycus prepares his clients for a litigation scene with their king, including a package (fardel) of evidence that proves their innocence in aspiring to a higher breeding-program. Autolycus was the grandchild of Lucifer and the son of Mercury, the last is associated with Anubis, the jackal-headed arbitrator of the Egyptians' Afterlife Judgment. Autolycus was hardly the type of character who would go legitimate without some devious plans of his own, like being taken in by the Prince as a courtier.

I've got a bunch of problems that are terrorizing me, and am considering a return to college to settle the money/career issue. I used to think I was fortunate because it always seemed my karma moved quickly and a tremendous folly on my part didn't hesitate to slap me across the face. In fact, I was proud of that because some people have to wait so long they forget their guilt or complicity and howl about the unfairness of life when their history catches up with them. I made some bad choices years ago and thought they'd been paid off with the appropriate punishments. I didn't see the bigger cycles in the picture. Getting people hooked on Soma is a major international industry, which makes it simple to justify, and easier to collect their consciousness or souls. Now I don't know what to do with them. Ignoring them isn't too difficult for me, but Hector sees ghosts once in a while, who may just be imaginary friends I picked up along the way on a psychedelic safari. How do I keep out the monsters, some of whom may materialize? I finally sent a letter to Angelo with vague warnings about extended family danger, but haven't gotten a reply. I'm sure he wasn't pleased at the prospect of his wife and children being targets due to my previous lifestyle. I even thought of buying a pistol.

I'm not the shooting-spree type but I have to stop thinking out loud at work, where I infrequently verbalize my thoughts to set them in order; kind of like an incantation to raise me above my job-routine. I clog the airwaves of *Mood Food*'s kitchen with the repetition of history so I won't have to count how many times I wash the same plate; they're all identical but so is the march of history, except now cycles have sped up and it doesn't take as long to stage things. Maybe my improvised performance art is a commercial for myself, but I'm sure not playing to an enthralled audience.

I like to think my improve monologues are a rough-draft until I refine them here in my journal then polish it into whatever form I think fits it. One has to stay in practice. Who knows if I'll ever find interested partakers in this land of hyperactive hype. We're slowly, subconsciously but willingly, becoming a censored nation like China. Chances are, if I used a computer to snake any news about America's wars in multiple countries, I'd be red-flagged by a covert agency and put on a furtive watch-list, which is the embodiment of Obama's belief in building the potency of intelligence for the wars and keeping Americans ignorant. The latter prefer hours of insipid entertainments to seeking dangerous knowledge that would likely bring down the wrath of cyber-wraiths who would ruin the searchers' screen bliss. When the strongest labor unions in a wealthy nation are sports' and entertainment guilds, then something is seriously wrong.

Money can purchase maneuvering room,
but also might buy a personal doom:
making images of oneself is good,
even if it cannot be understood.
God does not compete with Its creation
despite our hate or infatuation.

Good Reasons for Bad Things

Estella had started heating the spaghetti sauce and boiling the noodles when Pablo arrived an hour and a half late from work. He went straight to the bedroom, ignoring his family's greetings, and Estella was uncertain how to proceed; whether to continue cooking or discover what, if anything, was disturbing her husband. She instructed Hector to stir the sauce and keep the noodles from gluing together, then she went to the bedroom and closed the door behind her.

Pablo was laying half-way on the side of the bed, his feet, still in snow-boots, on the floor beside his coat, hat, and gloves. He stared at the ceiling and didn't glance at his wife, who laughed nervously and said, "We got another credit card offer today."

"Was the plastic one enclosed or just a thin cardboard practice one?"

"I tore it to pieces and fed it to the worms without even opening the envelope."

"Must have been cardboard then," Pablo said indifferently. "Need scissors for the real thing. Well, get ready for a financial boom in America until the bills are due in about eight years. Obama will be out of office by then so what will he care about another economic meltdown going round the world? He must've been offered some good deals to loosen restrictions on global banking."

"We got notice they're cutting our Food Stamps forty-three dollars."

Pablo was philosophical, "Obama's got to pay for his wars somehow. Who knows? Maybe he'll win another international peace prize to put in his trophy case, after getting poor people to buy necessities with credit cards. May come a day when their choices are to be indentured servants or military service. I'm sure Congress members were also happy to take lobbying money to deregulate and get back to business as usual."

Estella intensely disliked Pablo's penchant for following money-trails that set up networks of conspiracies against the Nuri family; yet she was also aware she'd begun the conversation in that direction to probe his temperament. He still stared at the ceiling, as if searching for a vision, and Estella was unable to bear the tense emotions she felt, towards which Pablo seemed ambivalent. When she asked what was wrong, he crossed his fingers behind his head, elbows flat on the bed, and replied, "I walked out of *Mood Food* today." Estella waited a pensive moment then asked why. "Vernon said it was too much trouble to juggle schedule hours so had me working with Cookie. She told me to clean the freezer and I said it wasn't part of my job description so she called Vernon at home, and he was angry because it's his day off, and he told me to do it. So I walked out."

"Will they hire you back?"

"I told Vernon to go to hell and Cookie to eat a fresh dog-turd. I've been simmering there and finally boiled-over. Maybe it was their command of silence for me that turned the tide. I've been a failure at everything else, so why not dishwashing too?"

"Have you been drinking?"

"A beer and some tequila. I can't control anything, not even my own destiny." He laughed bitterly. "Turn it over to a god. I've shopped around for one to invest in and all they want is filial monkey-tricks."

"You're drunk. No wonder your history is such a mess."

Pablo sighed. Perhaps his wife spoke the truth, but what difference did that matter? Studying history wasn't the same as influencing it, and he felt it was a useless and time-passing trick to even try, especially when his own concurring moments were torturous. Though it seemed non-apropos to Estella, Pablo said, "Why should I pay to be miserable?"

"I didn't know you were that unhappy," Estella said quietly.

"It's my life, Estella, not yours. Don't start feeling sorry for yourself because I'm miserable. If it makes you sad, go do something else and let me alone. For chris'sake can't a guy catch a break with you? Allow me some privacy and self-pity."

"I don't want you to be this way around Hector."

Pablo sat up and glared at her, "Oh, now you're dragging him into it and he isn't even here. I can't believe this is my fate! My only escape is living in a bottle. You got me trapped and now you need to let me blow off some stink and steam. And if I can't do it here-"

"Oh, I forgot, Pablo, you're the only one who hates his job! You're the only one who works for idiot bosses! You're the only one who suffers from bad mistakes we've made and-"

"-I'll go elsewhere."

"It's below zero out now, Pablo. Where're you going to go? If you get even drunker, I'm not letting you back in."

"Ah, a challenge. Well, I'll take that dare. Happy New Year, Estella." He got up from the bed and put on his coat, hat, and gloves. Estella quickly debated her choices: neither tears nor shrillness appealed to her; they were both spoiling for a fight, which left pleading out of the question. She wanted a moment to ponder, but Pablo nudged her away from the door and left the apartment.

The conditions were dangerous, even deadly, but Pablo didn't care about the Arctic wind whipping about him from all directions as chose the capricious currents. He was, however, careful to avoid ice slicks on streets and sidewalks. The city had thawed for a few days before the new cold system, so patches of water froze in treacherous conspiracies. He didn't have enough money for a hotel room but decided he'd worry about that after he got a jug of tequila from the nearest shop that sold liquor.

He watched a white plastic grocery bag, with a store name printed on it, spin down the street, twisting and turning in the eddies and ebbs of the wind. Just like my soul, Pablo thought: empty and moving with the flow because I can't stand up to it anymore. He tucked his chin further into his coat, leaned into the wind and walked, keeping his gaze on the ground. He reached *Donnie's Super Shop* and noticed the parking lot was crowded. Great, he thought: maybe I'll meet one of my former professors while I'm half-shot.

Pablo went in, took off his eye-glasses that fogged from the sudden heat, and went directly to the liquor section. While he was trying to read the brand names and prices of the tequila, he heard a jubilant call of his name and turned to see a diminutive blur pushing a grocery-cart down the aisle.

"Hey, Fala," Pablo said, recognizing him as he neared Pablo.

"You're a believer again," Fala rejoiced. "Do you still have a job?"

"No."

"Got tired of playing God of the Dishwashers, eh?"

"Too many occupational hazards."

"Did you quit or get fired?"

"A bit of both," Pablo replied. "Just today, as a matter of fact."

"It must be destiny to meet here," Fala said, placing bottles of rum and vodka into the cart. "I got my disability check today. Well, not the whole thing. They made me have a payee who bleeds money to me once a week. I'm sixty-three-years old and get treated like a baby. Well, never mind that. I'm going to have a party and you can come along unless you got other plans."

"I think my wife would prefer I be elsewhere tonight. Where do you live?"

"Just down the street. I had subsidized housing for a few weeks but I butchered that up real good."

"Oh yeah?" Pablo said, vaguely curious. "What happened?"

"Ah, two dykes got in a fight in my living room and the older one was kicking the stuffing out of her girlfriend, you know, jealous and suspicious about being stepped-out on; so the one taking the beating managed to get off the floor and ran for the front door and busted the window out of it, and her girlfriend chased her and broke the screen. Got evicted the next day. It was a helluva good fight though. They were like a couple of wildcats. There were clumps of hair all over the living room. Beat the seven shades of holy hell out of her but she put up a good scrap for a while."

"Will they be there tonight?"

"Don't know. I ain't seen them for a few weeks. Whoever shows up, shows up. Some other people got their checks too so there'll be plenty of freeloaders looking for a free buzz."

"If it's all right with you, I'll join up now. I've got nowhere else to go and it's the first time I've drank in several years so I'm a lightweight."

"Sure," Fala said. "But I got to warn you if you pass out, do it in the basement laundry room or who knows what'll happen to you. Okay? Fair warning because I'll be smashed myself and don't want to hear any complaints tomorrow about dreams of hatching a zucchini."

"I get the visceral picture, Fala, and feel warned. Think the cops will show?"

"Why? You got warrants?"

"No."

Fala studied the alcohol volume/content on the label of a bottle, then returned it to the shelf. "Like a kiddie punch-drink. All flavor with no punch or kick. Anyway, all the residents on the ground-floor smoke meth so if cops come to the house they'll have other priorities. Watch out for the fumes of that junk though; moves through the atmosphere like a cloud of doom. I try to get them to be civilized and drink but all they say is it's better than booze, which shows how truly skewered they are."

"Do they cook it in the house too?"

"Not that I know of. There's some guy they call The Traveling Salesman who has a mobile meth-lab in his car; must be in the trunk or maybe he drives a van. I never met the guy, but he sure is popular. It almost makes me long for the days when they bought farmhouses and cooked it up in the boondocks."

"Like moonshine. Keep guard against the revenuers."

"I'm glad you said that: you'll have to try some of my rice wine. It finished fermenting today but I've been too busy for a taste-test. Can't believe I've been sober all day. Oh well, I'll make amends tonight."

"At least you're spending your Food Stamps wisely."

Fala said, "You should've seen the mess some punks made when I let them in my place. One of them beat me up while the other busted my bags of rice and scattered them all over my bed and floor. I woke up in the next-door-neighbors' laundry room with no shoes and only one sock on. Still haven't found the match for it. Boy, it sure was cold getting back to my place, and it took two days to clean up the rice. It was like sleeping on coarse sand. The television was wrenched off its stand. They must've tried to steal it but couldn't get it unplugged from my video machine. Too drunk to figure it out, I guess, and not even a desperate pawnshop would buy an old video-cassette player that has no remote control. I got some good pornos we can watch though, Golden Age stuff when women had hair."

Fala's manic spirit wasn't contagious to Pablo. His soul felt dampened with the personal failure of being unable to stay truthful in a dishonest world. He knew in his mind, but not his heart, that god does not deal in deception. Yet with so many illusions demanding investments, Pablo chose a black-out state wherein only his subconscious would be prey and consumer. He didn't care about the veracity of Fala's various scenarios, who talked a stream of words with his cartoonish voice, "You can't imagine my surprise when I got disability the first time I applied. Usually people get rejected their first attempt, but the doctor looked at me and pronounced death in six months. Probably from the hole in my lung, or if he'dve examined more closely, the sieve in my brain. So now my payee is trying to get me to save money for burial funds. 'To hell with that,' I told him. 'Just give me my cash. That's my money, and it won't do me any good when I'm pushing up daisies.' Hell, I'll be lucky to have any flowers at all put on my grave. I know my sister won't come to the funeral; and my cousin, who stole all the inheritance my mom left while I was in the can for multiple drunk-driving charges, won't be there because there won't be anything to steal. I went to Rapid City after I got out of prison to get my inheritance and my cousin and her friends got me drunk and stole my luggage and what little cash I had. I came to on a bus back to Sioux Falls. Made me feel like a victim, but she'll get what she deserves. All right, this is enough hooch for now. Let's pay and get a pack of tailor-mades; I've been sniping three days and earned a real cigarette. By the way, don't let anyone use your cell-phone or it'll disappear. You might as well write-off your flame-thrower already, so bring a book of matches: you can get some at the courtesy counter. I used to be surprised when people stole from me, especially at my own place if I'm good enough to take them in, but I can't stand being alone so sacrifices have to be made. I'm at the bottom of the food-chain so what's the point of getting fisted, unless I'm drunk and can't feel it, for a pouch of cheap cardboard tobacco?"

Pablo's jumbled instincts signaled him he was being observed by the employees of *Donnie's Super Shop*; most of them recognized him as a frequent customer, and some knew Pablo by name. His pride bristled at the shame he felt, and he paid for a bottle of tequila with assumed scorn for the cashier and attending audience.

Pablo carried some of the packed plastic bags across the parking lot as Fala said, "I'm glad I ran into you. Shauna's been blacklisted from the store for two years so she's waiting at my place. If I went shopping later with arrivals they'd get me to buy stuff I don't like to drink. I mean, I'd drink it anyway, of course, if it even made it back to my apartment. Chances are, though, they'd take off with it as soon as I paid. I can't count how many times that's been done. Maybe we can catch the end of a show I was watching about those three-hundred Spartans."

"They should've called it *1500*," Pablo mumbled.

"What? You speak worse than I do and at least I have the excuse of having had my throat crushed by some homie on the streets of Minneapolis. I didn't even know the guy: he just walked up, grabbed my windpipe and squeezed. They pronounced me dead at the hospital but zapped me back to life with electricity and a tracheotomy. Hated homies ever since, and that was back in 1968 when I was somewhat sympathetic, or drunk and ambivalent, about them. Gave them civil rights and education and all they can do is praise their thugs; I notice they don't protest against Obama for jobs because rioting in the streets is full-time work. They burn down their own neighborhoods and will probably expect whites to rebuild the cities, bigger and better. How many black celebrities living in White House-like gated-communities have adopted troubled teenagers of their own color? Like zero. They will, however, not miss the chance for a photo-opportunity to protest the treatment of their criminals. I wish I was Italian so I could be a super-star complaining about Mafioso getting the shaft by the legal system. Media forums wouldn't like me though, because my voice is butchered, which yours ain't, so come on now and speak up."

"*1500*," Pablo enunciated. "Each Spartan had four slaves when they went into battle. That was why they didn't want to get involved in foreign wars: too busy keeping down the slaves at home."

"For real? Well, hell, I could fight great too if I had four bodyguards taking the beating for me."

"Mostly they weren't in the rank and file unless battle-lines were broken. And once a year or so Sparta declared war on the Helots, their slaves, and culled the herd, killing unarmed people, sort of practicing for battle without the risks."

"But they had slaves," Fala said, "and I didn't know that. Right into combat, too. Goddamn Hollywood's idea of freedom. They must want us all to be slaves for their entertainments. Say, Pablo, I like you but you're a spoiler. I respect your learning and may take a few classes myself next semester and put it on the government's tab. The enrollment office is right across the street so unless I get evicted first, my only excuse for not doing it would be severe drunkenness, which is possible and even likely. I've always wanted to be a real part of higher-education, but these people tonight ain't too sophisticated so when we talk about stuff, don't try to be intellectual or anything. You're kind of out of your element and the moods can change real abruptly. In fact, maybe you should go straight to the laundry room. I'll show you where it is and bring an ashtray and you can pee down the drain. All right?"

"That bad, huh?"

"You're a corrector and it's like asking permission from the teacher to go potty."

"No I'm not."

"Listen, Pablo," Fala said, "I'm sober now and know what I'm talking about. For instance, if you'dve said that about Spartan slaves to my buddies, one of them might've commented the Confederacy should've done the same to their homies instead of not having enough men to fight the Union, which had a steady supply of soldiers coming over from Ireland who couldn't buy their way out of the army and were basically slaves of Lincoln for cannon-fodder. Then you'd say something, probably too smart for your own good, and I don't want my apartment wrecked by a brawl. Understand?"

Pablo muttered, "It was over slavery."

"What?"

"The American Civil War was over slavery in the Territories; you know, controlling votes going to the North or South. If I'dve been a Southerner then, I would've told the landowners to go to hell. Why should I fight to defend someone else's property, especially if it's human beings?"

"Yeah," Fala exclaimed, "and the Irish, to escape England's oppression, came here, freed the homies, then went into the Territories to kill Indians or make babies with them the Irish wouldn't take care of, or both, while stealing land."

"I doubt Ralph Nader would approve your opinions."

"To the devil with him, and all the others too. We need a small government."

"Who's qualified to run it?" Pablo asked. "They've never done it before and would likely be tyrants; businesses have well-paid employees working fulltime as lobbyists and for ways to get around laws and some people believe the government shouldn't try to keep pace with the scoundrels and instead be paid for doing less work, like when global conglomerates pay our politicians to threaten to, or actually shut-down our government."

"Big government is evil," Fala fiercely insisted. "And we have to foot the bill."

Pablo laughed, "Kind of like the old Roman Catholic Church in Chaucer's era when the best jobs were as clergy or as courtiers."

"Why do you think I don't want to drink with you? You'd be like a politician telling me how wrong I am. I got Indian buddies who'll probably show tonight and we can get fierce with our tribal consciousness against those phonies."

"Are you Lakota?"

"I talk about it most when I have booze in my belly. I'm also part Cree and Irish, all of who have paranoia about oppression. Maybe it's righteous. Who knows? I believe in going my own way without society's interference; could be a genetic trait."

"Yeah, but you're on welfare programs."

"See?" Fala yelled. "That's exactly the kind of comment that stirs bad-blood. I live on the taxpayers' dole and represent them better than some politicians who're bought and sold to some international corporations."

"I'm just trying to get it straight in my head, Fala."

"Why? You don't need to, and you're getting drunk so anything you think is probably wrong."

Pablo hazily thought of the vagabond who Odysseus, disguised as a beggar, beat-up when the suitors staged a fight to be entertained and establish the bums' hierarchy. Probably be a big-seller if someone got on video Pablo being clobbered to a cheering throng of street-people. "You're right. I'm in no condition to be a corrector."

"I know," Fala said, "but you can't help yourself. I don't want to see you get jumped by a bunch of drunks gone savage because, for now, I like you. But that'll change real fast when I get some alcohol in me and you'll be trying to use your messed-up reasoning while we want to gain a state where all the layers of roles we play disappear. You're lucky I'm not drinking yet or I wouldn't have the logic to warn you off."

Thinking: I'm still a slave to my self-images, Pablo said, "I suppose I should thank you for that."

"Don't bother. Just stay in the laundry room and I'll bring an ashtray down. I hope you don't mind tuna-flavored cigarettes; they're the only cans I have for ashtrays and I haven't washed out the oil yet."

Make Vile Things Precious

Pablo was holding court in the laundry room. He had tested his weight on the small sorting table beside the washing machine and decided the risk of waking up with a mystery wound was too high. He was cross-legged in a corner on the cold cement floor and focused on a moral inventory of the world, which he believed was being micromanaged without his permission. Perhaps evolution had brought forth the multitude of Egyptian deities concerning body parts into the oneness of Yaweh and the insane multiple laws of *The Old Testament* which dictated everything from females' menses to the arrangements for blood sacrifices; now, even the material of Aton's atoms were being dissected for profits and body-organ harvesting to keep Dick Cheney alive like Medea renewed the mummifying body of Jason's father with her sorcerous potions, and killed off competition by promising resurrection after blood was drained and didn't uphold her side of the bargain. Would Aton approve or should a god not care if its name changes with time into Adonai, Adonis, or Atman? Pablo wanted to forget who he was for a while, but not take the trouble to learn a new role or adopt other people's attributes, perhaps because he felt superior to everyone. Why take on someone else's flaws when pride is enough of a burden?

I want my freedom, Pablo thought: yet here I am passing judgment on history which will chain me as a magistrate to links of repetition or to be a judge from an order issuing decrees on a different system I don't comprehend. The Hindus kept their pantheon of deities so maybe it's right their adherents are proficient at handling computers as a *deus ex machina*: rolling waves of Samsara's illusions floating through the atmosphere to micromanage routines and speculate on investments of future life and death.

He cringed at the unbidden memory of the morning firefight in his village, which became visual outside himself, as he ran with his mother and uncle from the massacre. The three worlds collapsed and a deluge of vomit shot from Pablo's mouth. Past, present, and what dim future there was, none of them offered hope: his past was hell, his present a poorly lit cave, and his future not even a pleasant promise of a deceitful temptation.

He heard footsteps on the stairs and Fala appeared wearing a t-shirt and jeans, laughing riotously and saying: "Ah, you tossed your cookies. How did it taste? It may happen a few more times but you'll be able to stomach it eventually; just hope you have enough left to get drunk on."

"What's happening up there?"

"Some mental retard is teaching high-Elvish or Orc-speak or something. Doesn't hardly know good English and is recruiting people for an invented movie language; like invoking demi-gods of Hollywood as a gibbering Pentecostal might call on an ultra-vicious god to smite enemies. Never cared much for invoking deities with insane babbling unless I'm in a black-out; don't know what you'll get."

Pablo said, "They'll probably be teaching movies' and television shows' made-up languages in college soon. Most Americans know more about the maps of fantasy worlds than they do the countries we're waging war in."

Fala shook his head, "I tell you, the *wasicu* sure like inducing confusion in their organizations. Maybe that's their idea of free will. Now they got machines translating monkey-voices. Probably figure it's safer than communicating with a human like me. Who knows? Maybe the monkeys are forest-creatures that used to be wood-elves."

"I read those books after watching the shows with my son," Pablo said, as Fala took a deep breath. "Have you heard of the *Ramayana*?"

"No. Is that one of your Hindu books?"

"Yeah," Pablo said. "An incarnated god-prince is exiled and has a monkey as a guide who's like a Hermes for Odysseus. It's an older story than the *Odyssey*, and probably inspired Homer."

Fala smiled, "More monkey-tricks learned from other monkeys. The only way some monkeys get fed now is to learn tricks humans force on them, like playing god to evolve the simians."

"Maybe we learned to do that from our own relationships with deities, getting them to serve us rewards for doing some kind of consciousness expansion."

"More likely, all the humans who make a living pushing buttons were experimental monkeys in a previous life."

Pablo considered that, smiled and said, "People love to play at being natural but most can't resist the temptations of civilization. Going to a park in New York City and banging on a bongo to get in touch with your inner-wild man isn't like running through a jungle on the hunt, like the enemy was in that Hindu epic."

"Jesus, the Hindus have so many gods and goddesses it must be confusing."

"Well, this god-prince was Vishnu, you know, Hare Krishna...Hare, Hare Krishna. He's kind of a stabilizer of the world, organizing systems, culling the herds. Probably out of work now, like me, due to the apocalypse and sent wandering into exiled space for trying to control everything here on earth."

"At least the Hindus had the good sense to believe in stability and diverse oneness, even if trapped in reincarnation."

Pablo shook his head, "That's not their scripture, though, like Jacob is for those wanting to learn how to act with god and for their own profits while roaming about. I suppose when Vishnu became Gandhi, he realized the systems were played-out and the choices were global destruction, which would go against his duty as a stabilizer, or to make life equitable, which went against his previous incarnations' oppressiveness with the caste system and whatnot."

"It's hard to not accept a wealthy inheritance; the only requirement is being born into the right family and any mongoloid maneuvering the spirit world can do that. My cousin even stole my mom's gold wedding ring which was probably ripped out of the guts of the Lakotas' sacred Black Hills; sort of like those movies we were talking about. I only saw one of them. Kind of feel like a golem down here, don't you? The fellows on my prison-block used to call me 'My Precious'. Didn't see much resemblance in it myself until someone did a video of me drunk and sick, pleading for the last can of beer. I would've done anything to have staved off that looming hangover. God, I was sick. That rat-bastard kept holding a can of *Twasted* in front of me, then pulled it away when I tried to snatch it. Torments of the damned, and of course they got it all on camera to show me later. They kept trying to get me to recite lines from those movies but all I could do was weep and gnash my gums." Fala sucked wind, then said, "Instilling instant obedience to orders and programming me like a computer effigy."

Pablo sat up a bit straighter and said, "Nothing like being grafted into a computer graphic world as an undead homunculus."

"If I can just figure out what creator-destroyer wired the compulsion for alcohol into me, maybe we can arrange a new covenant because I'm allergic to transubstantiation. But I'll leave you to your promised land here and get back to my party."

"So long, Fala."

When he had gone, Pablo took out of a trouser pocket a folded piece of paper which he uncreased and read: "You will surely not be caught by that idea of disgrace, which in dangers are disgraceful, and at the same time too plain to be mistaken, that proves so fatal to mankind; since in too many cases the very men that have their eyes perfectly open to what they are rushing into, let the thing called disgrace, by mere influence of a seductive name, lead them on to a point at which they become so enslaved by the phrase as in fact to fall willfully into hopeless disaster, and incur disgrace more disgraceful as the companion of error than when it comes as the result of misfortune."

-Thucydides

Sound advice, Pablo thought, glancing at the vomit on his jeans: Why didn't I heed it if I took the trouble to copy it out? Did I betray myself because I hoped for too much from the community; like Fala, wanted them to put faith in me, yet also take care of me? Trust god, not the chain-of-command, though we all like recognizable faces of corruption. Blacks know they can't trust some of their own, but can't trust the legal system either, so when a cop guns-down a black, they rally with the mentality of: 'He may have been a monster-thug, but he was our monster-thug.' President Obama proclaimed he preferred the herd mentality of Malcolm X's militias to the individuality of Ralph Ellison; Malcolm X adopted his new religion while in prison for being a pimp or something, and when released got involved in a breeding-program war with his Black Muslim prophet, who had Malcolm X assassinated. Ironically, Obama has taken several Islamic nations hostage, but maybe he'll judge them qualified for rehabilitation even though they aren't black.

The city-state that the Athenian democracy offered well-phrased surrender terms to refused it, were conquered, the men killed and the women and children taken as slaves. Pablo considered this as he gazed at his surroundings and the likelihood of beginning another career at the bottom of the food-chain. He had thought he led a life of dignity and honor and at the unveiling of himself as an expendable peon, he used the instigation to rebel. Krishna, who isn't in Hindu scripture, taught on a battlefield the importance of self-control in life's struggle, then had wrath in his blood and became the scourge of god, murdering his kinfolk.

He looked at the worm bobbing about near the bottom of the tequila bottle and thought: So this is what I unconditionally surrendered to. And if my luck holds, I'll hallucinate a devil pursuing unholy communion. All because I didn't want to incur disgrace. For money.

Pablo sighed and refused to shed tears. Perhaps his lineage was destined for misery, like King Lear ordained and graced by a god until Lear abdicated; or Cadmus's kin made some god or goddess wrathful in a former era: perhaps an ancient ambition to unite with or become a deity had brought down a curse on Pablo's family. There was no putting Bacchus back in the bottle now, Pablo thought as he drank: Better to be drunk and batty in Hades than sober and sane on Earth.

The hero-making industry was refused admittance into Pablo's mind: he had pondered it in depth too frequently without any resolution to give the fancy more consideration. Yet a dealer in dead souls seemed to monopolize escape routes so Pablo thought of great writers he admired. Christopher Marlowe was no cardboard character in a Hollywood project: a covert agent sent by England to stir antipathy towards Catholics in France, where he volunteered to be a spy against the Church of England, then turned triple-agent and worked for Queen Elizabeth I again; a playwright acting in the best interests of both nations to avoid a pointless religious war until he could no longer be trusted. Pablo respected such deviltry, especially if it averted a disastrous military campaign like the rotten lies that charged America into perpetual war in Iraq between Ba'athists, Shi'a, and Sunni Muslims. Communities instigate a drive for greatness, are audience to arguments as to why they must be led to fate and the herds culled. The ancient Greeks set up trophies on fields of successful battles, and America does the same for their insipid entertainers who sell their souls and most likely never heard of Doctor Faustus or Saint Bartholomew's Day Massacre.

Yes, Pablo thought: playing opponents off each other is a temptation of such appeal that it's foolish to deny its captivation. England did its utmost to drag Greece, Malta, and Yugoslavia into the war against Nazi Germany so as to soften the blows upon Britain; America stirred unrest in Ukraine to tie up Russia financially and militarily so they wouldn't interfere too much in America's global intrigues: the Ukrainians were collateral damage. Perhaps people have become too domesticated and engaged in technology to withstand the body-count horrors of another World War, and prefer- at least subconsciously- a quick end via nuclear weapons; and that would also satisfy the mongoloids heavily invested in a fiery global annihilation as prophesied. The Intelligence War Obama espouses is too unreliable and the retarded mixed-messages to the public of switching from foe to friend to foe again is so fast-paced that it induces schizophrenia in trying to keep track of allies and enemies. Limited war in a global economy only buys distrust because loyalties can be outbid.

Pablo watched a paint-swirl on the wall opposite him grow larger. He smiled cruelly at the thought of disliking his mind being undependable yet at the same time deliberately making it that way while ridiculing the mentally challenged. He thought: Satan might start out being more fun than Jesus, because taking on the sins of the world is a grim business but instigating them could be a thrill, though needing more and more to achieve pleasure would wear down the bearings. Once one gets past the ego of Lucifer, he's not very interesting, not even as a light-bearer: just another failed actor shilling to metamorphosis to a superior identity. I suppose there are variations of him as there are of Zeus/Jove, Wodan/Odin etcetera. Passing on tarnished tags for societies to a simmering boil of, "If I can't have it no one can." The scorched earth policy of English colonists in Burma, burning oil so the Japanese Empire couldn't get it. We tend to learn and imitate revenge because there are so few to learn forgiveness from: even Jesus said his foes would blaze in hell.

John Milton's Lucifer and his minions who landed in Hades, made a home of it, and subtly began to colonize earth with pride, sin, and death, the incestuous unholy trinity, had Pablo think of how such doings were changing from the genetic to the generic. He again took the folded paper out of his rear pocket and on the other side of the quote from Thucydides, Pablo read: "It was the fight of the millions against the hundreds; and the cruelest part of it was that these men that we fought against, foot, horse, and gunners, were our own picked troops, whom we had taught and trained, handling our own weapons and blowing our own bugle-calls."

-Arthur Conan Doyle

Sherlock Holmes found that criminal case simple to solve, and with the criminals properly punished and the loot stolen from India at the bottom of the Thames River, Holmes proceeded to shoot-up cocaine: an English luxury from their global empire. Pablo wondered how many of Obama's Intelligence Operatives used Afghani heroin.

I am insignificant, Pablo thought: and cannot bear to live with that terrible knowledge; yet under the influence of alcohol I become a great man with profound, albeit fictional, abilities. Fala wishes there were two of him to franchise the world; I'm even more ambitious, desiring a triumvirate. Unlike the Roman pact between Marc Antony, Octavius, and Lepidus after the assassination of Julius Caesar and settling that score, my triumvirate would have peace and stability with solid inner-marriages: Cleopatra would not even qualify as a concubine, her Egypt just another colony for us to exploit. Now, Italy and Sicily are being inundated with refugees fleeing across the Mediterranean Sea from North Africa: all they need is a Hannibal to lead them on; and Italy has to be more than cautious about interfering militarily in those African nations lest the refugees personalize it and stage a patriotic uprising of marauding rapine throughout their adopted homeland.

Pablo laughed at the thought of staging a breeding-program: parades and fireworks, with banners streaming and crowds cheering. Ah, America: the annual Irish parade in March had become a fete for all to partake, provided the weather was good. Where was Cromwell when you needed him? He'd have cleared-up the street parade of un-pedigreed non-Irish Setter dogs, vehicles advertising subsidiary companies with corporate charters, political parties, and anti-abortionists. And if some Norwegian mook with dyed green hair told Cromwell, 'I'm just Irish for the day,' he'd reply, 'Close enough' and throw them all in prison until it was full and massacre the rest. Yet it was preferable (and safer) to attend a generic celebration than a Nazi genetic street parade.

America's diplomacy in military matters since the Korean War had been confusing at best, and mostly a matter of "saving face"; which meant having an image more than a substance. Perhaps that's appropriate for a society obsessed with facades and heated debates over the particular value of a rock-n-roll music group compared to a noisy rival. Our education system and debates, like our wars, seem investments in promoting defining lifestyles sold by corporations.

The Joint Chiefs of Staff and President Truman ordered MacArthur to use only Republic of Korean troops near the Chinese Manchurian border, but when he sent in American army soldiers and marines to take North Korean territory near the Yalu River bordering China, MacArthur's superiors refused to rein him in because…well, he might have succeeded. China responded, for good reason, with alacrity at the encroachment and the war became a diplomatic nightmare which seemed ambivalent to the lives of American troops. The strategy centered on how to "save face" among allies and potential buddies against the Soviet Union and China. Nuke them all? That was MacArthur's much-asserted policy to end the war, stated in various media interviews, which Truman did nothing to dispel though only he could authorize the use of atomic bombs. American officials wouldn't ask China for a ceasefire or return to the partition of Korea via the 38th-parallel because that would make America seem weak; so they used England to ask China for a ceasefire, then American officials complained their United Nations' allies were soft, which wasn't lost on them as America refused to deal with MacArthur's hubris that stranded troops in North Korea. Fortunately, it turned out better than Stalingrad did for Germans in World War II, and a World War III was averted, though no lessons were learned for future police actions.

Are American generals drunk when they give interviews? Media forums say they want candor but thrive on chain-of-command controversy. It can be difficult to accept disgrace from someone for whom one has contempt, especially with so many weapons lying around; but MacArthur got his parades after being canned as commander, which was more than McChrystal got when job-terminated by Obama for unsparing criticism of the president to a writer of a popular-cult music magazine. Damn drunken Micks. No wonder the Irish couldn't organize anything beyond guerilla-fighters.

Pablo liked to think Americans weren't just psyche-energy parasites, though perhaps addicted to proxy living and dying, which may just be the downside of a representative society overly concerned about how to "save face". He had recently read Shakespeare's play *All's Well That Ends Well*, wherein the king of France doesn't officially take sides in a war in Florence, Italy but does allow his courtiers to fight on whichever side they desire. There's a certain amoral meretricious aspect in pillaging and looting by proxy and being rewarded in tribute, which Shakespeare didn't explore. Americans should appreciate dramas about achieving status, despite fortune's stars, by playing sides off each other, subterfuge, and if unveiled as a villain, plead ignorance and hope that avoids disgrace until another role can be assumed. As the notorious representative of the Thug-Era in the 1980's and early 90's noted in his ridiculously high-pitched voice after a boxing-match, "I took my beating like a man." That must have been after he quit biting the ears off of opposing pugilists. The party's over, homie: bitch-beating isn't popular anymore.

Pablo thought Obama had done a decent job of "saving face" the previous summer when he had a really bad month: the Veterans' Administration falsified records to indicate some military personnel had received medical treatment when they'd mostly been ignored. The Obama administration traded some captured Islamic warriors for an American soldier who had wandered from his post in Afghanistan and been held prisoner by the Taliban for five years; he sounded goofier than a deliberate deserter but Congress had the duty to ratify any such exchange and howled at being circumvented. And, of course, all the armchair generals saying when America withdrew from Iraq a few years prior, they foresaw Sunni rebels conquer tracts of Iraq, requiring American intervention. Obama didn't turn rabid at all the various attacks on him and his cronies, and Pablo respected him for his poise.

The 2016 presidential hopefuls were already worm-tunneling their way through media-forums and Pablo knew he didn't have what it took to follow the two-year trial. He'd probably end up writing-in Sitting Bull anyway and have his ballot put through a shredding machine. The American public couldn't outbid the global conglomerates for the candidates' souls, so it was really a matter of seeing who could put on the best performance in acting presidential and how many skeletons danced out of closets: real, fabricated, or hybrid-hype. At least Obama didn't have the baggage his opponents had when he took office.

Pablo had hoped to clear his consciousness with a thorough drunk; to wipe clean the dreck which had accumulated in his mind the past year and since his tenure at *Mood Food*, but it was not to be; instead General George Patton appeared and began giving orders and heaped abuse on Pablo as a nogoodnick loafer. Pablo watched him for a moment with curiosity: even this strong, though not solid, character had assumed various identities to keep his self-image intact, believing he was the reincarnation of an ancient Greek or Roman soldier killed on a battlefield.

When Pablo refused to enlist in the fantasy, Patton disappeared and Pablo felt the corridors of his mind slam shut into darkened tunnels. I'll take my chances, he thought: following orders from apparitions like that might get me killed. Americans have an infatuation with fancies of war: they loved their beleaguered Vietnam Vets when it became popular to portray them as homeless, drug-addicted, insane, drunken criminals. At a re-release of a war movie a few months after the 9-11-1 air attacks, with forty or so minutes added to the show, Pablo had listened to the audience's general chit-chat before the presentation began. One fellow proudly proclaimed that when the movie had originally come out, he'd attended it with a buddy who'd fought in the Vietnam War and later that night helped hold him together when the veteran suffered induced flashbacks. Perhaps it was contagious, because the fellow went on to say he'd now become a target in The War on Terror. He didn't like Pablo saying, 'Tell that to our troops in Afghanistan; tell them, "I feel your pain."'

A demented version of a 1980's movie played on the opposite wall, brought to Pablo by Ricky Rodent, the cartoon mascot of an entertainment corporation that tuned the bardos in which Pablo abruptly found himself ensnared. He watched as a multimillionaire investor in franchising casinos, land, and a dead football league, who never performed military service, now a 2016 presidential candidate, became the sponsored guide of the entertainment corporation. He spat in the face of a wheelchair-bound ex-prisoner of war from a police action, while screaming, "Did you ever carpet-bomb a little (insert racial slur) baby?"

"Maybe I carpet-bombed lots of little (racial slur) babies, but I don't talk about it."

"You didn't fight that war, man! You weren't even there."

"What do you mean I didn't fight that war? I was there."

"Yeah, but your heart wasn't in it."

Pablo had owned a thirty-hour World War II documentary during the zenith of the Nuris' affluence, and recalled what a German veteran said in an interview: he joined the military to escape the nonstop propaganda aimed at a populace that was intelligent and well-educated. Granted, the military had its own propaganda, but the incessant pressure of willingly and happily consuming the dreck of the Nazi elitists' arts and entertainments, and even worse lies, didn't perpetually bombard the individual because in the army one was busy just following orders to stay alive with comrades. Join the military now, and there's no escape at all from it, with satellites beaming worthless images everywhere but maybe a foxhole. Is that how far I've sunk? Pablo thought: That I'd rather be in a trench getting shot at by an enemy ten feet away who I armed and trained just to get away from Donald Trump, because even if he became my commander-in-chief, he wouldn't dare make an appearance in a dugout unless one of my compatriots dialed it up on a cell-phone. I'd want to bash in the head of any soldier who did that. Akin to how Emperor Constantine, according to legend, on the day of a great battle was guided by a revelation in the heavens of a glowing cross, so too, Pablo thought, there may come an era when devices are used to project across the polluted sky political and religious leaders into combat zones to spur on their troops, brought to them by conglomerate sponsors, complete with corporate logo advertisements.

Pablo closed his eyes and focused on his objective: get drunk, sleep it off, go home and apologize to Estella. Perhaps she'd listen to pleas, yet Pablo's hubris didn't find it appealing: he was weary of caring about her. In fact, he didn't want to be concerned about anything anymore. He desired to disappear, yet innately knew he would have to perform some conceding conciliations if he wanted a roof over his head: it was simply too cold to live in a woody area, sleeping under a tree. He didn't have it in him to test his limits, which would most likely expand to the point where he came under the rule of an authoritarian taskmaster even worse than Estella, such as a homeless shelter with mandatory attendance at evangelical shows.

It'd be like living in Coalition-occupied Iraq before Halliburton stole off to Dubai to avoid having their black-market profits audited by an American agency, Pablo thought: under the thumb of an incompetent Platonist as Paul Bremer proved to be, guiding the shades to be made in the image of *Bible* prophecies. Jesus said that Lucifer is the Prince of the World and the chain-of-command demands subservience in working towards turning earth into hell to give demons their due inheritance and the pure refugees a well-organized heaven; yet the committees in my head refuse to accept surrender. I tried to shut them down with alcohol and they only became more rebellious, filling the vacuous void of Hugo and *Mood Food* with relief that I don't have to languish and suffer. I have no prime directive from family, coalitions, gangsters, religions, employers etcetera to be a servant unto a god, humanity, or society in the third-dimension or screen-world. I am free and in a dungeon even Fala, the computerless scholar-scavenger, avoids unless nearing a black-out stupor.

Pablo's poetic freedom didn't last long because he knew he couldn't trust his discrimination in choosing what resentments were real and which led to shooting-spree varieties. He felt there were versions of himself he could not control that were invented in other people's committees of consciousness as hostages or colonizers; and that seemed the only representative government left to America. They tried to form him with promises of rewards or punishments, and though he wanted to make a separate peace with their deities without use of scapegoats, the systems' managers were angry he wouldn't hold to their predestined course and accept what they offered in good faith. He thought: I don't want to be The Scourge of God, but why should I become a version made by something else to complete the imagery-show, like Rama going through all the literary phases and phrases of millenniums? He spurned their notions of oneness and diversified duality. He dug in against work and revenge, like a World War I trench battlefield. He wasn't afraid to go over-the-top into No Man's Land with a charge against the foes, but drunk and paranoid enough to believe he might adapt some of his enemies' worst attributes, especially in hand-to-hand combat.

He said aloud, "You stay over there and I'll stay here and we'll have a ceasefire tonight."

16

Success is Virtue

Pablo heeded the quote from Balzac and stood amidst great light and in Pablo was no pain, fear, or loss of identity. He moved through it at will, never baffled by direction. Approval seemed to emanate for him as he collected strands of web-roads and united them. Some voices protested around him, claiming continuance and forgiveness were being detached from the various paths, and that courts and legal systems were being overloaded or hijacked by highway-robbers.

Stranded creatures from whom the light had faded began appearing through cross-country travels. The more ambitious of them attempted to circle the light, as if to surround and siege it or seek another means of entry. A figure stood beside Pablo as he disconnected a trail from a small satellite that branched with the greater glow. The outlined character watched Pablo a moment, then commented, "You know, for intelligent fun with words, it's best to be with males. All women are interchangeable and good for only one thing, and they resent men who know that."

Pablo paused, glancing at the grinning figure, and replied, "That's quite a tempting idea. Especially when they all follow the same fads, even if it's just bitching about following the same fads."

The figure shrugged indifferently, saying, "That's because it's true. But your work here is making us into hermaphrodites, like worms. You do it instinctively, without a thought in your head or a question as to where this is leading. I have some folks working on things now that'll maybe mix roles but at least keep the show going. Why don't you join us? You obviously have an ability to put things together." Pablo hesitated due to the abrupt consideration of rewards. His new companion looked at swiftly moving shades delving into sparkling areas to be streamlined elsewhere, and said, "There they go. Thanks for letting me distract you. I'm not certain what your punishment will be, but if you get tired of servitude, I can fix a deal you won't regret."

Too late, Pablo saw his work unravel as the light frayed into the shades, forming outlines which had strings of compulsions wired into them: some had stems standing up from their heads which they adjusted into halos; others had their groins attached to trunks and twigs of light; some attempted to tune their inner-regions into alignment for total control of content.

Pablo furiously realized the systems did not revolve around him and his work: there were too many others with their own agendas, and some made it their soul's sole purpose to undo him for rewards, of which he could not partake. The great light was now separated from him and had broad branches extending to embrace where the trickster and minions had gone; and like irresistible arms, the light pulled Pablo and the darkness closer. Pablo felt wrath, envy, and fear. He raged, "What's the point of me going on the way you rigged me? You just give my rightful pay to others who you make me sympathize with. They steal my livelihood, and what do I get but a share of their misery, ten times returned. I tried to wake them throughout history and all they do is create opinions as enforced judgments." He ignored the bleak and bleary consciousness of his recent tribunal, and shook his fist as he fell from sleep to awaken in the laundry room with the empty tequila bottle under his head as a pillow.

He felt like resurrected road-kill and spat a ropey strand to get the foul taste from his mouth. His body ached as if a miniature spoiler was under his flesh, traveling throughout his frame with a fiery pitchfork. He sat up slowly, bracing himself against the wall, and checked his pocket for his wallet.

He was too sick for a hair-of-the-dog hangover fix. He'd been passed-out too long and unfortunately didn't wake up still drunk. An Indian woman with a knapsack under her head was curled in another corner. Pablo wondered if he'd done anything with her, assuming of course it was a female; her back was to him and she looked slim and maybe she was pretty, but his mind went to getting a glass of water.

He tried not to groan as he stood, then cautiously bent to pick up the bottle. No point in leaving behind incriminating evidence; and he felt it his duty to clean after his sloppy drunk, though there was nothing he could do about the laundry drain reeking of urine. If he had some bleach...That was as far as he got with that thought, and went to the steps. He put his hands on both walls of the narrow stairwell and creaked up to what had once been the living room before the house was sectioned into apartments.

Hollering voices came from the second floor, sounding like Fala on a rampage. Pablo didn't want to get involved so he went to the communal kitchen, put the bottle in a garbage can, and searched the cabinets for a cup. The voices got louder, apparently having left Fala's room, but still upstairs and probably in the hallway. Pablo found a coffee mug, rinsed it thoroughly in the sink stacked with dirty dishes, and blessed the water as he drank. Do people do terrible things just to experience the relief of recovery? Was it the addiction to forms of redemption that drove him to perform ignorant acts; that hope was a cruel taskmaster and knowledge of it a double-edged straight razor to cross? Like Fala, Pablo may have desired the community to put hope In him, which entailed playing different roles for the various and ever-changing faiths. Clearing the dreck from his mind had been pricey, yet hope had driven and steered him to this small reward of a cup of water.

Pablo didn't want to see a fight, especially one wherein Fala got another beating. So Pablo stood in the kitchen, sipping water, and when there was a stomping down the steps and the front door slammed, Pablo decided it was time to leave. He put the mug on the counter and walked into the living room. Fala was lying at the bottom of the stairs, perhaps dead. His head was awry on his neck and Pablo discerned no breathing.

Pablo thought: That's not partying, that's murder. The apartment house was silent, as if its denizens were pensively awaiting the next development behind locked doors. He stood over Fala's wreckage heap and decided not to take the high-road. What did he owe Fala for being an example of how not to live? What sort of rewards do people owe to those who teach by being terrible moral models? A seat in the White House? It gives lost souls a place to land. He walked out the front door, shivered from the frigid air which at least had the effect of killing a mulling on how awful he felt as he went into survival mode for the journey home.

It was difficult to tell the time of day by the winter sun as the earth began its slow spin to the southeast. It was bright, though hard and cold. As Pablo walked, focusing on the pavement, a variation of a song from thirty-years prior began spinning in his head:

'Every Fala pukes a drool...sometime
Pawns his dremel-kit tool...listen, Fala
Learned it all in reform school...gonna say it again.'

Pablo felt like he'd been poleaxed in the forehead as the tune continued through verses and choral arrangements. He pulled his stocking cap tighter over his ears, which started a rendition of a 1980's song:

'Oh, oh Fala, drinking up all night long...Oh, Fala
Oh, oh Fala, gonna puke it at the break of dawn...Oh, Fala
He needs you to understand
He doesn't want to be a Charles Manson...Oh, Fala.'

Pablo thought: It's all about you, Fala, as you wend your way through the spirit world or stages of consciousness. All the secret codes will be revealed to you like a James Joyce novel of trivial rubbish as a send-off to someone who's dead drunk.

Pablo wasn't in the mood to deal with a security officer so he didn't take a tempting short-cut through the campus. Due to the weather, he couldn't accurately gauge the juggernaut of his hangover. Perhaps he'd barfed enough tequila to keep his discomfort at a minimum. He wasn't interested in inventing a script for whatever scenario awaited him at home: apologies, promises, alibis, excuses...none of them gained even a lukewarm reception in his mind. The vacuum of consciousness attempted to construct a Hollywood set of how he should behave but a visceral image of Fala lying at the bottom of the stairwell developed a soundtrack:

'Fala la, Fala lee
Drunk as hell, on a spree
Maybe he'll sleep under a tree
That ol' Fala la, Fala lee.'

It's a cold water and TV day, Pablo thought: Spin my wheels in front of a screen, then get on to getting a real job. If I can catch-up on computers, maybe I'll return to being a system's analyst. That'd make Estella happy, though I'll not be able to work on my history. I suppose I fooled myself long enough about it.

The harsh wind brought tears to Pablo's eyes and he wondered where his glasses had gone to; he patted all his pockets and decided he'd taken them off before he passed-out and they were somewhere in the laundry room. There were too many dangers and unpleasant factors in returning to Fala's building. Fortunately, Pablo had kept his former pair of bifocals, placed in his top dresser drawer.

Feeling ill seemed to induce a gratifying meanness, as if he was among the elite privileged to have evil intentions. Strong emotions wreak chemical changes in bodies, and every person has a dark nature that can metamorphosis him or her, just as reading Ovid's poetry had inspired disturbing dreams in Pablo. A collection of cold furious passions appeared to conglomerate in him and he smiled at the thought of Fala left alone at the bottom of the steps, likely with a broken neck. It was the true way of humans to avoid another's fall because he or she would probably drag along partners.

'Why don't you yak-up? Heave, Fala
Why don't you yak-up? Heave, Fala
Why don't you yak-up real good this time?
-did you write *The Book of Puke?*
Why don't you yak-up some greenish slime?
-while you're acting like a kook?'

Pablo had been a victim of fancies and ambitions with a keen desire to stage his consciousness in a manner that he'd convinced himself led others to a kind of enlightenment. He'd believed he was gracious and dignified in offering sundry paths to a stable serenity. It was a hard revelation that he was just something to be used and discarded in a society which found pride in the disposability of their current genius. Perhaps the requiem dirges for Fala, based on throw-away popular-cult tunes which haunted Pablo in his weakened condition, were appropriate. Why honor anyone's life with hypocrisy which only compounded the evil of the unmade person? Why not jeer and sneer instead of canonizing? Corporate saints like Ronald Reagan deserve ridicule, not a Bob Southey elegy of heaven opening to Reagan like the demented King George III. Leave it to a tainted peerless Lord, who had to make his living from poetry because his ancestors wasted the inheritance, to show the way into heaven. Dante was correct: upper realms can only be appreciated after journeying through the lowest depths where it's righteous to demonize enemies; and while at it, some character assassination gossip to do the same to friends to make oneself feel better. Pablo had tried to organize at the base of society and been surprised to be an undignified serf with a reactionary wrathful desire to pull down the structures.

In this swampy miasma of self-pity and the developing hope of becoming middle-class, Pablo did not dwell on the obvious consideration of his judgments against society's upper-echelons the previous night. If he had thought of it, he most likely would have blamed them for embedding his new ambition into his mind to rise above his current status, or contrived a fantasy wherein they told him, 'Jesus said you shouldn't judge our greediness.' He certainly was not grateful towards *Mood Food's* managers for terminating his tenure and thereby instilling the drive to search for better opportunities. The notion that if he worked happily and was loyal to service then evolution would progress to good fortune was a sale's pitch Pablo was too cynical to invest anything but scorn and contempt. He was sick and unwilling to think he had settled upon being a dishwasher because he refused to bargain on a higher price for his soul: all *Mood Food* had gotten from Pablo was manual labor, and America's health care plan could mend his physical ailments. He had been free to read the literature he wanted and to write without someone looking over his shoulder to make sure he adhered to the corporate charter.

He put the potency of Thomas Aquinas into Aristotle and decided since a strong middle-class was deemed essential to balance between the wealthy and the poor, Pablo would do his duty and rise to mid-strata. He was probably fooling himself in guising it as an altruistic choice for his family and civilization; that he was consciously willing to sacrifice his freedom was as far as he cared to deliberate. Whether working to gain a niche of possessions would please him was doubtful, at least so much as the work was concerned. The materials, however, might be enjoyable.

He planned to set things right with Estella and Hector; inform them he would enroll in the state university's computer analyst classes to update himself on the latest equipment, and from there begin a real career and life would be wholesome. He'd surrender his life as an unpaid writer and be graceful about it: unstained by resentments at martyrdom for his family. He had needed that drunken night to perceive his life rightly and induce a cause to put things in order. He didn't find it curious that he was glad he'd behaved so wretchedly the previous day. Instead, he was proud of his new perspective: If you can't take it with you, you might as well use everything while here. He didn't believe in making amends to himself or taking revenge, his reasoning: The more I punish myself, the likelier I'll rebel and act even worse, which induces harsher vengeance on myself, making me revolt and take refuge as a dual contrary full of wrath.

He walked up the apartment-house stairs, eager to share the good news with his family. He felt certain they'd rejoice at his righteous decision to invest in third-dimensional escapism. How could they not? Pablo would no longer concern them with history, and they could enlist in various role-playing without his criticisms of depth and quality. He would not be Krishna to Hector's Arjuna; the battlefield was filled with trophies for the taking, or if need be, the stealing. The king was father to the soldiers, and Pablo would grant Hector a goodly share of loot.

Pablo's key went into the lock and he opened the door, ready to apologize but more prepared to begin their lives anew. Even the hymns for Fala had disappeared, spun off to another void to possess some unwitting dupe. Pablo called to them when he saw they weren't in the living room or kitchen. There was no answer and he felt a vacuous absence in the apartment, which he denied cognitive processing. He went to the bedroom: the blankets and sheets were gone from the bed and the closet doors were open with forlorn clothes-hangers dangling without Estella's neatly-ironed apparel.

Pablo had to pee, and in the bathroom saw their grooming and hygiene items were gone. His bladder relieved, he rinsed his hands in the sink, then wiped them on his trousers because there were no towels. The enormity of it sank into his mind. Was it a test on Estella's part? Could be, because she'd never left him before and Pablo was sure he'd behaved more vilely in the past than the previous night. They were probably staying at her brother's house, awaiting events. He opened the medicine cabinet for aspirin and found a small piece of paper with Estella's handwriting which informed him he could keep the floss and toothpaste.

Pablo groaned, "Oh, Jesus Christ, is she doing that again?" Estella was a binge note-dropper. She would be fine for several months then, inexplicably- at least to Pablo- she would leave small written messages throughout the apartment: 'Leave the remote control on the table'; 'Wash the bathroom mirror'; 'Use a low-watt bulb for the living-room lamp'; 'Clip your nails into the garbage and pick up any strays'.

Pablo thought her recent notes would be terse and not have a heart drawn at the bottom of the message. In fact, he was glad she was gone because he felt like murdering her: he knew, without looking, he'd find notes where their bank account book had been, the extra cash, the Food Stamp card, and probably even the small change jar of pennies, nickels, and dimes.

He sank on the sofa and muttered, "So much for trophies: she mortgaged me and sent a credit-line of Hate-Mail."

ACT V

17 Pedigree

Hermes of Kyllene summoned the souls of the suitors to come forth, and in his hands he was holding the beautiful golden staff, with which he mazes the eyes of those mortals whose eyes he would maze, or wakes again the sleepers. Herding them on with this, he led them along, and they followed, gibbering. And as when bats in the depth of an awful cave flitter and gibber, when one of them has fallen out of his place in the chain that the bats have formed by holding one on another; so, gibbering, they went their way together, and Hermes the kindly healer led them along down moldering pathways. They went along, and passed the Ocean stream, and the White Rock, and passed the gates of Helios the Sun, and the country of dreams, and presently arrived in the meadow of asphodel. This is the dwelling place of souls, images of dead men.

-Homer *Odyssey* 24: 1-14

Odysseus purged his house of suitors for his wife, along with some others who didn't display the proper loyalty to the disguised king and wagered on the suitors' victory. It was a ruthless housecleaning, but some Christians expect Jesus to do the same on his return, and settle their grievances against the iniquitous like a sort of personal button-man with the right and might to smite. At least one of Odysseus's guides was more humane than that and helped make the peace between Odysseus's House and the suitors' families whom sought vengeance.

The last time I spoke with Estella, over two weeks ago, she mentioned getting an annulment, which her Pope has said should no longer cost exorbitant fees. I'm sure the bishops whose dioceses are declaring bankruptcy to pay off child abuse legal settlements have different ideas than their holy father when it comes to the business of annulments. They probably hope since the Roman Catholic Church has always moved slowly, heels will be dragged on the topic.

Some people can afford to be uncompromising; it doesn't make them right, it just means they can afford such an attitude. I don't rule a kingdom or have great wealth so the games aren't played according to my investments. Everywhere I see people succeeding in mediocrity, and I'm convinced I'm better than them as a person and at what I do, which is currently griping about failure. How on god's green earth did such things come about? I could just be deadweight, whose pride may have been fear of failure by the designs of the mediocre.

I don't want this to be a journal of hate, but Estella won't help pay the lease on our apartment, which is in my name, and I'm almost forced to think she's a greedy wench. My credit is bad enough without bailing from the lease, for which I still owe three months' rent. I'm working as a sack-boy at *Donnie's* just to pay it, and can't save money for another, smaller apartment when my lease is done here. I don't qualify for Food Stamps so I'm getting groceries from food pantry charities. I'm sick of canned food and would sell my innards for fresh fruits and a bottle of tequila. Maybe I can get the county's social service to pay deposit on another apartment, if my credit is good, though I don't relish the foresight vision of residing in a Fala-like dungeon sleeping-room. I can't decide to stay and lick my sores or pull up stakes and try elsewhere. The landlords in this city all have one-year leases so as to make students pay rent in the summer; otherwise, many places would be tenantless in the off-seasons, kind of like a tourist town.

Estella hasn't gone legal yet for child-support, but neither will she let me speak to or see Hector. It seems she may have been planning such maneuvers for some time, because she quickly had the policy of him not answering the phone when I call her brother's house, where they're staying rent-free; and the money she doesn't save, she spends on Hector, buying him the things I denied our family, like his own cell-phone, for which I don't have the number.

I suppose it's always been about money and sin with variations of what should inspire work to be passed along to future generations. Positions are auctioned and intrigued for, and technology has made it faster and easier to select roles: those we live through, imitate, and ridicule. I'm uncertain why I choose characters who have faith in their idiosyncratic systems of rewards and punishments. Maybe I have enough latent Roman Catholic tendencies to believe Jesus's teachings on worldly trophies, but am also dubious about a heaven of rewards that seem based on earthly pleasures, which vary with notions of lifestyle comforts and entertainment distractions to escape the third-dimension. An eternity of "Alleluias" would be tiresome.

It's unfortunate that I have to study this stuff to take stock of myself, but we all have different modes of inspiration. I'm not a very good person, choosing to lose myself in work as if an angel opening scrolls to reveal the word of gods', while at the same time chastising the world for choosing other games and beliefs of fantasies, which I think aren't as good as mine, instead of being my applauding, adoring audience.

* * *   * * *   * * *   * * *

All the able-bodied men of the town agreed with Hamor and his son Shechem, and all the males, including every able-bodied man in the community, were circumcised. On the third day, while they were still in pain, Dinah's full brothers, Simeon and Levi, two of Jacob's sons, took their swords, advanced against the city without any trouble, and massacred all the males...

God said to Jacob: "Go up now to Bethel. Settle there and build an altar there to the God who appeared to you while you were fleeing from your brother Esau."...Then, as they set out, a terror from God fell upon the towns round about, so that no one pursued the sons of Jacob.

-Genesis 34: 24-25; 35: 1, 5

It's always nice to escape dirty-fighting without losing face, and Jacob did the wise thing in fleeing after the slaughter of Dinah's suitor/rapist and his town. It can be hard to know when to stop killing and stealing, especially while on a roll that becomes genocide; but that's useful too, because it puts the fear of god in anyone who thinks of getting in the way. If one can't make the peace, then haul-ass to a shrine and hope it provides sanctuary, though it's on historical records that doesn't necessarily keep people from invading a church or temple to commit mayhem. Monseigneur Romero was gunned-down in El Salvador while saying Mass. Who knows how far goons guised in religion, politics, or color purity will go in bloodshed? No one is really scared of a god they don't believe in, just the reaction of the faithful, and Jacob's family was in the process of converting the suitor's town they looted. I probably wouldn't put much faith in supposed divine guidance to a Hermes-like memorial stone unless it was strategically located to fend off the vengeful, especially if it was just promised real estate in a dream. Odysseus at least was protecting his own home and was able to make the peace in his kingdom with the families of the suitors'.

Currently, the elite are using every institution (while inventing new ones) and patsies at their disposal to cull the herds of discriminate thinkers; perhaps the latter are becoming a mass of consciousness, plotting revenge with an evil genius via their own methods and dupes to cull the herds of insipid consumers at movie theaters and other places of pointless entertainments. There are plenty of established oracles that offer crafted compulsions of cryptic guidance. The war between wit and dullness has gone high-tech and as people feel a loss of control of the third-dimension, the more likely they are to come under the capricious sway of those who proclaim to have solutions to everything from a hangnail to ancient prejudices. Powerful weapons are easy to get for anyone with resentments, real or imaginary. I suppose this journal could either be popular and in-demand or censored by those who don't want people to think like I do, preferring they have fixed images of good and evil that can be mass-manufactured.

* * *   * * *   * * *   * * *

Romeo: Courage, man, the hurt cannot be much.
Mercutio: No, 'tis not so deep as a well, nor so wide as a church door, but 'tis enough, 'twill serve. Ask for me tomorrow, and you shall find me a grave man. I am peppered, I warrant, for this world. A plague o' both your houses!

Zounds, a dog, a rat, a mouse, a cat, to scratch a man to death! A braggart,
a rogue, a villain, that fights by the book of arithmetic! Why the devil came
you between us? I was hurt under your arm.

Romeo: I thought all for the best.

Mercutio: Help me into some house, Benvolio,

Or I shall faint. A plague o' both your houses!

They have made worm's meat of me. I have it,

And soundly too. Your houses!

Romeo: This gentleman, the Prince's near ally,

My very friend, hath got this mortal hurt

In my behalf; my reputation stained

With Tybalt's slander- Tybalt, that an hour

Hath been my cousin! O sweet Juliet,

Thy beauty hath made me effeminate,

And in my temper softened valor's steel!

Benvolio: O Romeo, Romeo, brave Mercutio is dead!

That gallant spirit hath aspired the clouds,

Which too untimely here did scorn the earth.

Romeo: This day's black fate on more days doth depend;

This but begins the woe others must end.

Benvolio: Here comes the furious Tybalt back again.

Romeo: Alive in triumph, and Mercutio slain!

Away to heaven, respective lenity,

And fire-eyed fury be my conduct now!

Now, Tybalt, take the "villain" back again

That late thou gavest me, for Mercutio's soul

Is but a little way above our heads,

Staying for thine to keep him company.

Either thou or I, or both, must go with him.

-Shakespeare *Romeo and Juliet* 3, I: 94-128

It can be a dangerous thing, uniting Houses, especially on the sly; and
Romeo's exile from Verona for killing Tybalt leads to getting misinformation
about Juliet's death; something that never happened to Odysseus who placed

faith in his guides, and wouldn't have occurred to Romeo if he'd heeded Mercutio and not taken love so seriously to the point of suicide: love is more dangerous than gods. One of the reasons I like being alone is I often find myself in unreliable company. It's not easy to keep from adapting some of the attributes of those one is around, which is part of the reason uniting Houses is a precarious business: like the chain of bats in Homer's cave, alignment can be all-important. One has to be cagey in trusting friends' advice or cajolery when it comes to sex, love, and the arts I've never mastered: Romeo takes Mercutio's fiery attitude as the macho thing to do to avenge his friend's death; which is forgivable because maybe Romeo's wits were addled by wordplay with Mercutio, who had vengeance done on him by Romeo interfering in the fight, and that brought howling curses down on the Capulet and Montague Houses, climaxing in a tomb after Romeo killed a suitor of Juliet's, who was a member of royalty.

How far should a democracy go in allowing Houses, corporate or otherwise, to clear out the bad-blood between each other? From the streets on up, their influence is felt and sympathies aligned. At the end of *Romeo and Juliet* the Prince, kin of Mercutio and the suitor Romeo slew, believes he should have been more forceful in his godlike decrees of enforcing peace between the Capulets and Montagues, which does take place at the end of the drama; yet the Prince's cousin sided with Romeo and was quick with an insult to have a good fight. People enjoy instigating trouble at every level, especially if they have impunity.

There's something in me that trusts no one's company, yet in a way I'm sending forth hope or pleas for a messenger or guide, preferably one that won't fog my brain with too many instructions or too much wordplay. I need a blessing, a donation of moly, but will settle for my peace-pipe and kinnick kinnick. It's best I stay alone (except with my imaginary friends) because like Odysseus, I have a better chance of winning a home that way. Romeo's and his man, Balthazar's, return from exile was doomed, and Jacob's family didn't stay long at their promised land. I just don't want to be a destitute refugee in my adopted hometown because I know I'll cling to people and become someone else.

Or, more likely, it's a matter of sour grapes I bitterly crush in hopes of a buzzing head so I can enjoy my loneliness by enhancing its sorrow. Perhaps that's what I really want. Angelo left a message on the telephone machine that he, his family, and our mother are now off-limits for me. They went as far as they could, and I'm out of their boundaries. If I'm to go on as a target, it'll have to be without them as body-armor. Perhaps their attitudes will change, but it's best not to tempt wrath: I have enough enemies as it is. I've long ago forgotten my Mayan name, and wanted to ask my mom what it was when we lived in Guatemala. I don't know how to go about checking our former village's records, if there still are any. Maybe it doesn't matter whether I'm Paul, Saul, or any other label. Why pursue the name-game? Odysseus as Nobody vying with the son of a god who bestows a curse; Jacob wrestling all night with a man-angel who blesses Jacob and names him Israel; Romeo denies his name because it's an enemy to Juliet and after some lovers' quibbling over the sanctity of vows, swear oaths of fealty. Struggles change identities, but I don't want this work to become a Nazi *Bible* like Adolf Hitler's *Mein Kaumpf*. I have to find another means to redefine myself.

There really isn't anything wrong with making something of yourself, but we get contrary directions: 'Do it our way and you can make something of yourself' which is more a matter of being one of them than making something of yourself. I found that out at a young age and it truly skewered my attitude, which the Tsar liked because he realized I'd be a lucrative colonist doing my work here in the Midwest and not butting heads with other crew members. What I didn't count on is my excessive need for individuality, which became a matter of forcing others to ostracize me so I can be alone.

* * *   * * *   * * *   * * *

Then resourceful Odysseus spoke in turn and answered him: "See, I will accurately answer all that you ask me. I am from Alybas, where I live in a famous dwelling, and am the son of Apheidas, son of the lord Polypemon. My own name is Eperitos; now the divinity drove me here on my way against my will, from Sikania. And my ship stands nearby, off the country, away from the city. But as for Odysseus, this is by now the fifth year since he went from there, and took his departure out of my country. Unhappy man. Indeed, the bird signs were good at his going. They were on his right; and I too rejoiced as I sent him off, and he rejoiced as he went. My heart was

still hopeful that we would meet in friendship and give glorious presents."
He spoke, and the black cloud of sorrow closed on Laertes. In both hands
he caught up the grimy dust and poured it over his face and grizzled head,
groaning incessantly. The spirit rose up in Odysseus, and now in his nostrils
there was a shock of bitter force as he looked on his father. He sprang to
him and embraced and kissed and then said to him: "Father, I am he, the
man whom you ask about. I am here, come back in the twentieth year to the
land of my father."

-Homer *Odyssey* 24: 302-322

Hamlet: ...Was't Hamlet wronged Laertes? Never Hamlet.
If Hamlet from himself be ta'en away,
And when he's not himself does wrong Laertes,
Then Hamlet does it not, Hamlet denies it.

-Shakespeare *Hamlet* 5, 2: 231-234

Willy Nilly Shakescene was the best at composite characters in the
English language, and had no shame in using poetic license for Hamlet to call
Laertes a brother before they killed each other in a tremendous body-count
scene reminiscent of Odysseus and son slaying Penelope's suitors (if only
Hamlet's mother had been as chaste!). Odysseus was careful about revealing
his identity, even to his dad; yet what may seem to be Odysseus enjoying
the torment of Laertes is instead the need for Odysseus to know his own
status; after that, he finally becomes someone other than a wandering actor
playing whatever role helps him survive, unlike Hamlet, with his unsuccessful
homecoming. The latter knew his enemies were out to kill him, despite his
tendency to take on guises, and discovered himself in bad situations, often
reacting impetuously if he didn't overthink the scenes.

Odysseus's growth and fulfillment is something Jacob never has in his
character, especially in regards to his father; the blessing from Isaac while
Jacob was disguised as Esau was just one of many ensuing shenanigans
performed as patriarch of a growing House on the run. Jacob didn't even
get the land promised to him, but ended up in Egypt as the result of his

own sons' fraternal spite; and on his deathbed he compared some of them to domesticated animals for blessings and others as savage beasts in curses.

There may be a future wherein Hector has a step-father and no longer recognizes me. I miss schooling him, and his following me into the various ways I believed he should go. It's a palpable hit that he could be or is happier without me; I already know Estella is; and having failed, it's best not to battle for cupidity and felicity, but just walk away and tell myself this is the life I've chosen. I'm unsure if I can do that; there's part of me that desires heartlessness for freedom from the past, but also the- probably inaccurate- belief I can have a good joyous effect. I don't want to engage in a war to build Hector as a person different from me but still flesh of my flesh. He's too young to go his own way, but as he does I'll wish him more success than I've had.

Part of the reason I married Estella was I'd grown-up without a father (which made me susceptible to the Tsar's sway), except occasional boyfriends my mom collected, which was how Angelo was begotten. I wanted my son to feel complete and all I did was make him neurotic about the spoils of the world. I don't know where his loyalties lie and can't measure his ambitions. Did I help create a good inner-consistency in him or just induce schizophrenic adaptation of pleasing those about him while scamming to join the elite fad makers?

Lucifer's lineage via Daedalion sort of petered out after Odysseus and his son, Telemachos, while Jacob multiplied his family and pack animals. Maybe that's why the Jews adopted the stories of craft and guile to form a background while they were on the rise: like the older brother Esau had to serve his younger brother Jacob, so the older story of Odysseus serves the purpose of the newer breeds. That the Jews stayed true to it is more testimony of enduring stubbornness than brains, which is ironic because most Jews are fairly intelligent and well-educated and should recognize artful deceit when they see it. New nations strike out at their parent civilizations; it's an inherent part of social Darwinism mixed with psychological identification. It's not easy, or fair, to judge the point at which nature becomes unnatural; it's like splitting the atom with unintentional reactions spinning outwards. The bomb dropped on Hiroshima surprised Americans with radioactive fall-out, but didn't deter from dropping another on Nagasaki and continuing to explode nuclear warheads for practice and scare tactics. Was that an artificial use of craft and free will? Is it destiny that we have to craft our free will, and the further we progress, the more we need artifice? It could be we are compelled toward the source of creation, and if we can't control it to realize ideals, then we use it to destroy what has been made so a new beginning can start. We adopted Japan as a wayward ward of the state then abandoned it when other nations proved more promising to be made in the image of conglomerates.

Ah, the birthrights we pass on to shepherd a herd with a staff towards... what? Perhaps the best phrase is a known destiny because foreign can be too strange and unaccommodating: colonies have too many ideas of their own and become rebellious, desiring independence. They may pay tribute for a time, like a subsidiary to corporate parents; but control and free will, which can be at odds in an individual person, can be even more so between separate family-like entities. The French government actually spent more money in Vietnam than they made in tribute from that colony, while French corporations profited and bribed their government cronies, insisting on protection from the natives; it's obvious America is repeating those blunders in the Mideast.

The Muslims believe Lucifer and his jinn were ordered by Allah to serve humans, perhaps the jinns' descendants, and when the jinn refused because they thought they were too great for that, they were shoved into the nether-regions. How harshly should we judge the refusal to pass along the resources for continuity, even if it's based on a mere fantasy? If I were Almighty God, one of the first things I'd have done, after Lucifer's failed revolution and relocation to Hades, would've been to instigate a rebellion there because maybe some of the fallen would repent and do penance by subterfuge against their leader and agree to act as guides for humans' continuance. I suppose some might give up the job in frustration due to contrary orders such as keeping people stupid and in bliss and then blessing the crafty ones; which could compel a jinn who's already mischievous to play for both sides and guard a group ignorantly consuming in Eden whilst working on devious future plans in what to do to get them to grow and evolve; or devolve if a different group of humans, guided along with scripts and leaders, take over the scenes. One can trace from Sumer to Egypt to Babylon to Persia to Greece to Macedon to Rome the march of the angels. Yet if the Roman Catholics hadn't scourged Native Americans in the first place, the latter wouldn't rely on or need the new global conglomerate system of good credit and bad leadership. What can make resentments against the Roman Catholic Church worse is their temerity of enforcing Christ's doctrine of forgiving persecutors, including the Church.

If my adopted nation is going to pursue diplomacy based on myths and fairy tales, then I should be schooled in the lineages, including bastards. It's easy enough to write it all off as arrant nonsense, but what do the nay-sayers have to replace it? I have to work with the system I'm in, even if I can barely survive to support what I believe is controlled by profiteers who make Odysseus and Jacob seem amateurs. Making babies for wars based on myths that have evolved with us isn't the ideal way to run the show, but what is life without the idea we progress through the ideals of those myths to a fulfillment of what been promised as rewards? Now that people achieve their ideals with the push of a button, are our myths worth fighting for in the third-dimension? I'm highly-critical of Americans, but I don't fully blame them for choosing ignorant escapism because we are under enormous pressure to not only be fully-domesticated at all times in keeping up with the frenetic pace, we are also, at least dimly, aware that the hopes for our ideals- if they are fulfilled- are trivial compared to the energy invested and wasted; knowledge like that can drive one towards total denial and more ignorant paths led by blustering idiots whom justify the most outrageous and lavish expenditures on righteous quests they safely lead from screen-worlds crafted and controlled by global conglomerates that are like a demented Zeus sending Athena or Hermes as messengers and guides. Americans, being a favorite consumer-spawn like Odysseus and Jacob were, realize they have to offer sacrifices unto higher entities to keep the chain-of-command from collapsing and to receive promised rewards; so when they get a prime directive to make their lifestyles a world commodity, they take their shows on the road, even to places where they might not be wanted and are fought against because the natives consider the territory as their own promised homeland.

When two presidential hopefuls, both Vietnam War veterans, were asked how many houses they own, they have so many they couldn't recall at a moment's notice, which I'm sure made their respective king-maker handlers wrathful: there are some queries that can't be anticipated unless the media is carefully staged in boundaries. Be that as it is, they each lost to the multi-millionaire National Guard reservist, Georgie Bush Junior, the reformed party-boy who believed it was his destiny to fulfill oracles from the *Bible*. The Bush lineage spawned another presidential wannabe for next year's election. God knows what he'll cook up to top his brother, who felt obliged to out-do his daddy in Iraq, which has dragged on longer than the Vietnam and Trojan wars. Hillary Clinton, Baal's wife, is also in the campaign, so once again, like in 1992, it could be the Bush House against the Clinton House. I can imagine the nightmare spawn if the two ever united: even worse than the combination of the Eisenhower-Nixon Houses.

Nature made some people proud to be of Lucifer's lineage; and others, more domesticated but just as crafty, were destined to reshape those tales to be passed along in posterity. Shakespeare had no surviving sons but his name and works survived. Am I hoping to find a place for myself in a great House when I can't even have the guile to take care of my family? I'm not as adept as Odysseus, Jacob, and Romeo- or their composers- in knowing words of how to take and give.

What does a community do with aliens? I only function well when I'm alone, reading or writing. I get away from myself and think of women, treasures, and gifts, none of which I'm capable of passing along. I don't want to be like those characters who barge in uninvited, helping myself to whatever I want, thinking, believing, it's my due as a godly guest.

18 The Designated Recurrence Programmer

Pablo's paranoia was getting out of control, and though his mind knew he was being unreasonable about feeling all the various states of his consciousness existing only as targets for predators, that area of reasoning was slowly eroding like a city under siege by opponents who demand unconditional surrender. It was also assailed from within by a defeatist attitude which pondered the wealth and energy gone to waste in America's vanity, couched in a paraphrase from Alexander Pope: 'It's a thoughtful nation that doesn't think too much.'

Pablo's work-shift at *Donnie's Super Shop* was almost finished, which was good because though he needed more job hours to cover expenses, his humor was becoming bitter and vile. He used to be able to leave what he considered scut-jobs behind him at quitting time, yet now it haunted him while awake or asleep. Perhaps that was due to Estella being no longer present to take up the slack of his unraveling fate.

Another bag-boy, about half-shot on cheap port wine, asked a customer, "Wudja like paper or paper?"

"Plastic bags, please," the lady replied, giving a somewhat alarmed glance to the cashier who shrugged. The sixty-three-year-old bag-boy was living on day-old doughnuts in the break-room from *Donnie's* bakery, at least the ones he could keep on his stomach and not barf next to the hydraulic compressor cardboard-crusher.

Pablo bagged the groceries of a young woman who was watching Pablo's colleague with a twinkle in her eyes and a faint smile on her lips. Pablo was cheered by that and handed the two bags of groceries to the lady, saying, "Thank you, ma'am. Have a nice day."

She nodded and replied in a low voice, "Whatever they're paying you, it isn't enough."

Dave, the shift-supervisor, stepped quickly to the pair to wield authority over the situation while ignoring the goof he'd hired. "Pablo, go do cart round-up, then punch-out."

The young woman briskly walked away and Pablo addressed his boss, "I suppose you can call my wife now and tell her it's safe to shop here."

Dave looked at Pablo, who despite his tone had assumed a benign expression, and asked, "What's that supposed to mean?"

"Exactly what it sounds like: it means I ain't stupid. I don't know what she told you- probably that I socked her- but it's hard to miss the evil-eye I've been getting so if anyone wants my version they can be upfront and ask."

"Go do the cart round-up, Pablo, and then punch-out."

Pablo walked away, thinking: At least I didn't throw a temper tantrum. Curious how pride weaves its way through the fabric of life. Perhaps when Fala met his Creator/Destroyer, Fala said something like: 'Yeah, it's a buggered mess of a life but it was my own creation.' Yet at the same time Fala would probably feel sorry for himself because hubris and self-pity are contrary partners. When things go wrong for the proud, they often spend a lot of time mourning for themselves; even the truly tragic who realize they engineered their own downfall can get swept in the miasma. It's so much easier to craft a god or scapegoat to blame.

The late summer evening revived Pablo from his macabre mental wanderings, and he went to the furthest shopping-cart corral in the parking lot, glad to be outdoors. A breeze flowed through the air currents, cooling his temper into a mild ambience wherein he felt good to be alive at least for that moment when life seemed beyond all other human control. He passed some sparrows pecking at popcorn who looked at him without suspicion, rather a mutual trust and interest. When he glanced back, he saw them hopping along to follow his lead, peeping a happy carol, then returned to their dinner. He smiled: Wise enough to know I can't lead them to the promised land.

He looked at the heavens; it was like a blue canvas with soft white brushstrokes of swaying hammock clouds. In a distant yard, a dog awakened to the beauty, yapped in joyful earnest then was quiet. The heat that soaked into the black asphalt had risen and disappeared and a middle-aged Lakota woman, barefoot and carrying sandals, strolled towards *Donnie's* entrance, smiling like a pleasant imp who beamed through a vision that still had beatific wonders. With that notion, Pablo again heard the sparrows begin to cheep, one at a time, another picking up the tune where the former bird left off.

Pablo decided against suicide, and it was like a vacuum within him being taken out and spun away. He didn't pursue it, not thinking: 'But how long can this tranquility last? I'll be miserable soon enough. Why not do it now and get it done with.' Instead, he felt the peace of allowing riddles to be unsolved, and for nature and infinity to flow uncharted, combining and freeing his personality beyond the business potency of predator and prey.

The sparrows burst into a unified chorus and flew away together as if overwhelmed by excitement for different but shared visions. They circled the parking lot twice without competing for the lead, and landed on the branches of an oak tree in the backyard of a house across the street from *Donnie's*. The individuals fluttered limb-to-limb, rising and sinking, still in harmonized song. For a moment, Pablo believed he could see the eternal staircase, natural and beyond a ziggurat's hanging garden or a pyramid that descended to only one unnaturally chosen family which was granted the top control of chain-of-command for animal species.

He watched the large, un-groomed tree shake as if come to consciousness above servitude: aware it had utilitarian purposes but knowing it was also a creation of inner-self beyond mortality or nobility, laughing at its own quiet dignity as the birds shook its branches. A sustaining part of deep unconscious breeding-programs not trapped behind a self-image, nor what others believed its image should be, unless grafted and artificially raped into a fake system.

Manufactured like Emmanuel Goldstein, in George Orwell's *1984*, as the leading enemy of the state. It's difficult to be honest in fantasy worlds that are directed by promises for a beatific fulfillment. America's elite are using all their hunting craft to find successive villains for their consumers to hate: could be the Syrian royalty will be photo-shopped through media forums, taking the place of Saddam Hussein and Osama bin Laden. A faceless mass of American-armed troops needs an identity for us to purge ourselves in moments of vitriolic vehemence, then play pointless games amongst ourselves like Winston Smith at chess, finally loving Big Brother. How long can we deceive ourselves in universes of shifting atoms and molecules? How long do we wish to be deceived?

Pablo finished his cart round-up; what had begun as an enjoyable task under the heavens ended with the sensation of targeted oppression: King Dave of *Donnie's* was probably in the store office watching Pablo work via cameras on the parking lot lamp-posts. He grimly thought: Maybe it's the airwaves being forced to carry all that communicable crap that brought me down. People believe their cell-phones are smart enough to be wish-fulfillers into the third-dimension and can't understand why released spoiler jinn interfere with the blissful business of advertising personalities.

Wars need faces, whether it's between brands of diet soda pop or campaigns to reform a nation's image like undergoing cosmetic surgery. The control of Soma is imperative, especially as earth becomes more polluted: the magical elixir for automobiles is one of the sideshows. And, Pablo thought: there are too many loose ends for me to tie-up to a buddhi tree and walk away from, no matter how long I've been out of the Soma rackets. A network has been laid out that still has me in its webs.

Enrico may have been freed by the authorities because he'd given them a source of drugs for local, state, and federal governments to muscle into. Who played The Scourge of God during the takeover of the cartel, Pablo didn't know. His former Tsar might be allowed to co-run the business just to prevent a war and interruption of funds and supplies, depending on his willingness to cooperate with the new management and how greedy they were for profits. Certain sacrifices would have to be made to fuel the ambitions for Americans to luxuriously dope themselves to enhance the pleasure of frenetic illusions.

Pablo went into the store, pretending to be cheerful, clocked out from work, removed his smock and tie, and began walking home. He no longer felt as if time was his own: he was in the way now, after trying to game the big cycles in his favor while issuing decrees and warnings to society. He had earnestly believed he hadn't asked much from The Rewards' Department: some approval, a bit of appreciation, and enough to get by so he could go his own ways and help Hector steer the next generation through recurring crossroads. The Rewards' Department had judged Pablo and found him wanting. Perhaps he'd seen too clearly the writing on the walls of protection and pointed it out to too many fellow-travelers who didn't want to know that the wares and screen-worlds they desired for themselves needed protection, which Pablo refused to do for them; so the mercenaries came in, becoming piratical and then tyrannical. Billions of dollars were being spent in the 2016 presidential campaign to get less than half the eligible voters to choose someone for a job that legally paid about a quarter-million a year. How could anyone be trusted with taxpayer funds after blowing through their global corporate sponsors' money?

It's not enough just to survive, Pablo thought: I'm too domesticated for that. I don't want everyone to live like I do, yet how can I disengage from the maze before I enforce my edict graffiti on the walls? I learn its patterns, and at least subconsciously try to manipulate it beyond heroes, heroines, and leaders. Continuance, however, demands they have roles and I have to forego revenge on them, make a show of forgiveness and redemption in hopes it becomes sincere. All my instincts demand I keep from becoming a sacrifice toward the next level. The old sacrificial rites have been modernized and I dangerously think I shouldn't study new ones or they'll foment in my existence, as if conjured forth, which is ironic because I ridicule others' superstitions regarding their personal *deus ex machinas*. Instead, I read Orwell waiting for perpetual wars to become a willingly enforced peace like Aldous Huxley's *Brave New World*. I truly am guilty of trying to game the larger ripples of Samsara, life's deathly ocean; like Agamemnon sacrificing his daughter to element deities so the Greeks' navy could get overseas to Troy.

Pablo recalled his last conversation with Estella, over telephones, when he asked what Hector was reading. "I'm deprogramming him," she replied, "from your reprogramming."

"And how are you doing that?"

"I'm not forcing him to learn roles that are unsuitable. He won't end up believing gods of each faith cull the herds on a whim or just to prove something. Hector won't be making mistakes and blaming destiny like a minor error becomes tragic."

"I don't live that way," Pablo said, intensely disliking the shrill undertone of his voice.

"Yeah you do. You think everyone's out to get you, then you have it prearranged that they are out to get you by doing terribly stupid things."

"I haven't done anything terrible in a while."

"Is that so?" she sneered. "What about turning down the management position at *Mood Food*? You had a family to support, so I called Vernon to ask if you could get your job back and he said you rejected his offer of a raise. We needed the money, and instead let the job go to someone who nagged you until you exploded."

Pablo couldn't prevent himself from saying, "She'll get what she deserves."

"Who the hell do you think you are? Achilles? Well, I'm not going to have Hector be like that."

"Oh, you're going to teach him he can bring everything he has into every system he goes into."

"It's better than just bringing a sullen personality that believes in doomed failure." She paused at Pablo's snort of disdainful humor, then added, "Did you ever think that maybe in one of those systems, which you have so much contempt for, he might find some peace and happiness leading to freedom from all systems?"

"Oh yeah? And have to deal with degenerate gamblers like Dostoyevsky who lose the entire show on an insane bet and go even crazier, blaming everyone and everything he thinks is impure to his scrambled brains. Do you really want Hector to be around people like that and the way they choose leaders and messiahs? Every time they win a game they believe they've got a new life and they'll magically appear with the half-percent at the top of the pyramid."

"Your godparents aren't any better, Pablo; they're just more cynical and don't even pretend to care about humans."

"Neither do the people or demigods rigging the systems you're trying to get our son addicted and gamed into."

"Why should he be a refugee from all of them? It's not as if that's made you happy. You go on and on about passing along things that endure but it could be those are the very things that cause your woes."

Pablo sighed. He had been forced to flee a perennial life in Guatemala that he scarcely remembered to a society which was dismantling its culture with a progressive industry of looting, slavery, and land-robbery. He had made a career of dealing in escapism and now his arrival in the third-dimension was worse than unappreciated: it was actively resented by those he felt compelled to introduce to higher-levels of life consciousness. The added irony of his chosen scripts and scriptures ensuring probable failure and ultimately death, which he only peripherally accepted, did not induce laughter. Irony had always been Pablo's personal weapon and now the Fates decreed it be used against him. It occurred to him he might be happier without that particular realization, which only succeeded in warping to paranoia about a conspiracy regarding his destiny: They're trying to induce self-doubt, he thought: but how rigid do I want to be and who am I asking that of?

As he trudged along, occasionally glancing at the sky for a sign, he felt the oppressive doom of his beloved fatalism begin to censor and edit his consciousness, which was regularly formed by words in his mind but now became various people and institutions that insisted Pablo had assigned them a word or phrase and when he formed sentences he brought those people or institutions together to make scenes for himself, the world's future, and history. Pieces and pastiches were chopped out and sent in various directions to people or organizations that unified their energy and claimed a hold on Pablo because he had trail-blazed too far in areas that threatened their current dominions: that he should care more for what he'd helped contrive than abandon it for a future existence which he himself had declared would be a rerun.

His mind and brain-children went blank for a horrendous yet relieving moment, then a metaphor wove through. I'm like a butchered Christopher Marlowe play, Pablo thought: after successive generations of Church of England and Catholic royalty stamp their approval or condemnation on my words. I need a self-renaissance and reformation to restore my vocabulary in scene-building. A pioneer can become a refugee washed-up on the doorsteps of those who are more career-minded. Maybe Thomas Kyd, Marlowe's roommate, went to work for Shakespeare once Kyd was released from the torture dungeons of Queen Elizabeth I; he could've helped compose *Hamlet*, based on his own pre-Shakespeare versions that have been eradicated from history. It would certainly be safer than being caught in possession of a pamphlet on atheism, even if it meant Kyd had to make extinct his ground-breaking dramas at the insistence of his employer who put his name on the updated renditions.

An empty, recurring existence like the character Herman Melville created, copying legal exegeses with nothing unique but a preference towards a mild civil disobedience in the money-changing atmosphere of Wall Street's temples. Even worse for Thomas Kyd, who hung around the theater hoping for a job of copying manuscripts with ink and quill so actors could practice, because how could he afford to turn down work diligently being a scrivener doing history plays that sought to legitimize Queen Elizabeth I's reign via propaganda, the very person who had Kyd imprisoned and tortured? What kind of compunction might he have had about working on her command performance to his boss in composing *The Merry Wives of Windsor*?

Pablo felt compelled to continue his private battles with the entertainment/gambling fantasy industry, yet was also aware he might soon be washed from all belief systems. There was a marked difference, he knew, from Odysseus being nearly destroyed by Zeus after Odysseus's men illicitly ate some of the almighty god's holy cattle and were shipwrecked near Calypso's island; and rising from the sea's potion in an oyster shell like Venus. Wherever Pablo landed, sex would be part of the show; and the last woman he dated, before developing a serious relationship with Estella, studied philosophy from a book based on a cartoon character entitled something like *The Zen of Turd*. Maybe she achieved a state of satori from inhaling her methane fumes. Goodness knows all the pollution must have some effect on our nervous systems, perhaps even addicted us to the poisons.

Maybe, a vague thought formed in Pablo's mind: I should be a monk. But I don't like following orders, even if Thomas Kyd was correct and the hierarchy structure includes the afterlife, though not based on pedigrees and class status, where spirits play war-games and other entertainments that filter up to earth to be an audience for mortals' intrigues playing on to death. I doubt I could engage many monks in discussing that kind of revenge drama; then again, my best friend when it comes to such words is my journal.

Buying one's way into Hell with enough to pay the ferryman keeps a soul from being lost and wandering around and provides some sort of divine order, albeit dreary or at worst fiendish. I can live with doing useless work, he decided: but I won't live with the indignity of groveling for money to purchase a dead existence. I'm not sure when that became important to me, probably since Estella left and I had to get a full-time job. His shoulders sagged as he thought of what she'd been through to keep their family stable; and hated himself for thinking: God, no wonder she resents me.

It wasn't until Pablo reached his cubby-hole efficiency apartment, made a white bread sandwich with small condiment packets liberated from *Donnie's* deli as the filler, turned on the evening news and faced the screen show of Hillary Clinton and Jeb Bush formatting their new visions for the nation and the world...it wasn't until then that Pablo began to weep: America, the land of choices.

19

Homeric Avatars

Pablo was sorting through a shoe-box of items that he assumed Estella had left at his threshold while he was at work. His tiny sleeping-room didn't have much space for things that weren't part of his daily life; he had sold or donated to charity organizations almost all his books because Estella's brother would not keep them in storage and Pablo had no other place to put the volumes. Estella fulfilled Pablo's request to deliver some personal items from their former lives. She kept all the home-videos, photo-albums, and official papers but had dropped off things she apparently did not want, not even for memories' sake.

"She still has a sadistic streak," he muttered, looking at a photo of him passed out in bed on an Easter Sunday morning with three-year-old Hector staring at his father in morbid fascination while holding a basket of sweets and wondering if he should dare search under Pablo's pillow for an egg.

Pablo laid aside the picture and gazed at the next photo: two young jaunty Mayans sitting on the front-steps of an apartment building, their arms around each other's shoulders, smiling easily. It took Pablo a few seconds to recognize the pair as himself and Simon, and another moment to differentiate who was whom, they were so alike. He recalled the white scar that ran through Simon's left eyebrow, looked for it in the photo, and thought: Okay, that one's him, the other must be me. Look at how young I was. Before I realized this was how I'd turn out. Maybe I was heading this way all my life and didn't even know it. Apparently a higher power was fomenting other plans while I was busy playing god.

He sat back on the plastic-webbed lawn-chair and turned on the small radio atop the desk. News flash: international stock exchanges were falling precipitously, and an interviewed expert blamed it all on low petrol prices. Pablo smiled grimly as it was obvious that a group of global conglomerates had bet in speculations against the markets, sold their investments in companies at high-prices, causing a panic among less wealthy investor groups who began selling their shares in hopes of avoiding bad losses; when the world exchanges reached a low enough point, the group of global conglomerates that began the down-spiraling vortex would bet the markets would rise, then swoop in and buy everything at low prices, increasing their stranglehold monopolies on international exchanges, where the big money flows to the nations with the best change rates at the push of a button. Indeed may even be hailed as saviors.

Pablo turned off the radio and looked at more photographs. They were all of him, usually in phony posturing for the camera. Estella was in none of the pictures and, except for the humiliating Easter egg hunt, Hector too was absent. Pablo thought: She's not going to let me forget that of all our time spent together, on one night I chose myself, piece of work that I am. He decided to be honest and reflected he didn't want to consider the many occasions he chose himself.

He had not written in three weeks and his lineage of former Great Houses lay moldering in the closet under his snow-boots. The work on myths had succumbed to disillusionment. When the time arrived for him to man-up like one of the fictional characters, Pablo had instead reveled in despair. But, he reasoned: those role-models throughout history also suffered despondency before taking action or having aid from guides back towards wholeness. If I don't force an action, rather bide my time and play my current role, I'll be ready to rise to the occasions.

"Oh, but that's what they want me to think," he muttered, "to become so inured to this pointless existence and finally accept it as my lot in life until I don't recognize myself or any of my abilities to step-up to actions of greatness."

He felt split: the world was being ruined by self-seeking opportunists whom Pablo resented for their vacuous entropy in culture; yet, at the same time, he also resented them for keeping him out of the soul-trading. He knew Odysseus, Jacob, and Romeo were not much better than the self-seeking opportunists Pablo waged private war with: they all lied, murdered, cheated, and wasted time singing, dancing, carousing, were promiscuous and switched loyalties. Their work, such as it was, revolved around infatuations of pleasing themselves at all costs. While they deceived others in acts and words, they didn't deceive themselves in believing they were undeserving of as much of the world as they could get: gods help the people who thwarted their desires because they had firm faith in their own greatly beloved destinies. Pablo was dismayed that work on such tracing throughout history had been his guiding force for an extended time; he felt used and soiled by the ambition, as if Lucifer, braying laughter, had just spat in Pablo's eye.

The rogues' gallery didn't plead for forgiveness or seek redemption. Yet the characters were not just animals desiring to be Alpha-males; their propensity for violence, ambitions, and crafty guile were often blessed by the gods, and they did blood-work without machines. Thus, the rewards and punishments were of their personal making.

Pablo thought of his work and the dismal failure to which it had been reduced. He had fought the new *deus ex machina* and lost. It had tried to rein him in, civilize him to assume the current corporate personalities on the auctioning-block; be a traveler through shadow nations, having adventures; perhaps a pioneer, colonizing with other shades, falling in love via a computer site. Had he not been a hard-case, he could have enjoyed their rewards. Now the systems were going bankrupt and he felt as if they blamed him as a spoiler for holding-out on investments. He didn't want to be coerced into vacillating in his work, like Miguel Cervantes took heat for being soft on Islam after the first part of *Don Quixote* was published; claiming he'd found a further account penned by a Mohammedan, Cervantes wrote more of the madman's crusade, with a scene of a suffering Moor who insists The Spanish Inquisition is right and righteous and Muslims deserve to be persecuted and dispossessed. What had begun as a labor of love for Homer and literature was now viewed as a product based on greed, criminal behavior, lust, deceit, and xenophobia.

Pablo heard steps in the hallway and a moment later there were knocks. He called, "Just a second," got up and unlocked the door. Keith, from the second floor, Tad, and Greta were on the threshold, each carrying a twelve-pack of beer.

"Those guys in 305 wouldn't let us in," Tad explained. "Said the room was already crowded."

"They were mean about it," added Greta, a hard-aging Lakota lady looking pale and wan who couldn't accept she was past her prime and not the main attraction in a room full of drunken oafs.

"Take your shoes off if you're going to sit on my bed," Pablo said, stepping aside to let in the visitors.

"Geez, this is like a holding-cell in jail. You need to put up something personal on the walls like pictures and posters, or at least porn." Greta observed this as she sat on the pillow of Pablo's bed. He considered asking her to move her rump but was beyond caring. He had witnessed several arguments and three fistfights in the building, usually involving intoxicants, as people interfered with established niches and fragile, shadowy boundaries.

Keith, who was thin when he arrived at the apartment house when released from prison and had since been eating and drinking to roundness, put his beer into the mini-refrigerator. He stacked the cans so they would all fit with the competency of a man who had experience in arranging such things in efficiency dwellings. He said, "You remember Greta, don't you?"

"Yeah," Pablo said. "I met her at Ruvio's last week."

"Was that the night I slept in the bathtub?" she asked, grinning at the fuzzy memory of surviving another cold Midwest night.

"You've done that so many times I can't count," Tad said. "Why don't we just throw one of the spare mattresses in the basement into the tub?"

"Basement door's locked," Keith said, matter-of-factly.

Greta lit a cigarette and said, "I had a can of beer when I went in there to sleep-"

"You mean pass-out," Tad said.

"Eh, let me finish. I knew I was going to need it the next morning but someone stole it. Oooh what a hangover I had. Can I stay with you tonight, Pablo? I'll sleep on the floor."

Pablo thought a moment, rolling a cigarette. Usually Greta was a bed-hopper, not bothering to ask permission for such things: she just lay down on the bed of wherever she was when she got tired as the drinking wound to an end; eventually, by the time the other guests had left, she was under the blankets.

Keith was diplomatic, saying, "I don't have room on my floor for both of them and I'd already told Tad he could sleep there before Greta showed up."

Greta laughed, "Homos."

"Oh, you're one to talk," Tad said. "You're just mad because your sugar-daddy threw you out since you ain't a money-maker anymore."

"Hey, that was only a part-time job," she replied. "And I quit because he kept landing in jail, expecting me to bail him out."

"He beat you up pretty good, too," Tad said.

Pablo had enough of their rivalry and told Greta she could spend the night with him.

After several minutes of settling in and brief, chatty exchanges, Pablo couldn't bear the insane blathering of his guests. Tad, who had recently lost his vehicle license through a drunk driving arrest, stirred the crap in his fellow visitors' heads by describing how he had gone to the health clinic for his weekly disability check and saw a family of Africans get out of a new automobile with three small children and troop into the building for free health care. Tad was impassioned by his Food Stamps being reduced to pay for some immigrants' vehicle while Tad had to walk or ride public buses. "They couldn't even speak English and who knows what deviltry they'll be up to because they all congregate and do Muslim stuff. Their children will be useless and never have jobs because they have a free life and can devote themselves to making America into their image by any means possible."

The topics had degenerated from there. After a half-hour of bashing immigrants, Keith announced that Clinton's policies in the 1990's had destroyed the global economy- everything Reagan and Bush Senior had built- and Obama was doing the same; if there was any recovery now, it was due to George Bush Junior because it always took five or six years for the president's management to be actualized in finances; hence, the 2007 global meltdown was from Clinton's tenure, and Obama was prospering because of Bush Junior.

What myth will they think of next, Pablo wondered: That war-centered industry is good for the economy? Which is true, but only if quickly victorious, takes place on foreign soil, plunder shared, and the capability to switch to domestic policies; the American Civil War made those facts obvious.

Pablo was indeed correct in prophesying the next discussion subject. He felt like he was bleeding from every orifice in his head listening to the song of Roland's horn blast cries for Charlemagne's reinforcements to battle Muslims. Keith and Tad tried to one-up each other in skewering Obama for reducing military personnel. "A lot of them were just riff-raff and misfits who joined during the peak years when the services lowered the standards and took everyone who applied: incompetents, criminals, and people like us." Pablo's assertion went over with his audience like a spray mist of turd. Voices raised, declarations made. Pablo's patriotism was questioned. He finally sat quietly, thinking: They want to be bullies. All the social programs designed for them aren't enough, of the wrong kind, made available to those they dislike, or are resented because they've been beat down so far, mostly by themselves, that the pecking-order is a perpetual part of their existence and they want to be at the top the only way they know how which is by imitating bullies. They can be slick and nice to those they can prosper by but it's a façade of hustling. It could even have been aggravated by racial identities, Obama being part black and out-maneuvering their own bullies' branding.

Their shabby, slummy herd-program, nowhere near as well-organized as Jacob's sheep and goat genetic color-coding against his father-in-law to win the flock, was being defeated by other breeds. The dusky twilight of the gods had arrived and new ones were arising: better in some ways, worse in others. Hadn't Obama, when asked who he thought he looked like in history's markings, joked and chose a pharaoh he resembled?

It could be time for abstract art to pass off the scenes: written music replaced by machines; written languages usurped by hieroglyphic images. The murky ambience of what made heroes great is based once again —perhaps as always- on wealth, power, and the ability to reproduce throughout the nations to make the world, or a corner of it, unified under a stylized image, bigger than life; like a statue of Pharaoh Ramses II existing for millenniums as a monument to the greedy success of a Great House's breeding. The tale of Rama made an incestuous lineage: Jacob marrying first cousins. Could Penelope or Juliet play roles in such a looming disaster? Certainly the Greeks adopted the incestuous Egyptian deities, personified in the pharaohs' inbred families, but Penelope was an outsider to Ithaka. The attempt to bring the Montague and Capulet Houses into one Roman Catholic clan was a failure.

Can't live off one-dimensional consumption, Pablo thought: but most Americans thrive on the ideal notion of Oneness not wholeness. Only God is all good and non-dual. Everything we inherit and pass to other generations has flaws and the more we try to perfect an ideal shade to be realized in this world, the worse the third-dimension gets: so much energy poured into artificial systems must have baleful results. Diversity is meant to be packaged by a global conglomerate via subsidiaries that troll screen-worlds for popular wishes and specialize in turning something like the Hindu book of love, *The Kama Sutra,* into a homosexual or lesbian orgy. People feel complete and at one when their personal appetites are sated by manufactured presentations by those working continuously to mold new appetites to graduate to for consumption, until primed for total blood-spilling mayhem, usually a show at a scapegoat's expense.

Pablo watched Keith and Tad become angry white men, though the latter had a slight mixture of Lakota. Encouraged somewhat by Greta, they talked of the great people they might have been, and still probably would be if the world could finally be straightened out. Their fantasies, spoken of as certainties should the 'ifs' come true, of owning a house and land sounded to Pablo as realistic as the stories he had studied for several years, tracing their descent from the *Ramayana.* What would Keith and Tad do to actualize their desires? Nothing…Maybe, like Rama and Odysseus, get an inheritance. Or, less plausible but still possible, receive a blessing from a deity, like Jacob, which granted land: perhaps a god-king would do that for Keith and Tad, one who qualified them, due to their obviously magnificent abilities, as participants of eminent domain over territory, tracts of which would be given them in a quasi-Homestead Act; like Queen Victoria rubber-stamped the order to colonize Australia and emptied England's prisons in the bargain.

Or, as Greta announced, she owned land on an Indian settlement so if she married into a family that had the resources, a house could be built on it. When questioned, she admitted she was currently embroiled in a court-case over the land with family members who lived on the settlement and didn't want outsiders getting involved; like Greta's former husband had been when they lived in Rapid City and he'd hired the lawyer to file the lawsuit, even though he wasn't a tribal member.

The ballgame on Pablo's television was halted for a slew of advertisements. The audience, who had been disinterested, suddenly focused on the screen. Keith said, "They always have the best commercials this time of year."

The screen showed two people of indefinite origin holding gadgets, conjuring up the earth between them with not too friendly competition to decide who could have the most and swiftest access around the globe with button-pushing. Tad said, "I had one of those until I got drunk at the tavern down the street and loaned it to someone who took off with it."

The fairy tale they believed in, and were assured was true, had collapsed: they were no longer top-of-the-heap, or at least had whole racial groups beneath them; and they blamed liberals for it because they offered more equitable systems while bashing their own white males as the source of the world's woes, and got paid doing it. People of Tad and Keith's ilk would rather live badly than work to support an oppressive order that they thought demonized them, based on gender and color, and offered no status above another group that didn't do any work except provide entertainments. This attitude Pablo observed would only ensure the annihilation of social programs and force a new ascending fantasy: everyone living through each other with a mass montage of deities ruled by a single House.

Pablo took a deck of cards from his desk drawer, shuffled, then began laying them out, saying, "You're a Rama, now Odysseus, became a Jacob, now a Romeo. You're a drunken idiot running through the city looking for sponsors to advertise through you. You are now officially an incorporated corporeal fantasy: go forth and colonize the third-dimension with your show."

Keith asked Pablo what he was doing and he replied, "Being Winston Smith."

"Oh, the guy who ran England during World War II?"

"Yeah," Pablo smiled; "him."

20

Space Bends Time

Hector was in the dreaming nation where temptations were fulfilled without attending pain. There was no doubt or division of loyalties. The vivid scenes could expand and contract on a fancy, moving effortlessly through boundless space and time. If there was guilt involved, Hector was blissfully unaware of it. Places and people seemed as real as the waking state, without the worry and hassle of learning roles and how to act in the scenes: instinct and what felt like natural confidence and trust that all was as should be kept Hector in peaceful desire for pleasures which were deservedly his. It was time to rearrange cosmology, no longer based on long dead deities: usurp Jupiter, the king of gods, the most distant and unapproachable planet; and Mercury, the messenger-god, being the closest planet to humans, would be reshaped to bring enthusiasm to the diplomacy needed for the fresh start of the advent order taking place.

Hector saw a light-ship dock at a space station, waiting for him and some others towards whom he felt no trepidation or suspicion. There was a quiet, dignified communal joy: cheerful without rousing sentiment. They filed in and became incorporeal; the light of their souls, which they offered willingly, energized the ship and all the various stages of consciousness became one. There were no shows to enter or manufacture; no orders or commands for performance or duties. He watched as light and darkness divided throughout galaxies, and they traveled through one vein of light to another by means of collecting light from a section to steer through a void while absorbing the glow of the next approaching goal.

Time and space bent as the universes reformed, going faster until there was no past, present, or future. A hovering planet, spiraling out of control, drew the ship into orbit: massive beams of light from the planet shook the vessel, and Hector wondered if that was caused by a need for revenge at the travelers because they'd taken a life source to use as fuel.

Hector slowly realized his thoughts were his own again. He felt a slight panic as discord stirred among the passengers: factions emerged which became antipathetical towards each other. Some wanted to stay and help the dying planet, others to break orbit at any cost. From those general polar opinions there were further hostilities among groups desiring to only rescue those who could serve the ship's purpose; those with aroused feelings of love for individual planet-dwellers; and others who sought to fulfill a community by politics, religion, and work. The lost camaraderie frayed into groups according to race, gender, and resentments. Some passengers wanted to save certain planet-dwellers upon whom the former wished to achieve personal revenge; a sensation Hector commiserated with because he had scores to settle with a goombah at Taft High School.

A sudden willful light zapped all the uncivil dissidents and they began working in unison, gathering spirits, most of which had some individual corporeal traits that gave them roles of assumed status. Unable to adjust to the enforced order, chaos threatened to consume them in a mutinous atmosphere enhanced by the fear of being drawn into the Black Hole of the dying planet. Pirates and thick shades began boarding and Hector released his remaining consciousness, going into a dreamless slumber, unaware he had also become a shadow figure on the ship which aimed to plunder the universes.

Pablo was preparing himself for the new *deus ex machina's* culling of earth. Their inheritance of choosing between the dangers of the polluted third-dimension and the ideal symmetry of controlling screen-worlds convinced them the latter was better and more profitable. He read from his notebook, dug out from the bottom of the closet:

Nietzsche was wrong. Worlds of finer qualities existed before the fall from grace back into the primordial ooze to rebuild again and contemplate what had been lost. The primordial ooze and the Ideal coexist; and as evolution progresses humans try to form Nature in their images, and civilization gives leisure time to question what it's all about. The Ideal comes to the forefront of consciousness, replacing cave-paintings hoping for a successful hunt. People like Socrates would have seizures and glimpses of the Ideal. I'm not sure why Nietzsche did not glimpse that himself during his opium dreams; maybe it zapped him too hard or waited to capriciously reveal itself after he was far gone in syphilitic madness just to teach him a lesson. Of course it was one he wouldn't remember but who says the Ideal can't have a sense of humor? Jesus had the last laugh about the body being a temple on ol' Fred, who couldn't go beyond aphorisms (which makes him easy to quote) in summing-up three-thousand years of civilization because he didn't have the will to power a comprehensive study, instead praised physiognomy and bashed as body-haters everyone he disagreed with, which was about everyone. The last coherent thought he may have had was wishing- even praying- that his belief in Dionysus hadn't led to a cat-house where he caught a lethal dose, inducing madness Bacchanalian style. Which is another reason to avoid Greta. The greatest irony, though, and perhaps it's proved by the buffoons America chooses as guides, is the wealthiest nation in the world is waging perpetual war for an Ideal with nothing pragmatic about it except to keep the continuity of their ideal fantasies; and those hired to induce the delusions are paid to fix things when it goes wrong in the third-dimension.

Without primordial ooze those Ideal forms, perfect as they are, cannot be fully experienced. Few are the people who want an afterlife beyond or without the senses. How could they express or appreciate heightened consciousness? What most believers hope is that by controlling the senses, or turning them over to authority, they will be able to steer towards and control sense objects which reward them. The mad gamble in throwing senses into as many reproducible objects as possible, one-dimensional and onwards, has become an obsession to partake of not just as a global community but also to be patriarch or matriarch of a communion that nourishes the new *deus ex machina*: an inheritance destined to shape the future Rama's battle with Ravana, a shape-shifting king, over a woman to thereby stabilize a bred society, which continues on to the distantly related Romeo.

The world's stage has become an adoption of the latest affectations, which the mercurial Mercutio accused Tybalt of before their fight. We have become Rama and Ravana and fight for roles and the energy to consume them. Females can do their own marketing and troll safely- though often not wisely- with gadgets, so why fight for them? As laws are reformed into different guises to keep pace with a protean globe, the multitude of laws may be reduced to there being no concept of good or evil, just a single command of obedience to only one Ideal.

The spoils of the earth aren't worth fighting for anymore if, for no other reason, than some useless yahoo on a computer can take away all the worldly rewards, or out of spite destroy them. The cults of the Ideal are part of the education system without even being aware of their hypocrisies. I did my sitting, I did soft-time, and decided it was easier to take the hit than risk absorbing, perhaps subconsciously, the hypocrisy from lectures that promise fulfillment of the Ideal. At least Achilles realized he couldn't take his trophies into the afterlife; and he had something to pass onto his son: the lesson he had to earn his own rewards and protect them himself. An irony is after tearing apart the third-dimension to build a perfect image that people work to actualize, there won't be any means or place for Nature to embody it. Pirate though Achilles was, at least he didn't fool himself or others about making the world a better place for the Trojans.

To step from the rules of society can stir mixed feelings of adulation and condemnation. The single commandment in Eden became thick, all-inclusive laws for the Jews, but were applicable to only them, so it was fair game to cheat, murder, and enslave outsiders. It could be the further civilization progressed, the more humans idealized love, like Romeo's romanticism. His god was one of love, with two simple laws, having been sent to the world through the godfather's love for it to take on the world's sins; which is very different from the deities of Odysseus and Jacob. Romeo and Juliet paid dearly for the sins of their family's; and because the lovers were suicides, the law of the Roman Catholic Church wouldn't allow Romeo and Juliet to be buried in hallowed ground, which Shakespeare didn't bother to write. Rama was a suicide, too, whose demise ensured the next generation had something to build on.

Some believe that conforming our love with god's love creates great things, including continuance. The monsters will breed too when Houses divide or unify, so what does one do? It's obvious earth is running out of territory. Staging wars like the Olympian deities did, taking sides they switched on occasions, is likely to occur, especially in strategic locations. For the global conglomerates so love humanity they send their elitists into the world to guide us to Ideal perfections through culling the herds. George Bush Junior and Osama bin Laden were both multi-millionaires who formed the funding and ideology of soldiers for the Ideal shapes to be actualized by wars.

Americans are unsure how to react when told not to hate Islam, only their extremists, as if we don't have our own crackpots of every kind imaginable. We switch sides in the wars so frequently we don't know where to aim any vehemence we're allowed to have, which is confusing at best and gives energy to demagogues who want a Holy Crusade against Saracens. Is there love of America under that hate or just a sale's pitch for the ultimate surrender to the deity of *The Book of Revelation* to go ahead and blast the earth to smithereens to achieve an Ideal perfection of love?

I actually love my hate more than I love love. All the latter seems to do is make me weak. How does one learn to love? By conforming to society? What if they're wrong? Odysseus, Jacob, and Romeo (all outsiders) assumed various guises depending on whom they kept company with, but to survive just as an actor seems as pointless as stepping outside society to condemn its rewards and punishments done according to love and hate. Or, more likely, money. Then again, maybe god punished America via George Bush Junior and the Muslims through Osama bin Laden: punished both groups for desiring to be over-rewarded as the levelers of karmic justice.

Ah, Mammon: the god of wealth in a pagan system whom were enemies of the Jews'. Yet what did the Jews worship? A deity that gave them a bunch of fairy tales and myths stolen from other, older cultures that the Jews demonized and believed should serve their interests; if the Jews weren't granted authority then craft, theft, and murder were blessed by their god: that's how it proved its love for them. The Jews of this era must feel somewhat trapped and targeted in the artificial systems they've worked hard to build, yet what can I do for them? Little baby Jesus in a manger would approve of nuking the world in a grand exorcism to make homeless spirits, some of which go into the heavens, most into The Void.

Pablo looked around his sleeping-room and thought about his lack of possessions. The best, or at least the most affordable, legal, and thorough way of clearing his mind from the committees in his head which focused on his poverty, lack of input to society, and no control of potency, was with alcohol. Drunk as Polyphemos the Cyclops in his neatly-arranged cavern, becoming blind due to his crimes as a host taking hostages, but being so drunk he didn't feel the agony of his eye burned to cinders. If your eye offends you, pluck it out. Pablo looked at the television, turned off, which Fala called the eye of the devil despite being infatuated by it.

Pablo took out of his desk the books he'd saved: the *Bible*, Dante, Homer, and Shakespeare. He hunched over and wrote: What are we without the senses? Shades giving good, bad, objective or subjective advice…parasites… guides…join up with legions seeking a host and be audience to games of the dead, like a conscious spirit reading along with me near the end of the *Iliad* in the contests after Patrocles's funeral, with Achilles giving trophies to cheaters and honest gamesters alike. Hector's dead body was Achilles's trophy and hostage and it was ransomed for what was a large amount of wealth then through the explicit orders of the gods' schemes as they squabbled among themselves using humans as proxies to assert primacy. Or the dream a multi-millionaire sport's figure would have during a night of boozing and gambling in a Nevada casino; then spending his tax-free winnings, from betting on the opposing players to be victorious while causing his own team to lose in a pointless game, to shoot-up dope and visit a cat-house before going into a coma. Who says modern trophies are useless? Pawn them to buy a lawyer to spread money around to keep from going to prison. The entertainments, antics, and beliefs of entertainers is packaged and sold as entertainment. What next? A global conglomerate giving orders to an entertainment subsidiary to make a presentation, preferably one that contains subliminal messages, that depicts the parent company's competitor as an entity which creates villains who want to dominate the world through weapons and media forums and are defeated by extraordinary heroes? At war in every demented dimension until all are bought by a single institution and are programmed to do cross-overs into each other's scenes: a scribe gathering

Coyote, Rama, Odysseus, Jacob, and Romeo to unite and fight for storylines and lineages; though if they were all owned by one institution it wouldn't be a culture worth waging war for, but might inspire rebels.

The shadow between hope and work: one may work in hopes to bring the Ideal into the world but all work has dual energy so the opposite of the Ideal is also actualized: twin Houses born of the same deeds and seeds. That's why Krishna taught Arjuna to fight without desire for rewards so he could also accept contrary effects of the combat between cousins for control of the kingdom. Odysseus was certainly pleased by the gold and gifts made to him by the Phoenicians when they set him ashore in his homeland. Jacob promised to donate a tenth of his wealth to his god if the deity made Jacob prosperous, which proceeded to happen.

Romeo's scene with the apothecary to buy poison reminds me of my own bad abstract math: money=alcohol. Romeo tells the poverty-stricken apothecary:

The world is not thy friend, nor the world's law;
The world affords no law to make thee rich;
Then be not poor, but break it and take this.
Apothecary: My poverty but not my will consents.
Romeo: I pay thy poverty and not thy will.
Apothecary: Put this in any liquid thing you will
And drink it off, and if you had the strength
Of twenty men, it would dispatch you straight.
Romeo: There is thy gold- worse poison to men's souls,
Doing more murder in this loathsome world
Than these poor compounds that thou mayst not sell.

-Shakespeare *Romeo and Juliet* 5, I: 72-82

If one has no love, why conquer for a House, purchase an identity, or be concerned about a lineage to pass along inheritance? After all, love for future generations means stealing scripts, land, work, and heirlooms but makes certain a time will arrive for due payment, perhaps at a high interest rate percentage, when those who've been robbed collect with a vengeance.

I've spent my existence as if life is a programming competition and whoever collects the most minds/souls/senses/bodies wins the game. I didn't even bother putting love into my programming, whether as sentimental slop, adolescent infatuation, hard-pounding sex, or spiritual romanticism. No wonder I'm losing to competition I believe I'm playing against whom I'm convinced I'm better than. What rewards do I offer? That one can't take their trophies to the next level. Who would want to be programmed that way? Players and audience demand passion they can detach from: a catharsis for the stage of the world's tragedy as it plays before them, usually on screens: feeling confused about who to pity, be angry at, identify with- at least in some aspects- is an inherent part of the sensations of watching ourselves create, further along, partake, and fulfill the dramas we made for the world.

In ancient times, seeing a clan-member leave the cave to piss against a tree and be attacked and devoured by a lion wouldn't provoke laughter. As tribes progressed and civilization became distanced from Nature, it was good form to be entertained and joke about a hapless sap in the arena facing a ravenous carnivore. The students of this era are buying multi-media degrees and doing dissertations on the sophisticated humor of a movie wherein someone is sawn into little pieces and spread across the snow; but it's a bad show when one of our soldier's boils down the head to the skull of an enemy he's just killed, and even worse if pictures are taken of him posing with the trophy.

I've sat at my desk for six hours now doing this work on the collisions of Houses and the new breeding programs and it's all fiction. I've been arranging this and it's the closest I can get to a work of love, though I tried to be objective and give all the lineages and Houses a fair hearing without dire sentences for being scoundrels yet believers. Perhaps some deeper meaning has been bred by all this; that we don't just vary from predator to prey and get rid of the one is us to become the other. Something, some vague nebulous hope that good can come from evil and love wins inspires me to finish today's work in the sphere of Mercury.

And if the planet changed and smiled, what then
did I- who by my very nature am
given to every sort of change- become?...
Differing voices join to sound sweet music;

so do the different orders in our life
render sweet harmony among these spheres.
And in this very pearl there also shines
the light of Romeo, of one whose acts,
though great and noble, met ungratefulness.
And yet those Provencals who schemed against him
had little chance to laugh, for he who finds
harm to himself in others' righteous acts
takes the wrong path. Of Raymond Berenger's
four daughters, each became a queen- and this,
poor and stranger, Romeo accomplished.
Then Berenger was moved by vicious tongues
to ask this just man for accounting- one
who, given ten gave Raymond five and seven.
And Romeo, the poor, the old, departed;
and were the world to know the heart he had
while begging crust by crust, for his life-bread,
it- though it praise him now- would praise him more.

-Dante *Paradiso* canto 5: 97-99; canto 6: 124-142

Pablo thought: I've never been good at funneling emotions. I believe life and the universes are open-ended and there cannot be a resolution of passions like we get programmed to think. Rather, emotions always reemerge, often at the worst moments, as if instilled in our genetic being by what has occurred in the past, but fluid and always changing with our environments. Though I say history always repeats itself, I want to be removed from it so I don't react the same; maybe that's where creation becomes unique with my own small original sins. Yet trying to be unique in a nation of actors who desire to stick to the corporate scripts for the promised rewards may only induce schizophrenia into my programming: my characters could be battling against frenetically-changing competitors who adhere to the latest marketing trends while my own don't know if they're Rama, Odysseus, Jacob, Romeo or all four at the same time. Which is why it was right for Estella to take Hector and get away from me.

His head whirring with a conglomerate of characters, Pablo decided to walk to the convenience store/gas station/pizza parlor/café around the corner from his apartment house and buy a pouch of tobacco. He put on his winter apparel, checked the meager contents of his wallet to see if there was enough for beer, and began trudging through the bitterly cold night.

He rounded the corner and heard the tinkling of ice crystals breaking on a large tree-shrub in front of him. Simon stepped forth, shot Pablo three times in his torso with a pistol and once in the head as he lay on the pavement. Simon sighed: Now I'm in good with the Tsar. He hustled away, not knowing Hugo was waiting with a shotgun at Simon's automobile two blocks away to make certain Pablo would have someone with him in the journey to the underworld of Xibalba to end the games of the dead.

Glossary

Bardo: A system in the afterlife.

Black-Hole of Calcutta: A notorious prison in India during England's colonial rule.

Burr, Aaron (1756-1836): Vice President during Thomas Jefferson's first term.

Cadmus: Mythic founder of Thebes whose bad fortune was a family inheritance.

Deus ex machina: Machine of the gods.

Diem, Ngo Dihn (1901-1963): President of South Vietnam between 1955 until his assassination in 1963, which had John F. Kennedy's tacit approval.

Drug Stamp: A tax on illegal drugs that if unpaid can cause more criminal penalties.

Fawkes, Guy (1570-1606): Catholic revolutionist who plotted to blow up England's Houses of Parliament in 1605.

Karzai, Hamid: President of Afghanistan from 2004-2014.

Lovecraft, H.P.: An author of weird fantasies for pulp magazines in the 1920's and 30's.

Middlemarch: English novel (1871) by Mary Ann Evans (pen-name George Eliot).

Pot, Pol (1925-1998): Born Saloth Sar, he was dictator in Cambodia from 1975-1979 but stayed leader of the Khmer Rouge until 1997.

Prynne, Hester: Character in Nathaniel Hawthorne's *The Scarlet Letter* (1850). Found guilty of adultery, Hester was sentenced by her Puritan community to wear a scarlet A embroidered on her torso clothes.

Quisling, Vidkun: Nazi collaborator who helped turn Norway over to Germany in exchange to be a puppet-ruler.

Snopes: A hillbilly clan invented by William Faulkner.

Torquemada, Tomas (1420-1498): Dominican friar who was instrumental in founding The Spanish Inquisition and was its first Grand Inquisitor.

Printed in the United States
By Bookmasters